Notes

from

the

Fog

Notes from the Fog

STORIES

Ben Marcus

GRANTA

Granta Publications, 12 Addison Avenue, London W11 4QR

First published in Great Britain by Granta Books, 2018

First published in the United States as a Borzoi Book by Alfred A. Knopf, a division of Penguin Random House LLC, New York, in 2018

Several stories were first published in the following publications: *Bomb*: "The Trees of Sawtooth Park"; *Frieze*: "Critique" as "Notes from the Hospital" (2013); *Granta*: "George and Elizabeth" (November 2015); *Harper's Magazine*: "A Suicide of Trees" as "A Failure of Concern" (January 2008); *The New Yorker*: "Blueprint for St. Louis" (October 2017), "Cold Little Bird" (October 2015), "The Grow-LightBlues" (June 2015) and "Stay Down and Take It" (May 2018); *Tablet Magazine*: "*Omen*" as "A Problem with the Sun" (2015); *The Thing Quarterly*: "Lotion" as "Prophecy" (Issue 21).

A CIP catalogue record for this book is available from the British Library.

1 3 5 7 9 10 8 6 4 2

ISBN 978 1 78378 282 6
eISBN 978 1 78378 283 3

Designed by Betty Lew
Offset by M Rules

Printed and bound by CPI Group (UK) Ltd, Croydon, CR0 4YY

www.granta.com

To my family:
Heidi, Delia, *and* Solomon

Contents

Cold Little Bird

It started with bedtime. A coldness. A formality.

Martin and Rachel tucked the boy in, as was their habit, then stooped to kiss him good night.

"Please don't do that," he said, turning to face the wall.

They took it as teasing, flopped onto his bed to nuzzle and tickle him.

The boy turned rigid, endured the cuddle, then barked out at them, "I really don't like that!"

"Jonah?" Martin said, sitting up.

"I don't want your help at bedtime anymore," he said. "I'm not a baby. You have Lester. Go cuddle with him."

"Sweetheart," Rachel said. "We're not helping you. We're just saying good night. You like kisses, right? Don't you like kisses and cuddles? You big silly."

Jonah hid under the blankets. A classic pout. Except that he wasn't a pouter, he wasn't a hider. He was a reserved boy who generally took a scientific interest in the tantrums and emotional extravagances of other children, marveling at them as though they were some strange form of street theater.

Martin tried to tickle the blanketed lump of person that was his son. He didn't know what part of Jonah he was touching. He just dug at him with a stiff hand, thinking a laugh would come out, some sound of pleasure. It used to work. One stab of the finger and the kid exploded with giggles. But Jonah didn't speak, didn't move.

"We love you so much. You know?" Martin said. "So we like to show it. It feels good."

"Not to me. I don't feel that way."

"What way? What do you mean?"

They sat with him, perplexed, and tried to rub his back, but he'd rolled to the edge of the bed, nearly flattening himself against the wall.

"I don't love you," Jonah said.

"Oh, now," Martin said. "You're just tired. No need to say that sort of stuff. Get some rest."

"You told me to tell the truth, and I'm telling the truth. I. Don't. Love. You."

This happened. Kids tested their attachments. They tried to push you away to see just how much it would take to really lose you. As a parent, you took the blow, even sharpened the knife yourself before handing it to the little fiends, who stepped right up and plunged. Or so Martin had heard.

They hovered by Jonah's bed, assuring him that it had been a long day—although the day had been entirely unremarkable—and he would feel better in the morning.

Martin felt like a robot saying these things. He felt like a robot thinking them. There was nothing to do but leave the boy there, let him sleep it off.

Downstairs, they cleaned the kitchen in silence. Rachel was troubled or not, he couldn't tell, and it was better not to check. In some way, Martin was captivated. If he were Jonah, ten years old and reasonably smart, starting to sniff out the world and find his angle, this might be something worth exploring. Getting rid of the soft, warm, dumb providers who spun opportunity around you relentlessly, answering your every need. Good play, Jonah. But how do you follow such a strong, definitive opening move? What now?

...

Over the next few weeks, Jonah stuck by his statement, wandering through their lives like some prisoner of war who'd been trained not to talk. He endured his parents, leaving for school in the morning with scarcely a goodbye. Upon coming home, he put away his coat and shoes, did his homework without prompting. He helped himself to snacks, dragging a chair into the kitchen so that he could climb on the counter. He got his own glass, filling it with water at the sink. When he was done eating, he loaded his dishes in the dishwasher. Martin, working from home in the afternoons, watched all this, impressed but bothered. He kept offering to help, but Jonah always said that he was fine, he could handle it. At bedtime, Martin and Rachel still fussed over Lester, who, at six years old, regressed and babified himself in order to drink up the extra attention. Jonah insisted on saying good night with no kiss, no hug. He shut his door and disappeared every night at 8 p.m.

When Martin or Rachel caught Jonah's eye, the boy forced a smile at them. But it was so obviously fake. Could a boy his age do that?

"Of course," Rachel said. "You think he doesn't know how to pretend?"

"No, I know he can pretend. But this seems different. I mean, to have to pretend that he's happy to see us. First of all, what the fuck is he so upset about? And, second, it just seems so kind of . . . grown-up. In the worst possible way. A fake smile. It's a tool one uses with strangers."

"Well, I don't know. He's ten. He has social skills. He can hide his feelings. That's not such an advanced thing to do."

Martin studied his wife.

"Okay, so you think everything's fine?"

"I think maybe he's growing up and you don't like it."

"And you like it? That's what you're saying? You like this?"

His voice had gone up. He had lost control for a minute there, and, as per motherfucking usual, it was a deal breaker. Rachel put up her hand, and she was gone. From the other room, he heard her say, "I'm not going to talk to you when you're like this."

Okay, he thought. Goodbye. We'll talk some other time when I'm not like this, aka never.

Jonah, it turned out, reserved this behavior solely for his parents. A probing note to his teacher revealed nothing. He was fine in school, did not act withdrawn, had successfully led a team project on Antarctica, and seemed to run and play with his friends during recess. Run and play? What animal were they discussing here? Everybody loved Jonah, was the verdict, along with some bullshit about how happy he seemed. "Seemed" was just the thing. Seemed! If you were an idiot who didn't know the boy, who had no grasp of human behavior.

At home, Jonah doted on his brother, read to him, played with him, even let Lester climb on his back for rides around the house, all fairly verboten in the old days, when Jonah's interest in Lester had only ever been theoretical. Lester was thrilled by it all. He suddenly had a new friend, the older brother he worshipped, who used to ignore him. Life was good. But to Martin it felt like a calculated display. With this performance of tenderness toward his brother, Jonah seemed to be saying, "Look, this is what you no longer get. See? It's over for you. Go fuck yourself."

Martin took it too personally, he knew. Maybe because it was personal.

One night, when Jonah hadn't touched his dinner, they were asking him if he would like something else to eat, and, because he wasn't answering, and really had not been answering for some weeks now, other than in one-word responses, curt and formal, Martin and Rachel abandoned their usual rules, the guideposts of parenting they'd clung to, and moved through a list of bribes. They dangled the promise of ice cream, and then those monstrosities passing for Popsicles, shaped like animals with chocolate faces or hats, which used to turn Jonah craven and desperate. When Jonah remained silent and sort of washed-out looking, Martin offered his son candy. He could have some right now. If only he'd fucking say something.

"It's just that you're all in his face," Rachel said to him later. "How's he supposed to breathe?"

"You think my desire for him to speak is making him silent?"

"It's probably not helping."

"Whereas your approach is so amazing."

"My approach? You mean being his mother? Loving him for who he is? Keeping him safe? Yeah, it is pretty amazing."

He turned over to sleep while Rachel clipped on her book light.

They'd ride this one out in silence, apparently.

Yes, well. They'd written their own vows, promising to be "intensely honest" with each other. They had not specifically said that they would hold up each other's flaws to the most rigorous scrutiny, calling out each other's smallest mistakes, like fact checkers, believing, perhaps, that the marriage would thrive only if all personal errors and misdeeds were rooted out of it. This mission had gone unstated.

In the morning, when Martin got up, Jonah sat reading while Lester played soldiers on the rug. Lester was fully dressed, his backpack near the door. There was no possible way that Lester had done this on his own. Obviously, Jonah had dressed his brother, emptied the boy's backpack of yesterday's crap art from the first-grade praise farm he attended, and readied it for a new day. Months ago, they'd asked Jonah to perform this role in the morning, to dress and prepare his brother, so that they could sleep in, and Jonah had complied a few times, but half-heartedly, with a certain mysterious cost to little Lester, who was often speechless and tear-streaked by the time they found him. The chore had quickly lapsed, and usually Martin awoke to a hungry, half-naked Lester, waiting for his help.

Today, Lester seemed happy. There was no sign of crying.

"Good morning, Daddy," he said.

"Hello there, Les, my friend. Sleep okay?"

"Jonah made me breakfast. I had juice and Cheerios. I brought in my own dishes."

"Way to go! Thank you."

Martin figured he'd play it casual, not draw too much attention to anything.

"Good morning, champ," he said to Jonah. "What are you reading?"

Martin braced himself for silence, for stillness, for a child who hadn't heard or who didn't want to answer. But Jonah looked at him.

"It's a book called *The Short*. It's a novel," he said, and then he resumed reading.

A fat bolt of lightning filled the cover. A boy ran beneath it. The title lettering was achieved graphically with one long wire, a plug trailing off the cover.

"Oh, yeah?" Martin said. "What's it about? Tell me about it."

There was a long pause this time. Martin went into the kitchen to get his coffee started. He popped back out to the living room and snapped his fingers.

"Jonah, hello. Your book. What's it about?"

Jonah spoke quietly. His little flannel shirt was buttoned up to the collar, as if he were headed out into a blizzard. Martin almost heard a kind of apology in his voice.

"Since I have to leave for school in fifteen minutes, and since I was hoping to get to page one hundred this morning, would it be okay if I didn't describe it to you? You can look it up on Amazon."

Martin told Rachel about this later in the morning, the boy's unsettling calm, his odd response.

"Yeah, I don't know," she said. "I mean, good for him, right? He wanted to read, and he told you that. So what?"

"Huh," Martin said.

Rachel was busy cleaning. She hadn't looked at him. Their argument last night had been either forgotten or stored for later activation. He'd find out. She seemed engrossed by a panicked effort at tidying, as if guests were arriving any second, as if their house were going to be inspected by the fucking UN. Martin followed her around while they talked, because if he didn't she'd roam out of earshot and the conversation would expire.

"He just seems like a stranger to me," Martin said, trying to add a lightness to his voice so she wouldn't hear it as a complaint.

Rachel stopped cleaning. "Yeah."

For a moment, it seemed that she might agree with him and they'd see this thing similarly.

"But he's not a stranger. I don't know. He's growing up. You should be happy that he's reading. At least he wasn't begging to be on the stupid iPad, and it seems like he's talking again. He wanted to read, and you're freaking out. Honestly."

Yes, well. You had these creatures in your house. You fed them. You cleaned them. And here was the person you'd made them with. She was beautiful, probably. She was smart, probably. It was impossible to know anymore. He looked at her through an unclean filter, for sure. He could indulge a great anger toward her that would suddenly vanish if she touched his hand. What was wrong? He'd done something or he hadn't done something. Figure it the fuck out, Martin thought. Root out the resentment. Apologize so hard it leaks from her body. Then drink the liquid. Or use it in a soup. Whatever.

Jonah came and went, such a weird bird of a boy, so serious. Martin tried to tread lightly. He tried not to tread at all. Better to float overhead, to allow the cold remoteness of his elder son to freeze their home. He studied Rachel's caution, her distance-giving, her respect, the confidence she possessed that he clearly lacked, even as he saw the toll it took on her, what had become of this person who needed to touch her young son and just couldn't.

Then, one afternoon, he forgot himself. He came home with groceries and saw Jonah sprawled on the rug with Lester, setting up his Lego figures for him, such an impossibly small person, dressed so carefully by his own hand, his son—it still seemed ridiculous and a miracle to Martin that there'd be such a thing as a son, that a little creature in this world would be his to protect and befriend. Without thinking about it, he sat down next to Jonah and took the whole of the boy in his arms. He didn't want to scare him, and he didn't want to hurt him, but he needed this boy to feel what it was like to be held, to really be swallowed up in a father's arms. Maybe he could squeeze all the aloofness out of the boy, just choke it out until it was gone.

Jonah gave nothing back. He went limp, and the hug didn't work the way Martin had hoped. You couldn't do it alone. The person being hugged had to do something, to be something. The person being hugged had to fucking exist. And whoever this was, whoever he was holding, felt like nothing.

Finally, Martin released him, and Jonah straightened his hair. He did not look happy.

"I know that you and Mom are in charge and you make the rules," Jonah said. "But even though I'm only ten, don't I have a right not to be touched?"

The boy sounded so reasonable.

"You do," Martin said. "I apologize."

"I keep asking, but you don't listen."

"I listen."

"You don't. Because you keep doing it. So does Mom. You want to treat me like a stuffed animal, and I don't want to be treated like that."

"No, I don't, buddy."

"I don't want to be called buddy. Or mister. Or champ. I don't do that to you. You wouldn't want me always inventing some new ridiculous name for you."

"Okay." Martin put up his hands in surrender. "No more nicknames. I promise. It's just that you're my son and I like to hug you. We like to hug you."

"I don't want you to anymore. And I've said that."

"Well, too bad," Martin said, trying to be lighthearted, and, as if to prove his point, he grabbed Lester, and Lester squealed with delight, squirming in his father's arms.

Do you see how this used to work? Martin wanted to say to Jonah. This was you once, this was us.

Jonah seemed genuinely puzzled. "It doesn't matter to you that I don't like it?"

"It matters, but you're wrong. You can be wrong, you know. You'll die, without affection. I'm not kidding. You will actually dry up and die."

Again, he found he had to explain love to this boy, to detail what it was like when you felt a desperate connection with someone else, how you wanted to hold that person and just crush him with hugs. But as Martin fought through the difficult and ridiculous discussion, he felt as if he were having a conversation with a lawyer. A lawyer, a scold, a little prick of a person. Whom he wanted to hug less and less. Maybe it'd be simpler just to give Jonah what he wanted. What he thought he wanted.

Jonah seemed pensive, concerned.

"Does any of that make sense to you?" Martin asked.

"It's just that I'd rather not say things that could hurt someone," Jonah said.

"Well . . . that's good. That's how you should feel."

"I'd rather not have to say anything about you and Mom. At school. To Mr. Fourenay."

Mr. Fourenay was what they called a "feelings doctor." He was paid, certainly not very much, to take the kids and their feelings very, very seriously. Martin and Rachel had trouble taking *him* seriously. He looked like a man who had subsisted, for a very long time, on a strict diet of the feelings of children. Gutted, wasted, and soft.

"Jonah, what are you talking about?"

"About you touching me when I don't want you to. I don't want to have to mention that to anyone at school. I really don't."

Martin stood up. It was as if a hand had moved inside him.

He stared at Jonah, who held his gaze patiently, waiting for an answer.

"Message received. I'll discuss it with Mom."

"Thank you."

Without really thinking about it, Martin had crafted an adulthood that was essentially friendless. There were, of course, the friends of the marriage, who knew him only as part of a couple—the dour, rotten part—and thus they were ruled out for anything remotely candid, like a confession of what the fuck had just gone down in his own home. Before the children came, he'd managed, sometimes erratically, to maintain preposterous phone relationships with several male friends. Deep, searching, facially sweaty conversations on the phone with other semi-articulate, vaguely unhappy men. In general, these friendships had heated up and found their purpose around a courtship or a breakup, when an aria of complaint or desire could be harmonized by some pathetic accomplice. But after Jonah was born, and then Lester, phone calls with friends had become out of the question. There was just never a time when it was okay, or even appealing, to talk on the phone. When he was home, he was in shark mode, cruising slowly and brutally through the house, cleaning and clearing, scrubbing food from rugs, folding and storing tiny items of clothing, and, if no one was looking, occasionally stopping at his laptop to see if his prospects had suddenly been lifted by some piece of tremendous fortune, delivered via email. When he finally came to rest, in a barf-covered chair, he was done for the night. He poured several beers, in succession, right onto his pleasure center, which could remain dry and withered no matter what came soaking down.

The gamble of a friendless adulthood, whether by accident or design, was that your partner would step up to the role. She for you, and you for her.

But when Martin thought about Jonah's threat—blackmail, really—he knew he couldn't tell Rachel. In a certain light, the only light that mattered, he was in the wrong. The instructions were already out that they were not to get all huggy with Jonah, and here he'd gone and done it anyway. Rachel would just ask him what he had expected and why he was surprised that Jonah had lashed out at him for not respecting his boundaries.

So, yeah, maybe, maybe that was all true. But there was the other part. The threat that came out of the boy. The quiet force of it. To even mention that Jonah had threatened to report them for touching him ghosted an irreversible suspicion into people's minds. You couldn't talk about it. You couldn't mention it. It seemed better to not even think it, to do the work that would begin to block such an event from memory.

The boys were talking quietly on the couch one afternoon a few days later. Martin was in the next room, and he caught the sweet tones, the two voices he loved, that he couldn't even bear. For a minute he forgot what was going on and listened to the life he'd helped make. They were speaking like little people, not kids, back and forth, a real discussion. Jonah was explaining something to Lester, and Lester was asking questions, listening patiently. It was heartbreaking.

He snuck out to see the boys on the couch, Lester cuddled up against his older brother, who had a big book in his hands. A grown-up one. On the cover, instead of a boy dashing beneath a bolt of lightning, were the good old Twin Towers. The title, *Lies,* was glazed in blood, which dripped down the towers themselves.

Oh, motherfucking hell.

"What's this?" Martin asked. "What are you reading there?"

"A book about 9/11. Who caused it."

Martin grabbed it, thumbed the pages. "Where'd you get it?"

"From Amazon. With my birthday gift card."

"Hmm. Do you believe it?"

"What do you mean? It's true."

"What's true?"

"That the Jews caused 9/11 and they all stayed home that day so they wouldn't get killed."

Martin excused Lester. Told him to skedaddle and, yes, it was fine to watch TV, even though watching time hadn't started yet. Just go, go.

"Jonah," he whispered. "Jonah, stop. This is not okay. Not even remotely okay. First of all, Jonah, you have to listen to me. This is insane. This is a book by an insane person."

"You know him?"

"No, I don't know him. I don't have to. Listen to me, you know that we're Jewish, right? You, me, Mom, Lester. We're Jewish."

"Not really."

"What do you mean, not really?"

"You don't go to synagogue. You don't seem to worship. You never talk about it."

"That's not all that matters."

"Last month was Yom Kippur and you didn't fast. You didn't go to services. You don't ever say Happy New Year on Rosh Hashanah."

"Those are rituals. You don't need to observe them to be part of the faith."

"But do you know anything about it?"

"9/11?"

"No, being Jewish. Do you know what it means and what you're supposed to believe and how you're supposed to act?"

"I do, yes. I have a pretty good idea."

"Then tell me."

"Jonah."

"What? I'm just wondering how you can call yourself Jewish."

"How? Are you fucking kidding me?"

He needed to walk away before he did something.

"Okay, Jonah, it's actually really simple. I'll tell you how. Because everyone else in the world would call me Jewish. With no debate. None. Because of my parents and their parents, and their parents, including whoever got turned to dust in the war. Zayde Anshel's whole family. You walk by their picture every day in the hall. Do you think you're not related to them? And because I was called a kike in junior high school, and high school, and college, and probably beyond that, right up to this fucking day. And because if they started rounding up Jews again they'd take one look at our name and they'd know. And that's you, too, mister. They would come for us and kill us. Okay? You."

He was shaking his fist in his son's face. Just old-school shouting. He wanted to do more. He wanted to tear something apart. There was no safe way to behave right now.

"They would kill you. And you'd be dead. You'd die."

"Martin?" Rachel said. "What's going on?"

Of course. There she was. Lurking. He had no idea how long she'd been standing there, what she'd heard.

Martin wasn't done. Jonah seemed fascinated, his eyes wide as his father ranted.

"Even if you said that you hated Jews, too, and that Jews were evil and caused all the suffering in the world, they would look at you and know for sure that you were Jewish, for sure! Buddy, champ, mister"—just spitting these names at his son—"because only a Jew, they would say, only a Jew would betray his own people like that."

Jonah looked at him. "I understand," he said. He didn't seem shaken. He didn't seem disturbed. Had he heard? How could he really understand?

The boy picked up the book and thumbed through it.

"This is just a different point of view. You always say that I should have an open mind, that I should think for myself. You say that to me all the time."

"Yes, I do. You're right." Martin was trembling.

"Then do I have your permission to keep reading it?"

"No, you absolutely don't. Not this time. Permission denied."

Rachel was shaking her head.

"Do you see what he's reading? Do you see it?" he shouted.

He waved the book at her, and she just looked at him with no expression at all.

After the kids were in bed, and the house had been quietly put back together, Rachel said they needed to talk.

Yes, we do, he thought, and about time.

"Honestly," she said. "It's upsetting that he had that book, but the way you spoke to him? I don't want you going anywhere near him."

"Yeah, well, that's not for you to say. You're his mom, not mine. You want to file papers? You want to seek custody? Good luck, Mrs. Freeze. I'm his father. And you didn't hear it. You didn't hear it all. You have no fucking idea."

"I heard it, and I heard you. Martin, you need help. You're, I don't know, depressed. You're self-pitying. You think everything is some concerted attack on you. For the record, I am worried about Jonah. Really worried. Something is seriously wrong. There is no debate there. But you're just the worst possible partner in that worry—the fucking worst—because you make everything harder, and we can't discuss it without analyzing your feelings. You act wounded and hurt, and we're all supposed to feel sorry for you. For you! This isn't about you. So shut down the pity party already."

When this kind of talk came on, Martin knew to listen. This was the scold she'd been winding up for, and if he could endure it, and cop to it, there might be some release and clarity at the other end. A part of him found these outbursts from Rachel thrilling, and in some ways it was possible that he co-engineered them, without really thinking about it. Performed the sullen and narcissistic dance moves that, over time, would yield this kind of eruption from her. His wife was alive. She cared. Even if it seemed that she might sort of hate him.

He circled the house for a while, cooling off, letting the attack—no, no, the truth—settle. Any argument or even discussion to the contrary would just feed her point and read as the defensive bleating of a cornered man. Any speech, that is, except admission, contrition, and apology, the three horsemen.

Which was who he brought back into the room with him.

Rachel was in bed reading, eyes locked onto the page. She didn't seem even remotely ready to surrender her anger.

"Hey, listen," Martin said. "So I know you're mad, but I just want to say that I agree with everything you said. I'm scared and I'm worried and I'm sorry."

He let this settle. It needed to spread, to sink in. She needed to realize that he was agreeing with her.

It was hard to tell, but it seemed that some of her anger, with nothing to meet it, was draining out.

"And," he continued. He waited for her to look up, which she finally did. "You'll think I'm kidding, and I know you don't even want to hear this right now, but it's true, and I have to say it. It made me a little bit horny to hear all that."

She shook her head at the bad joke, which at least meant there was room to move here.

"Shut up," she said.

This was the way in. He took it.

"You shut up."

"Sorry to yell, Martin. I am. I just—this is so hard. I'm sorry."

She probably wasn't. This was simply the script back in, to the two of them united, and they both knew it. One day, one of them would choose not to play. It would be so easy not to say their lines.

"No, it's okay," he said to her, climbing onto the bed. "I get it. Listen, let's take the little man to the shop. Get him fixed. I'll call some doctors in the morning."

They hugged. An actual hug, between two consenting people. A novelty in this house.

"Okay," she said. "I'm terrified. I don't know what's happening. I look at him and want so much to just grab him, but he's not there anymore. What has he done to himself?"

"Maybe he just needs minor surgery. Does that work on 9/11 truthers?"

"Oh, look," she said to him softly. "You're back. The real you. We missed you."

They talked a little and snuggled closer to each other in bed. For a moment, their good feeling came on them—a version of it, anyway. It felt mild and transitory, but he would take it. It was nice. He was in bed with his wife, and they would figure this out.

"Listen," he said to her. "Do you want to just shag a pony right now, get back on track?"

"I don't know," she said. "I feel gross. I feel depressed."

"I feel gross, too. Let's do it. Two gross people licking each other's buttons."

She went to the bathroom and got the jar of enabler. They took their positions on the bed.

He hoped he could. He hoped he could. He hoped he could.

He was cold and insecure, so he left his shirt on. And his socks.

They used a cream. They used their hands. They used an object or two. During the brief strain of actual fornication they persisted with casual conversation about the next day's errands. In the early days of their marriage, this had seemed wicked and sexy, some ironic ballast against the animal greed. Now it just seemed efficient, and the animal greed no longer appeared. Minus the wet spot at the end, and the minor glow one occasionally felt, their sex wasn't so different from riding the subway.

It turned out that there was a deep arsenal of medical professionals who would be delighted to consult on the problem of a disturbed child. Angry, depressed, anxious, remote, bizarre. Even a Jew-hating Jewish child who might very well be dead inside. Only when his parents looked at him, though. Only when his parents spoke to him. Important parameter for the differential.

They zeroed in on recommendations with the help of a high-level participant in this world, a friend named Maureen, whose three exquisitely exceptional children had consumed, and spat back out, various kinds of psych services ever since they could walk. Each of the kids seemed to romance a different diagnosis every month, so Maureen had a pretty good idea of who fixed what and for how much goddam moolah.

When they told her, in pale terms, about Jonah, she, as a connoisseur of alienating behavior from the young, got excited.

"This is so *The Fifth Child*," she said. "Did you guys read that? I mean, you probably shouldn't read that. But did you? It's like a fiction novel. I don't think it really happened. But it's still fascinating."

Rachel had read it. Happy couple with four children and perfect life have fifth child, leading to less-perfect life. Much, much, much, much less perfect. Sorrow, sorrow, sorrow, grief, and sorrow. Not really life at all.

"Yeah, but the kid in that book is a monster," Rachel said. "So heartless. He's not real. And he just wants to inflict pain. Jonah wouldn't hurt anyone. He wants to be alone. Or, not that, but. I don't know what Jonah wants. He's not violent, though. Or even mad. I don't think."

"All right, but he is hurting you, right?" Maureen said. "I mean, it seems like this is really causing you guys a lot of pain and suffering."

"I haven't read the book," Martin said. "But this isn't about us. This is about Jonah. His pain, his suffering. We just want to get to the bottom of it. To help him. To give him support."

In Rachel's silence he could feel her agreement and, maybe, her surprise that he would, or even could, think this way. He knew what to say now. He wasn't going to get burned again. But did he believe it? Was it true? He honestly didn't even know, and he wasn't so sure it mattered.

The doctor wanted to see them alone first. He told them that it was his job to listen. So they talked, just dumped the thing out on the floor. It was ugly, Martin thought, but it was a rough picture of what was going down. The doctor scribbled away, stopping occasionally to look at them, to really deeply look at them, and nod. Since when had the act of listening turned into such a strange charade?

Then the doctor met with Jonah, to see for himself, pull evidence right from the culprit's mouth. Martin and Rachel sat in the waiting room and stared at the door. What would the doctor see? Which kid would he get? Were they crazy and this was all just some preteen freak-out?

Finally, the whole gang of them—doctor, parents, and child—gathered to go over the plan, Jonah sitting polite and alert while the future of his brain was discussed. They told him the proposal: a slow ramp of antidepressants, along with weekly therapy, and then, depending, some group work, if that sounded good to Jonah.

Jonah didn't respond.

"What do you think?" the doctor said. "So you can feel better? And things can maybe go back to normal?"

"I told you, I feel fine," Jonah said.

"Yes, good! But sometimes when we're sick we think we're not. That can be a symptom of being sick—to think we are well."

"So all the healthy people are just lying to themselves?"

"Well, no, of course not," the doctor said.

"Right now I never think about hurting myself, but you want to give me a medicine that might make me think about hurting myself?"

The doctor seemed uneasy.

"It's called suicidal ideation," Jonah said.

"And how do you know about that?" the doctor asked.

"The Internet."

The adults all looked at one another.

"How come people are so surprised when someone knows something?" Jonah asked. "Your generation had better get used to how completely unspecial it is that a kid can look up a medicine online and learn about the side effects. That's not me being precocious. It's just me using my stupid computer."

"Okay, good. Well, you're right, you should be informed, and I want to congratulate you on finding that out for yourself. That's great work, Jonah."

Martin watched Jonah. He found himself hoping that the real Jonah would appear, scathing and cold, to show the doctor what they were dealing with.

"Thank you," Jonah said. "I'm really proud of myself. I didn't think I could do it, but I just really stuck with it and I kept trying until I succeeded."

Martin could not tell if the doctor caught the tone of this response.

"But you might have also read that that's a very uncommon symptom. It hardly ever happens. We just have to warn you and your parents about it, to be on the lookout for it."

"Maybe. But I have none of the symptoms of depression, either. So why would you risk making me feel like I want to kill myself if I'm not depressed and feel fine?"

"Okay, Jonah. You know what? I'm going to talk to your parents alone now. Does that sound all right? You can wait outside in the play area. There are books and games."

"Okay," Jonah said. "I'll just run and play now."

"There," Martin said. "There," after Jonah had closed the door. "That was it. That's what he does."

"Sarcasm? Maybe you don't much like it, but we don't treat sarcasm in young people. I think it's too virulent a strain." The doctor chuckled.

"No offense," Martin said to the doctor, "and I'm sure you know your job and this is your specialty, but I think that way of speaking to him—"

"What way?"

"Just, you know, as if he were much younger. He's just—I don't think that works with him."

"And how do you speak to him?"

"Excuse me?"

"How do you speak to him? I'm curious."

Rachel coughed and seemed uncomfortable. They'd agreed to be open, to let each other have ideas and opinions without feeling mad or threatened.

"It's true," she said. "I mean, Martin, I think you have been surprised lately that Jonah is as mature as he is. That seems to have really almost upset you. You know, you really have yelled at him a lot. We can't just pretend that hasn't happened." She looked at him apologetically. "Aside," she added, "from the scary things that he's been saying."

"Is it maturity? I don't think so. Have I been upset? Fucking hell, yes. And so have you, Rachel. And not because he thinks the Jews caused 9/11 or because he threatened to report us for sexual abuse for trying to hug him, which, for what it's worth, I spared you from, Rachel. I spared you. Because I didn't think you could bear it."

Rachel just stared at him.

"What you're seeing is a very, very bright boy," the doctor said.

"Too smart to treat?" Martin asked.

"I think family therapy would be productive. Very challenging, but worthwhile, in my opinion. I could get you a referral. What you're upset about, in relation to your son, may not fall under the purview of medicine, though."

"The purview? Really?"

"To be honest, I was on the fence about medication. Whatever is going on with Jonah, it does not present as depression. In my opinion, Jonah does not have a medical condition."

Martin stood up.

"He's not sick, he's just an asshole, is what you're saying?"

"I think that's a very dangerous way for a parent to feel," the doctor said.

"Yeah?" Martin said, standing over the doctor now. "You're right. You got that one right. Because all of a parent's feelings are dangerous, you motherfucker."

At home that night, Martin stuffed a chicken with lemon halves, drenched it in olive oil, scattered a handful of salt over it, and blasted it in the oven until it emerged deeply burnished, with skin as crisp as glass. Rachel poured drinks for the two of them, and they cooked in silence. To Martin, it was a harmless silence. He could trust it, and if he couldn't, then to hell with it. He wasn't going to chase down everything unsaid and shout it into their home, as if all important messages on the planet needed to be shared. He'd said enough, things he believed, things he didn't. Quota achieved. Quota surpassed.

Rachel looked small and tired. Beyond that, he wasn't sure. He was more aware than ever, as she set the table and put out Lester's cup and Jonah's big-kid glass, how impossibly unknowable she would always be—what she thought, what she felt—how what was most special about her was the careful way she guarded it all.

No matter their theories—about Jonah or each other or the larger world—their job was to watch over Jonah on his cold voyage. He had to come back. This kind of controlled solitude was unsustainable. No one could pull it off, especially not someone so young. Except that his reasoning on this, he knew, was wishful parental bullshit. Of course a child could do it. Who else but children to lead the species into darkness? Which meant what for the old-timers left behind?

Dinner was brief, destroyed by the savage appetite of Lester, who engulfed his meal before Rachel had even taken a bite, and begged, begged to be excused so that he could return to the platoon of small plastic men he'd deployed on the rug. According to Lester, his men were waiting to be told what to do. "I need to tell my guys who to attack!" he shouted. "I'm in charge!"

At the height of this tantrum, Jonah, silent since they'd returned from the doctor's office, leaned over to Lester, put a hand on his shoulder, and calmly told him not to whine.

"Don't use that tone of voice," he said. "Mom and Dad will excuse you when they're ready."

"Okay," Lester said, looking up at his brother with a kind of awe, and for the rest of their wordless dinner he sat there waiting, as patiently as a boy his age ever could, his hands folded in his lap.

At bedtime, Rachel asked Martin if he wouldn't mind letting her sleep alone. She was just very tired. She didn't think she could manage otherwise. She gave him a sort of smile, and he saw the effort behind it. She dragged her pillow and a blanket into a corner of the TV room and made herself a little nest there. He had the bedroom to himself. He crawled onto Rachel's side of the mattress, which was higher, softer, less abused, and fell asleep.

In the morning, Jonah did not say goodbye on his way to school, nor did he greet Martin upon his return home. When Martin asked after his day, Jonah, without looking up, said that it had been fine. Maybe that was all there was to say, and why, really, would you ever shit on such an answer?

Jonah took up his spot on the couch and opened a book, reading quietly until dinner, while Lester played at his feet. Martin watched Jonah. Was that a grin or a grimace on the boy's face? he wondered. And what, finally, was the difference? Why have a face at all if what was inside you was so perfectly hidden? The book Jonah was reading was nothing, some silliness. Make-believe and colorful and harmless. It looked like it belonged to a series, along with that book *The Short*. On the cover a boy, arms outspread, was gripping wires in each hand, and his whole body was glowing.

Precious Precious

It was late in the wretched season, and there was a sweet chill in the halls at Thompson Systems, where the future was getting fondled by some of the most anxious and self-regarding minds of Ida Grieve's generation.

Tonight a bunch of them were at drinks, because death was coming, and Foster, the wunderkind, whose official title at Thompson was Beekeeper, had ordered some nasty brew called Mud. It oozed up his glass and clumped in dark nuggets along the rim. When they asked the waiter what was in it, he seemed forlorn, as if he might soon bleed out on the carpet.

They watched him shuffle away, perhaps to go find out, or perhaps to throw himself from a cliff.

"Oh no. It's like we just sent him to the principal's office," said Foster. "Hey," he whispered toward the bar. "You're not in trouble. You didn't do anything wrong. We love you."

"Do we really love him, though?" said Aniel, a little too loudly. "I mean, we don't. In some ways we hardly think of him as human, or people like him, even though we know not to admit that."

"Jesus, Aniel," said Foster. "Apparently we don't really know not to admit that."

...

At the table were the brooding engineers — Mort and Bummer and Cerise — youngish and facially steamrolled from all-nighters at their terminals, and if they were rich they still dressed cheap and drank cheap and lived in cheap, bullshit apartments up in the hills. Maury Beryl was there because he was always there, sipping some cloudy fizz, sometimes swishing it in his mouth, as if he might spit it in someone's face. Ida felt that she could be sad around him, not that she'd tried. One day, maybe. She'd spill her moods over Maury Beryl and see what happened.

Sitting next to Maury was Harriet, about whom nothing could be said, or thought, or felt. Except that Harriet pushed a certain button of Ida's that very nearly seemed like the size of her entire body. Harriet had to be met with force, or else you just became her backup singer.

A mysterious young man named Donny Wohl sat at the end of the table. He was possibly still a teenager, despite his pretty mustache, so Ida was afraid of him, even though he was strangely beautiful and she thought about him sort of a lot when she was alone. And alongside Donny, or maybe just accidentally sitting nearly inside Donny's pants, and accidentally soothing a terrible itch of his under the table, Ida guessed, was Royce, who cock-blocked ideas in the pitch room at Thompson. It was Royce's job to pump discouragement into the Thompson intellectual climate, through the tiny pink valve in her face. Ida felt reliably like shit after every encounter with Royce. To drink with Royce, though, that was different. She was competitively bleak, and even though she seemed to be indifferently molesting Donny right now, taking her turn with the little love child, Ida was glad she was there.

Foster took careful sips of his drink and tried to smile. A watery brown stain crested up his mouth.

"I will not even remark on the kind of grin you have right now," said Aniel.

"Maybe the dirt is from somewhere and kind of, I don't know, amazing for you," said Harriet, pinging the glass with her finger. "The Dead Sea. Some legendary, healing mudflats." She studied the menu.

"It doesn't taste *terrible*," he said. "I was expecting cream."

Aniel got up and sniffed the drink. He struck a snobbish, wine-tasting face.

"It's a superfood, dude," he said. Aniel was older, which meant thirty-two or so, with all the shame that that entailed. He dressed young, but fancy young. Fifth Avenue Skate. He always seemed so well laundered.

"I was reading somewhere that certain regional soil samples have more protein than meat," Aniel said. "Per cubic whatever."

"Oh yeah. Read that too. In *Scientific American,* last August. That's totally right."

This was Bummer, a compulsive affirmer. Whenever Ida needed agreement at work, an ally or a second or a foil, a fall guy or a fool or a friend, or even just a live human being who bled on command, she sought out Bummer, but his inability to produce conversational friction had melted him into a puddle, contained, if barely, by a few odd bones.

"I don't know," said Harriet. "I could see that being true. If animals were buried in that soil, there'd be some protein in the sample. Vestigial."

Ida laughed. "*If?* Isn't that what soil is, ultimately? A compost of the dead? So, Foster, you're really just drinking your grandfather."

"No need to make it personal," said Foster. "And my grandfather is still alive, so that's gross." He'd abandoned his drink and was glancing around. For help, maybe. For an escape.

Royce whispered something to Donny, and Donny's face registered nothing. Donny was staring, it seemed, directly at Ida, and she squirmed in her seat. Activity seemed to accelerate under the table, as if Royce were solving a Rubik's Cube without looking.

Ida wouldn't have minded watching, without the table blocking their doings, but just in a casual way. Not sexual, exactly. Almost as you'd watch a short documentary at the museum. With others, on a bench, in a cool, dark room.

"I wish there was a more obvious way to make money off of that idea," Maury said. "That the earth is simply compacted corpse material. A kind of condensed, spherical dead body."

"Money!" shouted Bummer, and then a few of them repeated the word in different foreign accents, until they'd reduced it to a pirate's growl. Ida wasn't sure just how ironic they were being, and they probably weren't either.

"Actually," said Mort, and this set off a chorus of groans around the table.

"What? I was just going to say that that's the plot of a science fiction novel. Really. I'm not kidding."

"We know that, Mort," said Harriet. "That's what's so depressing. That you are reminded of a book and now we have to hear about it."

Cerise suggested that it wouldn't hurt to hear the plot. That Mort deserved a chance.

Foster said that it might hurt. It had hurt before. "In the Middle Ages they described the plots of books to people as a form of torture."

"Okay. Okay," said Mort. "I'll be fast and you will thank me. So the earth keeps swelling in circumference as people die and rot, adding to the mass of the planet. Right? Then it gets too big for its orbit and things go, uh, pretty wrong. I mean. There's a company, called The Company, I'm not even kidding, that has to keep people from dying. They have this old, wet—"

"Shut up already," said Harriet. "I didn't come to a reading. Jesus."

An obituary had just been written for their industry. And not just their industry—Thompson was a think tank that had turned into a make tank, which meant it was essentially just like any other company—but industry itself. Selling was old-school. Selling was done. The world may as well have worn black. The experts all signed off on it. The only thing left to fight about was the timing. Dead tomorrow, dead in a fortnight, dead before the solstice. A kind of rubbernecker's thrill had resulted, even if Ida would be watching her own spectacular crash. They'd all be out of jobs. The whole idea of a job would be washed from memory. People would wander in the snow, which they couldn't recall the name for, bleeding. Customers would no longer pay for anything. Customers had more power than ever. The word "customer" was, in fact, offensive. It was probably racist. You had to court these people personally, go to their houses and lather them in cream, rub their backs. That's what they were all talking about now. What this would look like. Who would scrub in and chase the danger.

"Who volunteers?" asked Maury, cracking his knuckles.

No one spoke.

"I gave my last massage in ninth grade," said Cerise. "Hit my quota early. I am pretty much done touching others. In that way."

"We are too obsessed with people," said Harriet.

Royce laughed. "Because they are the ones with the money?"

"And too obsessed with money. We are so obsessed with new products, new go-to-market strategies. What we need is to reinvent the customer. That's where the next major disruption will take place."

"The customer is always in flight," mumbled Aniel.

"Oh dear god," Royce said to Harriet. "Really? I truly hope that you are not getting paid for the things you say and do. I hope you are a secret intern, sent here to test us, to see how we respond to fatuous drool. Please, please tell me that you make no money for your ideas."

"Okay, Royce, if that's what you want to hear. I make no money for my ideas. But I'm only saying that to comfort you. You seem afraid and I don't want to scare you. Anyway, it's sort of true. Weirdly, since you are hardly ever right. 'Money,' per se, would be the wrong word—not nearly strong or frightening enough, too bound up in specific meaning—for what they heap on me in return for my services. I *used* to make money. A filthy amount of it, and I stashed it in a sock the size of your whole house. But then, well, 'raise' isn't the word for what happened. There is no word for the kind of promotion I received. And now I've left any category you could even remotely comprehend. I'd have to physically carve a new gutter in your brain for you to understand any of this. With a surgical knife that would blind you to look at. But I still enjoy being your friend. I'm not so advanced that I can't recognize what good people you are. Here's to good people, who remind us of our origins."

Harriet raised a glass, but the toast had few takers.

"That was funny at first, but then it got really long and tedious," said Royce, who was using Donny as a pillow.

"Whereas I feel that it started out tedious and then grew sickening," said Ida. "And we still don't actually know what she gets paid."

Harriet smirked, rubbing her fingers together to suggest currency.

"Speaking of people," said Aniel. "There are a few of them I'd like to lick. Not at this table, though. No offense."

It was getting late, and everyone started to look around at what, and who, there was to be had in the room. Or denied. It was that time of night, but maybe it was always that time of night. There was a collective obligation to try to find moisture, but they were often slow to suit up, sluggish to the starting line. They got tired. They felt slightly sick. Sometimes hooking up took so much *work*. In the end maybe they preferred to be alone. And yet even that didn't scratch at the distant craving, not really.

Ida went home with Mort that night. She'd survived his mild trespasses a few times, and the embarrassment she'd initially expected over sex with a young, hairless engineer never really ignited. Maybe that counted for something. Sometimes, at the end of drinking sessions like tonight, each ashamed and regretful to an equal degree, Ida guessed—since they didn't really stoop to disclosure—they stumbled into each other's territory, *Little Rascals* style, providing a certain service. One day, supposedly, a Kind Friend could give them what they needed, and clean up after, and possibly even flush the shame from their systems as well. But for the time being they still had to endure the company of other fleshy need machines, human spouters and little bags of weepery. Mort was younger, and softer all around, but Ida didn't mind consorting with him because he was erotically polite and nonthreatening and he devoted most of his fornicational energies confirming that everything was all right, as if each new timid push into her, his face ballooning above her like a parade float, might have suddenly changed the ethical terms of their encounter. Which, Ida thought, who knows, maybe it did?

Was it okay, was she okay, did this feel all right, did she mind, was it uncomfortable, did that feel nice? Would she like something else, something different, maybe even a person different from him, which he could possibly try to arrange? Ida pictured Mort on the street, half-naked with his sweet baby legs, soliciting civilians to come up to her apartment and make really, really nice. Mort would do that for her, even if it was secretly for him, to gratify some bottomless need to be solicitous and helpful. The desire to please and please and please. It was all a bit selfish, when you thought about it.

Was it okay, was she okay, did this feel all right? These were the questions a person deserved, Ida thought, but for some reason she only ever heard them naked, and even then not so often. Mort was a good egg, but that was just it. He was no more than that. Smooth and fragile and easy to take for granted.

Tonight Mort was especially soft, for which he blamed his diet and a deficiency in some vitamin buried deep in the alphabet. So there'd be no game of Bible study. He stared down at himself as if he should be able to troubleshoot the issue. "I did a cleanse and I'm fairly certain that I have not had an erection since then. I've been feeling weak and depleted. I probably should have done a run-through at home before coming over. I've just been too busy."

"You didn't connect it to your, uh," Ida asked, trying to be funny, pointing at the stupid thing on his wrist that barked his inner workings at him all day long.

Mort looked at the watch and didn't laugh. His wallpaper was of a cartoon bear, rubbing its belly.

So he'd managed to rid himself, through diet, of his male burden? Ida wondered. Could one say "manhood" anymore? It seemed problematic, but Ida wasn't especially sure. A good deal of the language was mired in lunacy and it sometimes seemed better not to partake. When talking about sensitive matters, or, really, when talking at all, it was safer to just breathe loudly, in different accents, adding a little bit of body English with your face — then the transcript could never come back and fuck you down into the mud. What proof would there ever be? You had only sighed. You just kept sighing and sighing. How could anyone be offended by that? Even biological terminology had taken on a wobble and when you messed up and said something out loud, you dated yourself. You prepped yourself for the dumpster. It was a little bit like using your own tombstone as a sandwich board.

So Mort was soft and she was tired and the night was late, late, late.

"I'm sorry," Ida said, in her flattest voice. It was stone-cold, she knew, but maybe Mort didn't even catch the shade. His self-punishment techniques were too powerful. She was mostly relieved not to have to get sweaty with this remote coworker who often smelled like her third-grade homeroom teacher, which confused things a good deal, but she felt some vague pressure to take the situation personally. Torn a little bit. You know, he was impotent because of *her*. She had not inspired a proper baton. It was difficult not to play along and pretend that if only her ass had a steeper switchback, or her breasts didn't spill to the side, Mort would be seesawing away at her with a diamond cutter. Except they'd consummated before, over the past few months, and her fun happy body, which she loved and loved with all of her blessed heart, oh yes she did, hadn't changed much in the interval. It hadn't spoiled or fallen apart or grown discolored or sloughed off a mild, gray powder from its lower parts. Nope, it sure hadn't. So whatever and whatever and whatever to this young gentleman with his lifeless baby wiener.

She patted Mort on the back. Cleanup would be easier tonight, but what the hell was she supposed to do with this naked person sitting on her bed, on the verge of feeling sorry for himself? Mort was too polite to openly emote about his misfortune—young sensitive men had turned into such exemplars of emotional restraint!— but he parked on the bed as if it was here that his problem would be fixed, and Ida knew that no such thing was in the cards. Must. Get. Sad. Man. Out. Of. House. Now. She'd had her quota of emotions for the week, caring for her mother and father, and right now her store of pity, or really anything else, was empty. She wanted to feed a little, get high, and maybe let the bathtub faucet thunder down on her and finish her off.

Thompson Systems demanded regular physicals of their employees, maybe so you didn't die at one of their cubicles and cause a lapse in productivity. Ida's number was up, and in the course of a routine exam, she was prescribed a legacy drug called Rally. Not for moods, she was told, but possibly for the lack of them. This was not a new drug, the doctor stressed. She was to please not think for a moment that she was taking anything new. Sometimes only the older, forgotten drugs could touch that sweet spot, explained her doctor. And we do need our sweet spots touched, Ida had said back, laughing a little too loudly, though the doctor looked at her with boredom and said that the pills were especially hard to swallow. Don't assume, he told her, that just because you have taken pills your whole life, that you can take these. It's not that simple. He paused. She wasn't sure what to picture. She couldn't picture anything, just a field with dead people in it, for some reason. It wasn't that the pills were so large, either, the doctor explained. They were just, trust him, really hard to swallow.

Ida signed in as a fake customer on the Thompson server—one of the hordes of false identities they cultivated in order to spread praise about themselves, along with a certain kind of low-key criticism, in order to build brand authenticity—and did a quick land grab on the drug, but instantly got bored reading about it. It had changed and ruined people's lives, they loved and hated it. They were indifferent and sad and happy, near death and reborn. Some of them said that if you let the pill sit in your mouth for too long before swallowing it, rather than dissolve it grew larger. It could choke you out, but it also taught you to be a person. Others said it didn't work and still others complained, at length, about the packaging. It was so soft and it crumbled into your hands and you'd never wash it off. As in ever. People seemed to agree that the drug could take years to kick in, a lifetime. Although some people claimed to be buzzing and cheerful and deeply changed after just one dose. An antidepressant for the afterlife, someone called it. Not a happy pill, no way. Not even really a pill. It works in your sleep. It might not affect you, but could leech over to a friend. Drugs like this, claimed one customer, were only for people who didn't think they needed them. It wasn't really a drug. It was more of a bomb, but it had no fuse and would never detonate. You never really swallowed it. You just held it inside you for a while. If you were lucky. We exist to give safe harbor to these pills, someone said. Your body is the bottle. Chemically the drug seemed kind of mild. More like a food than a drug. More like a sample of wind, trapped in a vial. Supposedly they were working on a cream.

Ida filled her prescription and took her bottle of Rally tablets home. With a toothpick she daubed some butter on her pill and it went down fine. But soon it had risen back into her mouth—it felt like a small insect crawling up her throat—and she had to take it out and butter it again. After that it stayed down, and as much as she wanted to claim some change over the next few weeks—to her mind, to her moods, to anything—she noticed nothing different whatsoever.

The next time Ida visited her mother at the nursing home, she asked her about Rally. Her mother had been a physician's assistant before she retired, and would maybe have heard something, or seen this drug in action. It turned out that her grandfather had taken the same medication, which was called Forlexa back then, for his issue, which could only be described, after a long silence on the part of Ida's mother, as estrangement.

Not the official diagnosis, Ida guessed, but still, it possessed a certain diagnostic elegance.

"Did it work?" Ida asked.

Her mother again paused, and it seemed she'd forgotten the question. Her clarity could be fleeting. Clearly she was thinking. And thinking and thinking. Her face strained so, and Ida felt bad about putting her mother through this. It wasn't so important. She didn't need to know. But another part of her was curious about how her mother's thoughts sounded now, given the change. Or maybe how they ever sounded.

Of course at work they had talked and talked about a system of capture, an extraction tool, for thoughts. This was a big R&D area for companies like Thompson. The last frontier of privacy, blah blah blah. How hard could it be to finally reach into people's faces and claw away at what they were thinking, and to turn that noisy chatter into a cogent transcription? Really stupendously hard, it turned out. But probably not entirely totally impossible. Probably just a matter of time, even if that meant that they'd all be dead and the world would be dead, just a cold and lifeless rock, but it would still happen. Maybe. Ida saw the appeal, and she'd done some grunt work on a mock interface, mostly just color blocking, building a palette, that might have been part of a black cloth project along those lines. She was on such a *don't*-need-to-know basis at Thompson that she might as well have been wearing a blindfold. In the end, though, she didn't want to live in a time when such tech came online and her own thoughts were on offer to the shimmering seals with human genitalia who seemed to encircle her with questions, punching straws into her head to draw out what little she had left. Her so-called thoughts. Her precious precious. She'd have to jump off a building, and she wasn't in an especially big hurry to do that. Not always, anyway.

"Well, I would say yes, I suppose, it did help," her mother answered finally.

"You suppose?"

"Grandpa never left us, no matter how much he threatened to. He remained. Sometimes he sat with us, far away, and you could very nearly set him on fire without him noticing. In fact I remember him burning. I do. Burning very prettily right there in his chair." She pointed at the wall.

"Mother." Ida touched her hand.

"But his distance from us, emotionally, became less threatening. How do you measure emotional distance? Miles? Days? That's almost always the question, I think. I never asked Grandma about it. But because my father stayed I would say the medication worked for us. That's what we all always said, anyway, and I guess that's what I'm saying now."

Her mother looked at Ida, bewildered.

"Is that what I'm saying, sweetheart?"

"Yes, Mom," said Ida. "That is. That's what you've said."

"Oh good." She grabbed Ida's hand. "I made sense, didn't I?"

"You did. You absolutely did."

"I want to. I so want to. You know that, right?"

"You always will to me, Mom."

Her mother looked up at her with such kindness. Her eyes, though, showed something else, and she looked around as if she'd lost something.

"What is it, Mom? Are you okay?"

"Oh yes, oh yes," she said, but she seemed nervous in front of Ida, or shy.

"I was just thinking, dear, that you are almost as beautiful as my daughter. I would very much like for you to meet her. She visits me here. She's coming soon."

She used to correct her mother, but she'd since been advised not to, and sometimes, lately, her mother's phrasing made a strange sort of sense to her.

Ida smiled and took her mother's hand. "I would like that, Mom. I really would."

Together they stared at the door, but the only person to finally come in was the nurse, who said she had to swap out garbage cans because there was sort of a problem with one of them, and that problem, as it was poured out of her mother's garbage can into a paper bag, was certainly nothing that Ida ever wanted to see again.

After work the next day, across town, Ida brought a spoonful of soup to her father's lips.

"You think I'm an imbecile," he said, staring past her hand at the TV.

"I don't."

"An idiot, at any rate. Don't insult me."

"No, Dad."

"You look at me with utter disgust."

Ida stroked her father's forehead. He still had his hair. He had a broad, smooth forehead and if he could be made to stand upright, and dressed in a suit, he would be so handsome.

"Are you tired, Dad?"

"Of course. Why wouldn't I be?"

It was a good answer. Ida was tired, too. Did anyone, when asked, ever say they weren't?

As usual, her father was watching the news, but, as far as she could tell—from the colors on the TV and the old-fashioned clothing the newscasters wore—it was news from a good while ago. Did they show reruns of such things? Maybe this old news was suddenly relevant again?

"What's this, Dad?"

"Just what it looks like. It's a funeral. You have to listen very carefully."

Ida couldn't really understand the men on the screen. They spoke a foreign language, like one she might have learned in high school and since forgotten. She looked at her father and marveled that he seemed to be following this. He was utterly engrossed.

It seemed like a standard newscast. Four men at a table, a wireframe globe spinning behind them. Ida tried to settle in and just be there with her father, to relax and enjoy his company and do something with him. She had so much to do, so much to do, so much to do, but it was useless to think about it. She tried not to look too carefully around her father's room. The bed, the little chair—far too small for anyone who might ever visit him—the window that needed to be cleaned. She focused with all her might on the TV.

"These men are not happy," her father said. "They can't say that because they will lose their jobs. Just look at them. They are holding it in. They always do that. They don't say what they think, so they're scared. No one is fooling me."

"You're probably right."

"Probably? C'mon."

She sat with her father and held his hand, which was heavy and dry.

Then her father said, "That one over there, the white man. I tell you what. He's going to die. The rest of them don't want to admit it, but he knows. Just look at him. He knows."

Ida studied the one her father referred to. He had on a white suit, with white hair, but his face was bright red and sweaty. It was likely, given how old this show was, that this man was already dead. Perhaps his children, too, were dead by now. Anyone who loved or knew him. Or quite old by now, anyway, maybe in a room just like this one, sitting with someone somewhere. Hopefully sitting with someone.

It was getting late, and Ida probably knew better, but she had to try.

"I saw Mom yesterday," she said.

"I've seen her before."

"Well, I saw her yesterday. You know, when people matter to us we see them more than once. We make a regular habit of it."

"I kicked the habit."

"She's doing well."

"She always does well. That's her specialty."

"Well, but she hasn't always. She's been sick, she's had some struggles."

"You mean something didn't go your mother's way? Boy, I'd have loved to see that. What a spectacle. What a rarity. Woman fails to get her own way. World collapses."

"I think illness is in a sort of different category."

Her father didn't respond for a long time.

"Illness is the only category," he finally said.

It had gotten dark out. Her father didn't like the overhead lights, so Ida had given him a little lamp, but she didn't see it now. Whatever she brought in, a lamp, a radio, a vase of flowers, it was always gone when she returned. She used to leave some money in his drawer for outings, in case he wanted something, a piece of candy, a soda, but he would give it away or forget about it and then it too was gone. Only his clothes remained. His sweater, his robe, his pajamas. She had tried to replace the pajamas once but he had grown surly when he put on the new ones. He tore at himself and yelled, accusing her of trying to strangle him. He insisted that she get rid of them.

She tried to speak to the nurses. She knew they were overworked, exhausted, poorly paid, and that they had families of their own. She understood that. But when she asked them if there was something to be done, even if she paid extra, so that what she brought her father, even just the chocolates she knew he liked, might not vanish so quickly from his room, what they told her was that if she, Ida, were around more, if she visited more often, that sort of stuff was less likely to happen. You're never here, they said to her. We never see you. Who knows what goes on in there?

Something seemed wrong with the picture on the TV in her father's room. There were numbers unlike any Ida had seen before—so much prettier than the old ones. They floated over a young man's face and formed a beautiful pattern: a flower, a galaxy. Was that Donny? The sound was down low, or her father's room simply drank in speech until only a foreign garble swirled around, but when the man spoke the numbers seemed to pulse, to breathe.

She'd fallen asleep again. Oh, god. Who knew how late it was and she was afraid to check her phone. Because of calls and texts she didn't want to receive, and actual human hands that would grab her and pull her down deep into the mud. Quietly she gathered her things, kissed her father's forehead, and crept from the room.

"You don't say good night?" asked her father. He was wide awake and he sounded cross.

"Good night, Dad," she whispered. "I gave you a kiss."

"I know that. I'm right here. I was here when you did it. I'm the person you kissed."

"Okay. Okay." She was whispering, even though there were loud voices in the hall, in the other rooms. No one anywhere was much trying to keep it down, despite the late hour. "I will see you soon."

"When, honey?"

"Whenever you want, Dad."

"Well, tomorrow works for me. Tomorrow and the next day. I'm free."

"Okay, I think I can do that." She had meetings upon meetings upon meetings for the rest of her life. Her calendar was dark with obligation.

She returned to his bed and gave his hand a squeeze, then leaned down to drop another light kiss on his forehead.

"A second kiss?" said her father. "I'm not sure that was warranted."

And as Ida drove home, winding through the empty city streets out across the old highway and into the hills where she lived, she couldn't help but think that her father might be right.

Sometimes Ida would forget, and she would appear at the office on Sundays, her face strangely delicate on her head, a visitor to her body. She would stare through the glass at the vast lobby of Thompson. The doors to work were locked on the weekends, of course, and after standing there a while, the intruder alert, which certainly went by a blander name, shot a jolt of current into Ida's legs, sweetening them with pain, and she backed away onto the sidewalk.

If there was a movie playing, Ida bathed in it, alone in the back of the theater. The movies these days were troubling. Children go searching for parents, lost in the snow, and do not find them. A boat's faulty navigation system leads it to an island not on any maps. The island turns out to be, well, everyone knew how these things went. A terrible place. A really unimaginably terrible place.

Here it was, summer, but something was off. In the air, on the faces of people. Just wherever you looked. The city of Chicago, if you could still call it that, was quiet on the weekend, pretty gusts of powder blowing around buildings, unmanned sweeper trucks docked in their charging pads. The restaurants were mostly open, but without too many other customers Ida felt odd bothering the staff.

Today she braved a diner, and sat and ate alone. She had a dark soup and some toast, and she listened to the prettiest piano music from the restaurant's little speaker. Music from under water, from another world. Or maybe just from the next room. But when it came time to pay she couldn't find her server, and no one answered when she politely whispered into the kitchen. She called out *Hello, hello,* until it started to sound strange. She peeked into the kitchen and found no one. The diner had emptied out and it was getting dark. Maybe they'd all gone home and forgotten to charge her, forgotten to lock up. That was a lot of forgetting. It was possible, maybe, but it didn't feel right. She never carried very much cash, so she crept out as apologetically as she could, thinking that she should write a note, or that she might come back. Before leaving she turned to face the kitchen, in case there was a surveillance camera. She shrugged and made a series of gestures that, she hoped, might tell the whole story here, if that were even possible. She wanted to pay, she really did, but there was no one left to pay, and she had no money, and everyone seemingly everywhere had vanished.

For most of the night she walked the city, until that magic hour when the streetlights are given a rest, and the early risers are not yet chewing up space on their way to the great, savage feed. A text came in from Mort—up really early, or maybe, like her, having not yet gone to sleep. He'd been texting her a lot, and now he wanted to come over. He kept referring to a rematch. "I have finished my training," he wrote, "if it pleases Madame."

It sort of didn't please Madame right now. Not really. She sent back a few little emojis, indicating that she was tired and busy, and she threw some other ones in that might make him feel better, some warm and bright little animals, smiling from ear to ear with wet human mouths.

Mort wrote back that he understood, and Ida figured that that was true. That was what was so wonderful about him. Mort probably understood far better than she did.

When June came there was a summer party at work, which meant that gray-faced cubicle worms tried to straighten their backs and stand at the punch bowl without crumbling into powder. The parents among the workforce clustered together, no doubt checking the coarseness of each other's hair shirts. Ida suddenly found herself inside their crop circle.

They were young, still in their twenties, if barely, but their prison was real and gleaming, and even though they sang pretty songs from within, generally you knew to steer wide, clear, and away, tying yourself to a mast if need be. They were afraid to be alone. They wanted reinforcements.

People with kids tended to look at Ida with a mixture of envy and derision, which wasn't so different from how she looked at herself. Right now one of them had singled her out. "I say this as a friend, as someone who just, like, completely loves you, I mean just as you are. You are amazing. Really. But you are nothing without kids. I'm sorry, it's true. I'm so sorry!"

"Hear, hear," a few of them said. "Well put."

"I wish," said Ida. "Nothing still seems like a long way off."

She looked down at her hands, made little fists, held up her fingers as if she'd never seen them before. Hadn't one of the big-time philosophers thrown himself from a window in order to prove that he existed?

"I don't know. I look at pictures of myself from *before*," said one of the parents, "and those pictures look, like, fake. Like they've been Photoshopped? I mean, who was that person? I am fairly certain that in most important ways I didn't really exist back then."

And now? Ida wanted to ask, looking at this smiling, tired bag of sauce in front of her. You're sure you exist now?

"Well," said Ida, trying to detach from orbit and find a childless friend elsewhere, someone to perhaps eat big, scary drugs with, "I do look forward to it some day. A child, wow. I know it would be, it might. I know that I." Ida pictured herself cramming bread into a grown man's mouth, or bathing an aging, unconscious wolf, waking up to terrible shouts. Parenthood?

They were smiling and nodding at her, showing teeth and possibly looking to pounce. "You will," they said. "It does. We know. They just absolutely do. It is not at all, and it just isn't and it isn't and it isn't. We fucking swear to you."

Later in the party her phone buzzed, and she got a text from Donny.

The text read, "Do unto others, as much as you can. Just keep doing and doing and doing, until they can't breathe. Until they stop moving."

"Okay," she wrote back. It didn't sound so bad. "Where are you? Please help."

He texted back: "The call is coming from inside the house."

She stood on her toes, scanned the room, surveying and dismissing one disappointing face after another, but no Donny. It surprised her how much she wanted to see him. She checked room after room, but nothing, and as she started to leave, not so happy with this game, Maury barreled up, pawing some undertouched parts of her, drunk as fuck.

"Jesus, Maury, please. You're totally groping me."

"I know, Ida. I know I am!" He smiled in a way that wasn't so endearing. It kind of creeped her out.

"Okay, well, stop it. Stop it. Stop it. It doesn't feel good."

Her voice surprised her.

"I did something terrible, Ida. I must confess."

Must you, though? she thought. She really didn't need to know whatever crummy deviance he'd allowed himself. Wasn't there a service that absorbed your dirty secrets for a fee? She'd pay, for god's sake. Did you have to test a friendship with such material?

For some reason he held up his phone. "I pretended to be some-one else. I couldn't help it. That was me, just now."

She wanted to say, who else would it have been, when she figured out what he was trying to tell her. And then, as she was pulling her-self away from him, she felt something tickle in her throat and sud-denly it was too late. The pill slipped from her mouth and landed on the carpet between them, like a lost piece of bone.

"Oh my god," she said.

Maury just blinked at her.

She grabbed the thing and made her excuses and got out of there. Fuck him, anyway. If he hadn't been harassing her she wouldn't have coughed the stupid thing up.

Ida was tired in some new kind of way. Cooked and done and smeared all over the road. She almost slept in her clothes. She couldn't bear getting undressed. Her teeth and face would have to wait. She would clean them in the morning. So much washing would just happen another time, and everything would be fine. Jesus. Like a four-month bath. A retreat to an underwater cave. A vow of silence, a blood transfusion, followed by a four-year sleep. She opened a window, hoping to hear something, a bird, a siren, voices. Too much room tone in her own house, room tone that could just kill a girl. But nothing was out there. It was a perfectly quiet night.

Her phone buzzed as she crawled into bed. Another text from "Donny."

"Mine comes out sometimes too," the text read. "Smiley face. (Sorry, I don't know how to make emoji symbols!)"

"Oh. Thank you. Is this Maury?"

"Hi. I'm sorry I lied. And I felt so bad when your pill came up. I hate that! Sometimes after I oil my pill I dip it in sand. I know that sounds weird. But it works! What kind of oil do you use?"

Ida snuggled into bed. It was a lot more pleasant dealing with

Maury this way, or at least it wasn't repulsive. The bar had gotten lower. "Sometimes when I cough one up," wrote Ida, "I wonder if it's that day's pill, or one from before."

"Oh my god, I have wondered that too."

"Have you ever thought of marking the pills before you swallow them?"

"No I have not!"

"Then you could know."

"That's true," wrote Maury. "You would definitely know. Tag those little guys. Name them. That way you would never lose track. I would hate to lose one. I think I would feel sad."

Summer burned out early and a little bit of icy wind curled over the city. Ida was breathing into her hands before too long, dragging herself from work to home, work to home. She saw her parents when she could, and if they didn't always see her, at least they felt her next to them. Or they felt someone, a body, a person, who spoke and touched them and smiled when she could.

It wasn't a romance that started with Donny, so much as a cluster of unrelated encounters after work, usually close to silent, in which it became easier and easier to meld her body with his. Donny was lithe and graceful and so endlessly mysterious, which maybe only meant that she no longer knew what to think of anyone. He hardly spoke and they didn't laugh together and she felt no need to reveal herself to him. But his silence made her feel good and safe, and she looked for him, more often than not, to mute some larger ruckus that seemed to be stalking her no matter where she went. She worried that when she undressed him she'd find, instead of the usual gray meat that made up a man, a small golden animal in place of his groin, or a fairy, or just some moss. In all the best ways he didn't seem human.

"I'm not someone you want to be investing any feeling in," he told her one day, with the brightest possible smile. "Try to look right through me. There's someone behind me and he's coming for you, I'm sure. I'm just in the way."

"Okay, Donny," she said. "I appreciate the advice." It's as if you're already not here, she didn't say. It's as if I imagined you.

"Ida," he said.

"Yes?" She looked at his clean, young face.

"For now, there's nothing better than this."

He crawled on top of her and she could feel him breathing. He was so light, so thin, so small, no more than the weight of an extra blanket or two, really.

For now, for today, for this very minute, it was certainly okay, she thought. It would do.

It was October, her father's birthday, and she showed up on a Saturday afternoon with chocolates, the ones littered with the kind of salt that looked like shards of glass. She brought flowers for his night table, and new clothing, too, but she didn't show it to him. It could wait in his closet, and if it vanished maybe that wasn't so bad, as long as it ended up somewhere, covering someone, keeping them warm or dry or cozy.

"I always thought that if I worked in a think tank, I would drown," her father said, sucking on a chocolate.

"Yes, well. That is a danger, Dad."

"You think I don't know what you do."

"I don't think that."

"Yes you do. You think I don't know and you think you can't talk about it and you think I won't understand. Don't insult me. I'm not an idiot."

"No, Dad, I know that."

"You think I've already died. You visit me here like you're visiting my grave. You come to sit at my grave. You even bring flowers. But here I am. Look. I'm right here."

Her father was a beautiful man, really. Tall and fine-featured and still elegant in his nursing home bed.

"I see you. I'm very happy you're alive."

"This isn't a grave, it's a bed. There's a window. No one has a window in their coffin. No one can look out their window at a parking lot or a hill. No one has sheets and a pillow in their coffin. You don't get to sit up and eat a sandwich."

"I know that."

"Do you see a tombstone in here?"

"No."

"Feel free to look. I'm not hiding anything. Take a look around."

"I don't need to, Dad. I believe you."

"Think tank."

"I know."

"You don't work at a think tank."

"You might be right, Dad. Sometimes even I don't know what I do. They don't always tell us what things are for."

"No one will ever tell you what something is for. For Christ's sake. We don't get that information. Don't expect that."

"I guess I shouldn't. But I spend my life there. It's okay if you don't know. You don't work there. But what about me? Shouldn't I know?"

"What about *you*? Don't start to get sad. That's not what this is about, being *sad*. Your sadness isn't the issue here, Ida. That's a distraction. Don't change the subject."

Her father was right. It could be heavily distracting. She finished feeding him, patted his arm, and left his room for a little while. Maybe some air or some sun or an area free of people would be nice, if such a thing existed. There were hallways and hallways in this home, with room after room, and if she ever made a mistake, and looked inside one, really looked, she saw people in beds all alone, connected to bags, mouths agape, struggling to breathe. She saw men in ill-fitting gowns, sprawled on the floor. Women with no hair, sobbing in their chairs. Now in the hallway she kept her head down, watching her feet, and soon she was outside, where there was a little bit of lawn ringing the parking lot.

The light was funny today, catching surfaces just so. Little sparkling things glimmered from the grass, from the parking lot, everywhere. Like jewels that had dropped from somewhere, which was stupid, she knew. Probably just little stones, maybe washed up over everything from a recent rain. She thought she might sit down, but there was her car, just waiting, and maybe she'd had enough for the day. Maybe it was time to go. She'd visited a little bit, and it was possible that her father would fall asleep soon, anyway.

A nurse approached Ida just as she was reaching for her keys.

"You here to see your father?"

"Yes I am. How are you today?"

Maybe if she showered this person with kindness, something would unlock in the tough, ungiving dispositions of the nurses, and maybe they'd look after her dad better when she wasn't around.

"If you're here to see him, why are you outside?"

"I just came out for some air."

"There's air inside. There's air everywhere. That's what the world is."

"I know."

"He can't see you if you're out here. You can't see him. You might as well be at home."

"I'm going back in."

"You weren't, though. You were going to leave."

"No."

"Don't tell me. I see your face. I can read your thoughts. You think I can't?"

Ida scanned up at her father's window. He would never be looking out. He didn't do that. He didn't really stand up anymore, although he did love his window. But she wouldn't want him to see this just the same. He wouldn't understand, not that she did either.

"Anyway, there aren't too many thoughts to read," the nurse said. "Just one big one. I gotta get out of here. I gotta go. Where's the door. That's the only thought anyone has ever had. In all of history. It's not just you."

For no reason that she could think of, Ida told the nurse that her mother was also in a home.

"Everybody's somewhere," said the nurse.

"She's at the Sullivan Gardens."

"That's a place."

"I go back and forth."

"How else would you do it?"

"My mother and my father."

"I don't imagine you'd visit any other kind of person in a place like that."

"No, I guess not."

The nurse almost smiled at her. "I know you're leaving, so you can go ahead and leave. I'm not going to stop you."

"I might have to," said Ida. "I don't feel so great."

"Your father will die soon."

"I know."

"You won't be here. Chances are. People are never here. They know not to be. People aren't stupid. They wake up that day and they know to stay away. You don't go into a burning house. You feel the heat. You keep walking."

"So it's not just me."

"Nothing is just you, dear. Trust me."

"I'd like to try to be here. When that happens."

"You'll get a phone call. It might be me calling you. It might be someone else. I make the phone calls when I'm here, but I'm not always here. If I'm here, I'll call you. We have your number. Your number is first. You're the emergency contact. But it won't be an emergency. The emergency will have already happened. It will have come and gone. I'll say hello, and I'll ask to speak to you. You'll probably say that it's you on the phone. Some people, fancy people, say This is *she,* or This is *he.* And that's when I say, It's about your father. That's how the call will go up to that point."

"Okay, well, I guess it's good to know this. I appreciate the information. May I ask your name?"

"It's Lorraine."

Ida took the nurse's hand. "Lorraine," she said. "I am really pleased to meet you."

The nurse pulled back her hand. "Don't be pleased. If you get a phone call, and the person says that it's Lorraine from Sweethill Village, then it's me calling, and you should never be happy to hear from me."

"Okay."

"Don't be happy when I call."

"I won't be," said Ida. "I promise."

And then, in her throat, Ida felt the familiar crawling, the little pill surging up, filling her mouth. This time she managed to get her hand up, to block it from getting out, but she had to double over and clench her teeth together.

Then she felt the nurse's hand rubbing her back, so softly, so gently, that she relaxed in some way that startled her, and her mouth opened and the pill rolled out onto the asphalt.

Ida and the nurse looked at it, shining like a perfect white tooth. It was hard to imagine that it had been in her stomach all day. It looked perfect, even cleaner and whiter than when she'd swallowed it.

"It's okay," the nurse said. "You can leave it there."

"I'd better not."

"Leave it. Trust me. Just look around for a minute. Everyone else is leaving theirs. It makes the world look prettier. Why keep something like that for yourself?"

Those shiny things in the grass, the glittering crystals in the parking lot, the glinting everywhere she looked. Like the tiny white skulls of birds. Tablets strewn everywhere, glowing at her feet.

Blueprints for St. Louis

It was winter, which meant that a pelvic frost had fallen across the land. Or maybe just across Roy and Helen's apartment. And, in truth, the frost had long since matured into a kind of bodily aloofness, just shy of visible flinching when they passed each other in the halls, or when they co-slept in the intimacy-free bed they'd splurged on. Why not have the best sleep of your life next to the dried-out sack of Daddy you've long taken for granted, whose wand no longer glows and quivers for you and for whom you no longer quietly melt? You had to track the erotic cooling back into summer, or the prior spring, and, well, didn't the seasons and the years just dog-pile one another when you tried to solve math like that?

Helen wasn't particularly concerned, because, whatever, there was a clarity to the coldness, right? And screw Roy if he'd fallen down a brightly colored porn hole, pummeling himself to images of animated youngsters slithering around nude, in grown-up crotch gear, in a cartoon fairyland. Internet histories weren't her favorite literary genre, but she knew how to read them. Anyway, if her husband's use-case viability on the marital graph had taken a nosedive, then so, too, had her own burden. She had her friends, she had her work on the memorial, and she had the showerhead. When she and Roy first got married, whenever ago, Helen's mother had told her that if people don't visit, you don't have to host. Period, full stop.

And even though Helen's take on this advice now was off-label, it applied just fine to her touchless union. The body unloved, the body unhandled and unseen. The body as a ghost in training for whatever soiled world came next. Anyway, wasn't left-alone the best place to wind up?

Maybe old age and the cold blue death of the groin would solve that. Maybe Helen would inherit a sweet and useless Roy, post-pornography, sitting politely behind a drool cloth, swaddled in food-stained sweaters. She'd feed him until he cooed and maybe sometimes they would run out of gruel and she would watch his hunger grow, watch his eyes turn small and sad. Would it be so terrible? The sexual urge would be merely an embarrassing spasm of the past. They'd been friends once, before they'd gotten into designing memorials for unspeakable catastrophes. Intense and respectful partners in their architectural firm. Mutually committed cattle prodders of each other's darker, stranger brains, torturing out each other's best ideas, before the chemical repulsion and bed-death had struck. Maybe by old age they'd return to form, be ideal dance partners again, if only they could stay alive long enough.

The problem was today and tomorrow and the next huge bunch of days, the entirety of their middle age, really, which shouldn't be just a rotten footbridge you had to navigate, with a creepy old troll beating off underneath it. Roy was technically handsome, but he preened, and he moped, and he fished for so many compliments that Helen was fished out, empty, unable to spray any favorable speech over his prim, needy body. Lately he'd been taking himself to the gym with more ambition and lust than he showed for their collaborative design work, and he was all cut up now, a strange, Photoshopped musculature slipped over his bones like a bronzed wet suit. She should have wanted to handle the new body he'd built, use it to snuff out her baser urges, not that Roy offered it to her, but she asked that he keep it covered. In loose-fitting layers, please. It stank of his not-so-hidden effort to attract a mammal outside the home. To sport with it and lick its fur, no doubt. Plus, she had tolerated her husband better when he wasn't such a vain custodian of the ephemeral—one mustn't fawn over that which will rot, someone important probably once said.

What consumed them both right now was the situation in St. Louis, for which their firm had been ceremoniously commissioned to design the memorial. Months after the bombing, the city was still digging out. Thirty dead souls, the news had said when it happened. But everyone knew that number wasn't real. It was low by a couple of decimal points. For days, the toll did not breach a hundred, which seemed impossible. Where did these cautious estimates come from? Maybe from actual bodies. Maybe this meant that the other, more plentiful dead were simply nowhere to be found, in the same way that wind can't be found. What you did was you factored in the missing, and privately you did not call them "missing." Thousands of people had not suddenly left their homes that morning and vanished to the mountains. When you watched the footage of the bombing, the dark slab of glass folding over itself like a blanket, then erupting into a pale brown flower of smoke, and you calculated the typical occupancy, not just of the office tower but of the surrounding plaza, with its underground restaurants and shops, its perimeter of cafes, along with the time of day, the number thirty was a violent piece of wishful thinking, heavy, heavy, heavy on the wish.

"10k+," Roy had texted Helen from wherever he was the day it happened.

He wasn't wrong. It emerged that explosives had been buried in the foundation of the tower when it was being built, two years before, by some slithering motherfuckers on the construction crew. Stashed down there the night before the footings were poured, apparently, and then triggered when the building was finished and stuffed to the gills with people. In burning daylight, a time of high commerce, maximum human traffic. Not a government building, so far as anyone knew. Just as dense a cluster of people as any in the Midwest, excepting one or two zones in downtown Chicago. And so, and so. They had the perpetrators on video, brutes in hard hats. Except that they were skinny and they laughed a lot and were often seen hugging one another. Four of them had walked off the job on the same day, before the building had even started to rise up out of the concrete. How that very act—quitting in a group, never to be seen again—hadn't been some sort of security trigger was beyond Helen, but whatever, hindsight was a foul drug. And now everyone was asking, Who were these men and where had they gone? Oh, please, Helen thought, whenever this particular investigation blistered onto the screen. The St. Louis Four. The villains of Missouri. Can we please not believe that finding these men will matter at all? Please?

"Terrorism" wasn't really the term anymore. Helen found that it soured in her mouth, like a German word for some obscure feeling. "Tax" seemed to be a finer way to put it. A tax had been levied in St. Louis. In New Orleans last year, in Tucson three years back. Et cetera. A tax on comfort, safety. A price paid for being alive, for waking up. Occasionally the tax collector came. Not just occasionally. Quite a lot these days. You could run out of breath trying to name all the cities that had been hit in this country. The collector came, and people were subtracted from space. Buildings withered into rubble. One's imagination needed to frequently dilate in order to accommodate the ways and means, and otherwise-smart men and women were busy with their scuffed and crummy crystal balls trying to figure out what was next, and how, and how. As if this forecasting ever . . . oh forget it. Soon you knew not to be surprised, and this awareness was chilling. A low hum could be heard during the day, the night, at all times. You walked in a space that might not really be there. There was no longer anything proverbial when it came to danger, nothing to invent, no more fiction of dark days to come. The dark days were here. They were now.

In light of this, it was somehow Roy and Helen's calling to honor the site with a memorial. Or to try to, to actually compete for this kind of work, squirming through town halls and public debates, spinning a story about their vision, which was only ever a humble story to the effect that nothing anyone did could ever be enough. Their track record so far wasn't the worst, which was not much of a feel-good fact for either of them, even if a sort of undertaker's renown had attached itself to their firm over the years. They made their mark by designing large public graves where people could gather and where maybe really cool food trucks would also park. There was money for this, and money for this, and money for this. Hooray. Except that now Helen found it hard to view any other kind of design commission—for a vanilla-white office building in their own downtown Chicago, for example—as anything other than a future headstone, a kind of sarcophagus that would briefly house living, glistening people before they were lowered into the earth or scattered out over the lake in a burst of powder. If you were an architect, you designed tombs, for before or for after. What was the difference?

Helen kept a map pinned above her desk because she thought she might see something in the pattern of fallen cities: a story. Detectives did this to solve crimes. She thought it might tell her what to build. But sometimes, when she and Roy marveled at it, it seemed to them like a coloring book that hadn't been filled in all the way yet. Sure, there were some spaces still to shade, whole cities left strangely untouched, but not that many. And there was always tomorrow.

St. Louis should not have been high on the list of targets, maybe not on the list at all, but that seemed to be the point these days, in the year of our sorrow. The years and years of it. A new and unspoken list of vulnerable sites had emerged: sweet zones, soft parts of the American body that could be knifed open and spilled out by the most skilled urban surgeons the world had ever seen.

Six months after the St. Louis attack, Roy and Helen had been invited to submit a proposal, and they'd gone through their usual tangled brainstorm, smoothing over the sharper ideas of their junior staff, whiteboarding a design that would appear sufficiently nonthreatening in the space, a kind of tranquilizing maze of low walls and open rooms for visitors to throw themselves around in and grieve. Roy called it the sanatorium aesthetic, and he wasn't that far off.

One day, as the deadline loomed, they walked along the lake, which was flat and black, even as the wind pounded them. They started, brokenly, to drill down toward what they might possibly build, what it would look and sound like, what sort of feelings they were trying to create. Usually you had to dance around the stakeholders to determine the emotional bolus of a work, as they called it. But the stakeholders for this project? Only the entire population of the United States of America.

Helen didn't want to aim high, she started to say, so much as she wanted to aim into a kind of hidden space. "I don't want you to be able to picture it when I talk about it," she told Roy. "You shouldn't be able to photograph it. I mean, like the lake—you wouldn't even want to photograph it. You shouldn't be able to draw it. That's my problem."

"Gosh, that really is your problem."

"I don't know," she said, gesturing at the sky, which was not particularly pretty or interesting that afternoon. It was not the kind of sky you would ever take a picture of, and Helen found that compelling. "Is there a better memorial than that? The sky?"

"Ha," Roy said. "It's good. It's moody. Maybe it's a bit obvious, though?"

"Isn't the sky just a gravestone," Helen said, "and we're all buried under it?"

"Oooh. Not bad. I see what you did there. But, no offense, why are we talking about this?"

Helen had to do this, to think too grandly or wrongly in order to maybe get closer to what was called for. "It's almost like," she said, "what if you had to design the afterlife exactly as you really think it is. Not something aspirational, some bullshit heaven. Not a religious fantasy. The truth."

"Yeah?" Roy said. "As in . . . oblivion? You want to build an oblivion theme park?"

He didn't care about any of this right now, Helen could tell, and maybe he had a point.

"I assume you don't believe in, well, anything?" When she thought back to their first conversations in grad school, prickly and intense and flirty, she wasn't sure if this had ever come up. Was that possible? She had adored and then admired him for so long and now she knew him inside and out, and she felt she understood him to the core. Was it possible that he harbored private, unknowable ideas about his own death and whatever might happen after?

"Okay, let's assume that you're agnostic," Helen said. "We die and there's nothing."

"Sometimes there's nothing before you die," Roy cut in. "Don't forget that. A foreshadowed nothingness."

"Okay, let's say that you want to make an experiential piece that invites people to inhabit that sort of emptiness. How do you do it?"

Roy looked up. "How? As in, how do certain midwestern architects make a credible design of the one, true afterlife? Jesus, Helen. Are we really having this conversation?"

He seemed to give it some thought, but there was something unnatural about how theatrically he pondered, as if he already knew what he was going to say but was pausing for effect. This was the Roy who spouted off at arts panels, who was about to spray fine, floral bullshit across the auditorium.

"I like the question," he said. "It reveals something important, and I see where you're going with it. If you make a space like that you connect visitors with the dead, which is a pretty big artistic win."

Helen winced. *Big artistic win.*

"In the end," Roy said, "the question falls apart because the answer is just too easy. It's too obvious. Why not just kill them? Then they'll get the real and true afterlife. Who needs to simulate anything when you have the real thing? Someone already designed death. We were beaten to the punch."

He smiled at her and very nearly seemed to be gloating.

Okay. God. "This isn't a battle of wits, Roy," she said. But then she wondered if maybe it was, and that was what was wrong. Partly. When one person thinks it's not a contest.

They stopped and looked out over the lake.

"I was hoping we could produce work without a body count, though. A modest goal."

"Oh, you mean because too many people have died already?"

"Jesus, Roy."

"None of this works if I can't be honest with you," he whispered.

"There are other reasons that none of this works," she said.

"Helen, I was joking. I was trying to be funny."

But why? She didn't say. To what end? And aren't we supposed to be doing this together?

"I don't know, Roy. Can we think about a tranquil space, not heavy on physical material, not oppressive and thick, that isn't just a New Age wank space with wind chimes and shit? Can we do that?"

Roy admitted that this sounded good, that this was something they could shoot for.

The memorial planning went on for weeks. They mocked up models, strung wire through their studio and tuned it to different tensions, just to explore suspended structures that might allow for a subterranean feeling without actually trapping people underground. Haunt the viewers but don't stress them out. And almost every day, sometimes in the afternoon and sometimes in the very early morning, they walked the city together, looking at space and light, growing ever more certain of what they didn't want the memorial to be.

Roy was kind and gracious, suppressing his own ideas while generously fielding every wild and unbuildable notion from Helen, perhaps knowing that her interest in reality, in plausibility and practicality, could be low. She couldn't help herself; she went on and on about the mourners. They were still here, she was saying, in this world, but they were conflicted. They were pulled elsewhere, to the place where their loved ones were. Wherever that was. Survivors lived in both places. That was what she wanted this monument to say. She wanted it to feel like that, the tension between two worlds.

"That's some Schrödinger's cat bullshit," Roy said. "And I love it. That's what I want, too. That's exactly right."

For a little while they walked arm in arm, and for a little while things seemed different. But what had they really agreed on? Helen wondered. What were they even talking about?

All the while Roy must have known that there was no building design behind this idea, that time was really upon them and something had to take shape on paper. The office was waiting to pounce at their go-ahead, and he needed to ring the bell. Helen realized that he'd been slowly laying the groundwork for his own plan, which maybe he'd had in his head all along. It was simple and obvious and probably inevitable, and he told it to her in pieces, over the course of a few days. It was to be a hollow square glass museum, low on the plaza, with a center that could not be accessed or even seen. A black void where the building and the shops had been. Right. There were details and details and details, and a narrative had to be written, because, well, yeah, but this was a square with a hole in it. To Helen, it resonated just a wee bit of other memorials, built and unbuilt, which was probably shrewd, on Roy's part. He wanted their work to get the go-ahead, whereas sometimes she suffered the classic ambivalence of an architect. Maybe her designs had a kill switch on purpose.

They went home and had dinner, and that night Roy was already calling it a lock, commissioning renderings, and speccing out site maps and plans and all the work that had to happen even to get this thing ready for the review board.

There was really just one more thing to deal with for now, and they had both been dreading it.

They had to finally sit down and look at bids from the pharmaceuticals, which were fighting their way onto the proposal, vying to be the providers of the chemical component that every memorial these days was more or less expected to have: a gentle mist to assist the emotional response of visitors and drug them into a torpor of sympathy. Not garment-rending sympathy, but something more dignified. A mood was delivered via fog. Discreetly, and mildly, with microdoses misting through carefully arranged spouts, the way an outdoor mall in the summer might be air-conditioned. You didn't see it and you didn't smell it. You strolled through a field or a plaza or a series of dark, marble tunnels, whatever, sipping the sorrow-laced air, and, when you finally departed, a kind of low-grade catharsis had been triggered. You were bursting with feeling. Big artistic win.

It was sponsorship and it was gross, but because it was essentially invisible, and because people genuinely seemed to seek it out—attendance had undeniably spiked—Roy and Helen had been looking the other way and letting it happen and now they really didn't have a choice. It was an inevitable shortcut, or even a stage of evolution, in architecture, assisting the public's reaction and securing that most prized of currencies: human fucking feeling. How to create it, how to create it? And why not use all the help you could get?

But here was Roy saying that he didn't want to agree to anything yet, and to hell with these companies for trying to leverage a sacred memorial with their goddamned money. "Maybe we only consent to a zoned dispensary this time," he said. "There should be an area, cordoned off, where the feelings are more intense."

"Intense how?"

"Like harder, more honest."

"Oh, some feelings aren't honest?"

"None of them are, Helen. It's fake, right? It's a drug spout in the ground. Or it's a gas stream pulsing from the ass of a mechanical bird flying a figure eight around the burial ground. Isn't that the idea, that we can't make people feel exactly what we want with our work, with what we make, so we poison them instead?"

"Poison."

"Sure, it's poison. In high enough doses."

"Like water, then. Like oxygen."

"Exactly like water and oxygen. A perfect comparison. You just read my mind."

"I couldn't help it. The door to your face was open and the text was scrolling inside. Impossible to miss."

Roy shook his head. "On the other hand, why not put people in a more pensive or reflective state? Why not even stoke their anger a bit?"

"Because those are the moods they bring to us. Those are the moods we correct."

"Okay, do you hear how that sounds, Helen? We correct their feelings? Really? I guess I'm just saying that right now we are therapists. We are not designers. We try to make people feel better."

"You make that sound dirty."

"I guess I'm not sure why we're even arguing about this," Roy said. He sounded defeated. "I don't think the ingredients are within our purview. I don't think we can edit those parameters."

"Not with chemicals, we can't," Helen said.

"Meaning?"

"Look, I don't care how happy or blissed out or in touch with the one true good earth you are, if you walk into a certain space, situated on a certain site, and that space has been shaped to the nth fucking degree, your mood, if we want it to, will freaking collapse like a lung."

"I don't know. Drugs are stronger than buildings."

"Maybe we make our buildings more potent, then," Helen said. "We increase the dosage."

Roy smiled at her. He raised an empty hand in a toast. Such a small and delicate hand. "Cheers," he said, and he softly pawed the air.

After they won the bid, with a forty-eighth-iteration proposal that was mildly tolerated by all—a black granite labyrinth, inset with dark transparencies, as if panels of the stone itself were made of glass, which, however badass that would have been, they weren't— Roy went out to St. Louis. Roy was the face, the body, the organism. Maybe he had sweet young people he fucked; Helen couldn't be sure. He caught the temperature of the place and tried to decode the deeper desires of the city, which could then be met or thwarted so that the appropriate tension might infuse the final project. He photo-documented and did flyovers and he stuck his finger into the client's collective rotten body to determine where the hard command center was. These kinds of projects often blew up in your face. You were fired while you slept. So Roy, with his temper and his charm and his fit little body, stayed out there and fought like a mongrel to keep them in the game.

Helen spent that time getting lost at the drafting table, sketching mostly, working from the gut, ignoring what she knew in order to make way for what interested her far more—what she didn't know. For instance, she knew that she felt tremendous sorrow for the dead and thought about them often, if vaguely. What she didn't know was why she wasn't crippled with grief, stupefied at the scale of the atrocity, unable to move or speak. This was a mystery. She wanted to draw a purely empty space, which wasn't as easy as it sounded. Heavy lines were required, of all things, and not just for framing the so-called void, as people in her profession loved to say, but for actual fucking substance. She had to ready the space for haunting. Purity was called for. This was a tombstone for a city, a funeral for a feeling of safety that was now gone. Leaving a blank page was not the same thing. That was a cop-out, and, anyway, you couldn't shit on the client that way. Partly because she herself was the client, and Roy was the client, and so was everyone they knew, and everyone they didn't. Now you had to view the world, the air itself, as something that could be torn away to reveal an eerier sort of place. Maybe that sounded like bullshit, but sometimes, sometimes, this process—if followed strictly and without concern for hovering meddlers—led to a wild, unstable kind of vacuum that you were not always prepared to be sucked into, Helen thought, even if you thought you were curious, even if you thought you couldn't be shocked.

That was what she tried to draw, and that was sometimes what she and Roy tried to build, even though "build" was a strange word, and you sounded like a punk if you said "erase" or something pretentious like that. *Like, in my work, I erase the landscape in order to reveal the true terrain of the world.* Yeah, uh, no. Maybe it didn't make sense, any of it, but it didn't have to. Sometimes it just had to sort of look pretty and make you sad and thoughtful. That was Memorial Theory 101. In the end, no one cared what you thought, or said, about a memorial you made. That sort of verbal posturing was for students and the simperingly boneless teachers who floated over them, gushing endless praise out of their open necks.

Roy phoned from St. Louis, early in the process, and even though a working design had been approved, the understanding—Helen's understanding, anyway—was that certain, uh, changes could still be made, and these changes could, caveat, significantly alter and enhance and improve the original, shit-sucking plan, which she suddenly thought might better belong, in miniature, on the wall of a Starbucks.

What Helen envisioned, she told Roy, was a series of soft columns swelling out of the plaza, but almost imperceptibly. You almost wouldn't even know they were there.

"You know how there are some people who think that if they could only sharpen their vision they would see ghosts?" Helen asked.

"I didn't know that," Roy said. "Interesting."

The plaza itself, Helen went on, would be poured from a spongy material, so that visitors might feel as though they were sinking as they walked along. Playground rubber, maybe? The columns would be slab-like, but ephemeral—Helen emphasized this word: "You know, very nearly not there," she told him—fabricated out of a kind of stable, nearly elastic, she didn't know how else to put it, *smoke.*

"You can admire them as sculpture—they will be beautiful, and up close the smoke will reveal a texture, sort of like porcelain, with streaks and veins and imperfections in the surface. But, from farther away, they may just look like clouds. Rogue clouds that have fallen from the sky."

Roy was quiet for a while. She thought she could hear him typing. "That sounds nice," he finally said. "Aside from wondering how this remotely relates to the approved plan, am I supposed to be asking how you'll achieve this?"

"Other than the obvious way?"

Roy was rummaging at the other end of the line. Talking to someone or watching TV. Helen listened into the room and listened and listened, on the verge of hearing something clear. Maybe he was falling from an airplane. She wasn't even kidding. There was so much wind around him.

"I mean, how serious are you?" he said. "This sounds maybe more speculative? Which is cool. Which is, you know, I know it's part of your process but I'm living in reality right now. I'm in an actual hotel room, in the actual real world. I'm talking to the board, or, really, they're talking to me, very sternly—they are literally holding my hand like I'm a child—and I'm talking to the mayor and the city and the state, and in my downtime I am having nonconsensual elevator sex with the donors, who are huge hairy creatures with indeterminate genitalia, because they get to have whatever little thing they want from me."

"How nice for you."

"I don't have a choice, Helen. Seriously, how possible is this, your sticky smoke? Are we really spitballing this idea right now, at this fucking late date? Am I supposed to be telling people that this is what we are doing?"

"Well, whatever you do, please don't refer to it as sticky smoke. It sounds like a carnival attraction. With a little bit of work, we can find some seductive language. That's never so hard."

She wanted to laugh. *Never so hard.* Finding seductive language was the hardest thing in the world. There wouldn't be language for this. Not in her lifetime.

"Jesus, Helen. The tech—and you know this very well—doesn't allow for what you're talking about. I mean, right? Suddenly I'm the bad guy because of physics?"

Helen sighed. "That's not why you're the bad guy, Roy."

They covered other topics, because they had a stupid business to run, and so many details to haggle over—zoning and permissions and negotiations with contractors, along with political tensions that Helen couldn't even fathom—and then, just as they were saying good night, Helen said she needed to ask him a question.

Roy was still distracted; he would always be. Some muscle in his face produced the word "yeah," but otherwise nobody was home. After finding out what he needed to know from Helen, he'd moved on to gather information from other sources. This was Roy spreading himself so thin that you could see through him. At least in person he knew to tilt his face into postures of interest, taming his little mannequin body. So Helen was silent for a while. She heard the same dull murmur in the background. A voice or a bird or the wind, or just some subvocal turbulence on the phone line. It was almost pretty.

"What?" Roy said, suddenly impatient. "What do you want to ask me?"

"I just wanted to know . . . who's that with you?"

"What?"

"Next to you, Roy. Just look. In the bed. Touching you while you talk. What a curious creature. Who is that? I'd really like to know."

As she said this, she pictured someone, something, crawling over her husband's body. The most gorgeous living thing.

Roy said nothing. Maybe he turned off the television, or maybe something else caused a rapid drop in room tone, because now the sheer silence was staggering. It was shocking to Helen. Like, you'd need a machine to achieve that kind of quiet. The world had been scrubbed of noise, just because she'd said a bunch of words. That was what a spell was, maybe. Had a mere sentence of hers ever had such an effect before? She could hear Roy breathe; she could hear the churn of his body.

"I don't know what you're talking about, Helen."

It wasn't like she expected a different answer, or particularly cared. Confessions and denials were equally troubling. Answers in general were so often disappointing. Was there any speech at all that didn't, in the end, cause a little bit of dejection?

"No, I guess you don't," she said.

"I mean, if I could show you, I would."

"Show me, Roy. Switch over to video. Show me the room and the closets and the hallway. That'd be great. Thanks."

"Uh, okay. I'll have to call you back. I'll call you back."

She laughed out loud, but it came out a little bit off, like a shout.

"Good night, Roy," she said. "Sleep well." And she hung up.

The apartment was cold and she couldn't wait to crawl under the covers. "Oh, and by the way," Helen said to no one, as she readied herself for bed. "You can bleed smoke into a clear skin, no problem." She laughed softly. It was not as strange as it might have been to be talking out loud to herself. "You'd want to use a large-field polymer, of course. Totally transparent and ridiculously thin. I guess it's a kind of windowpane balloon, in a way, but its contours can be fixed nonspherically, which gives it any shape you want, including tufts and wisps and whatnot, like a cloud. A sort of scientific version of a balloon animal. Low-tech, really. And what you get is a shape made of smoke with the barest hint of skin—a person, a column, a cloud, anything. You could even make a maze, and fill the walls of the maze with dark black smoke.

"So, yeah," she whispered, turning out the light in her empty apartment. "That's how you'd do it, if you were to do it. The physics aren't an issue. But honestly I'm not sure anymore that that's the way to go."

It was late and she was very tired. She could hardly even hear herself, as she started to fall asleep.

"I just can't honestly say that it's the right idea for this particular project."

When Roy returned from St. Louis he didn't come home. Helen wouldn't have minded seeing him, to shake hands maybe, to perform some soft footwork that might approximate closure, but Roy had apparently made his decision, and soon some sweethearts from the office came for his things, operating with a list, leaving behind only an old pair of shoes. The transaction was either respectfully nonverbal, Helen thought, or calmly hostile. Was there much of a difference? It was interesting when a set of feelings went so unspoken for so long that they drifted into the unknown. Did they expire or fester? Maybe one day she'd find out.

Construction was under way on the memorial, and the opening wasn't that far off, but rather than hover in St. Louis and fret, micromanaging the construction of their sorrowful mall, as she'd started to think of it, Helen stayed in Chicago and took walks along the lake. More often than not she ended up in one of the older graveyards of the city. For research, she told herself. Because wasn't that really all they did anymore, build new graveyards? She had no family dead in these places, no one to mourn. Everyone she grieved these days was unknown to her, which made her grief seem more like self-pity. Was that true of all grief? Who the hell knew. She toured the marked paths and cut across the grass when she could, because that was where you could start to feel something, however fleeting. Sometimes there were woods to traverse and then she'd burst out into a patch of graves on the other side. More dead to consider. Folks who died long before she was born. Cemetery design had not changed in some time. The aesthetic was pretty resilient. Maybe it wasn't an aesthetic. Just an instinct for shelter. She marveled at the sight lines, at the effortlessly endless rows of dead, each name, each life, hollowed out in space.

Of course it was too late. You couldn't simply plant grass in St. Louis and design the simplest of headstones. There were too many dead. A technical problem. But a headstone could shrivel into a narrow granite pin, with a name inscribed vertically. Didn't that solve the issue? Of course it didn't, because no one even knew what the issue was. And whatever slick and welcoming thing she and Roy built for the plaza, there would still be a graveyard beneath it, the way there is a graveyard beneath everything. It would just take generations of people to find it, clawing down into the earth year after year until they touched stone.

A fog of birds passed over the Eberlee Plaza in St. Louis on the morning the memorial opened.

Helen sat at some distance from the ceremony. Roy had said that she was, of course, expected to be there, and here she was, alone on a bench with a perfect view of what she had wrought.

The birds didn't go away. They swished and darted and soon struck a steady, gliding orbit over the plaza, a kind of dark and clotted halo, like barbed wire in the air. Had they come for the sweet sedatives that were no doubt pumping into the area from underground cylinders? Would the dosage be too strong for a bird, and was there any concern about this? Was anyone in charge of the most basic shit?

Helen sat, by chance, just across from the long, snaking plywood wall of the missing. The weather over the last two years had done a job on the wall. It was mostly stripped of posters by now. The remaining posters were scarred and wind-bleached and almost impossible to decipher. On a few, the photos had eroded but the text had endured, so there were blank sheets that simply said "Missing," with a white space below, as if it were the white space itself that had vanished and could no longer be found.

When the ceremony began, she saw Roy. He looked good. Half the size of the large, sweaty men who surrounded him, as if he were a child being herded by giants. He was shaking hands, talking, laughing, and several times, as Helen watched from the bench, she saw Roy applauding vigorously, even though no one, as far as she could see, was speaking or performing. It was just her husband, alone in the square, clapping his hands as hard as he could.

Mostly Helen watched the birds, which seemed bizarrely determined, certain of something that she would never know. There was a theory of bird vision that came to mind: that birds saw the world through a grid, bisected down to the finest detail. Not a mosaic so much as a shattered image, with white tracers boiling in the spaces in between, or so Helen imagined, so that all the bird really saw was a kind of luminescent netting. Aglow or afire or whatever. No need to poeticize it, but still. Sort of hard not to. You didn't see the mouse, if you were a bird, but a mouse-shaped mesh of light that contained it. She was butchering the science, she knew, but this was the general gist. A kind of shining wire bag we're all trapped in, which might explain some things, right? Or, Helen thought, deepen the mystery. It was a structural view of space, and it treated objects as an afterthought. Objects described the light, not the other way around. Yes, it was speculative, since, whatever, it posited the sensory experience of a goddamned bird, but it seemed to have been endorsed by some of the more distinguished eggheads from expensive, self-regarding universities. One particular scientist claimed that this bird vision revealed the true, unmediated world, something that we humans couldn't handle. We humans! Helen thought. Us! Is there anything we *can* handle? Our desire for sense and order, our sentimental belief that we are not hurtling through space in tiny pieces, has served as a kind of biological propaganda for our visual apparatus, leading to the sentimentalized, so-called whole-world on view in front of us.

In other words, fear, and more fear, and, yeah. Wouldn't there one day, just by chance, Helen thought, be a little person who came along and didn't feel afraid? Someone who saw this world of speeding pieces just as it was? Wasn't that bound to happen, and what on earth, she thought, as she watched everyone walking past her into the mirage, was taking so long?

2

The Boys

It happens. A close relative dies. One who lives elsewhere. And then some time has to be set aside, even if no such thing is possible. Because of work, because of a lack of funds when it comes to traveling. And also because of one's own dear family at home, a husband and two daughters, who need to be fed and petted and listened to and tolerated. Even just ignoring them or quietly loathing them takes its toll.

In this case the family member was my sister. She was in for a routine surgery, or so I was told. And you have to wonder what surgery is ever routine. As you live your life, you will, on occasion, be cut open and explored. It is what life is, part of the routine. Perhaps we should not be surprised. A knife will slice you open and some wunderkind wearing gloves will reach into the wound, with corrective fingers, one expects, and grope around. This is what killed my sister. The wunderkind reached too deep, reached the wrong way, the body crashed, and everyone wore black.

My husband brought me flowers. The kids cried, although they hardly knew her. My own reaction was delayed, to this day, really. It may never come, at least not in my lifetime—which doesn't mean I didn't love the hell out of her. Of course I did. Of course of course of course. I was her sister and she was mine, always—or so we had said long ago. We'd sort of stopped saying it. We had our own lives to chisel up. In some small way I was stirred to action. I had just been so bored, and now someone had died and I was needed and maybe we'd all be knocked out of our habits into a better, realer world.

I flew out to the so-called mountains where my sister and her husband lived with their children. Two little boys who spent their lives in toy helmets, so far as I could tell. They were not allowed to wear them to bed, but this turned out to be a struggle, a bit of a battleground, and some nights, with a mother newly dead, they won this war with their father and went to bed all suited up, ready to survive a nighttime clobbering. They had a game they played, and it involved sticks — store-bought sticks with lights and triggers on them. The helmets kept their heads safe. Without them they'd have killed each other already. When I was near them I almost felt like I should be wearing one myself. I'd met my nephews before, of course, but they seemed to regard me as an animal they could not ride. What was an aunt even for? What did I mean to them? I supplied presents that suffered too much from an educational vibe, and no goodies, and my fun factor was decidedly low. Where had my fun factor gone? Had I ever had one? Their world must have been filled with people like me: curious beasts lacking in magic, unable to entertain them. Could we be eaten? Could we be killed for pleasure? It seemed they had yet to decide.

I didn't have boys myself, and I'd like to think that my profound indifference to them had influenced the moment of conception of each of my two girls. It is not that boys were filthy, or brutish, or dumb and unsingular. One might have said that of anyone, of any age, of any gender. It is, as they say, a routine assessment of the human being. It's just that little boys always seemed terribly expendable, a product of nature that was meant to exist in excess, so it could be endlessly culled by other forces. Boys themselves seem to know this. The so-called death wish is apparent in their behavior, which is often entertaining, but only from a distance. Some creatures have a low survival rate, and so the world produces far too many of them, and as they fight among each other to live they grow more savage, more base, more dull, and the winners, the survivors, are distinctly unappealing little beings. Which isn't to say that some of them don't turn out lovely, with smooth, unknowable bodies, and voices of debilitating power, and a kind of broad indifference to remote suffering that allows great historical changes to take place.

The first night, I sat with my sister's husband. He'd always been a mystery to me, but perhaps no more so than anyone else. He used his moods as weapons, and you kept your distance. I don't mean that he was angry or aggressive or mean. It was the opposite. He had an alarming level of good cheer, a machine-honed smile, and whenever you saw him you felt overwhelmed by it, rebuked that someone in the world could be so profoundly happy. He wanted to hug and hold you and beam at you. He wanted to shout with joy, even, which was always alarming. What did it say about the rest of us, who moped and shuffled and mumbled and were always on the verge of quiet tears, or had spent so long shielding our emotions from view that the emotions themselves had finally been snuffed out and could not be detected, even by the proprietors themselves? It was like he, Drew, was running for office, even though the government had shut down and no one was voting and very likely the entire world had gone cold and dark. He was running a solitary campaign and there was no one to notice how insanely happy he was.

He was not so happy tonight. We drank wine and talked. I learned a great deal about his relationship with my sister, Sarah. She was the sweetest. She was the best. She did everything. She never complained. But sometimes she could be very quiet, Drew explained. Days without noise, as if she'd lost her voice. Was that so bad? I asked. I mean, we don't always need to disrupt the room tone, just because we can. Speech is so overused. The language will grow meaningless if we abuse it. Let's leave words alone so they won't erode. Maybe it's already too late.

"You're not quiet," he said. "You never had that problem."

Drew looked at me long and steady. This was the most we'd ever talked to each other since he started dating Sarah. We poured more wine. One of the boys came down, rubbing his eyes. He stood next to me and grabbed my arm, tugged at it, his thumb in his mouth perhaps to keep himself from shouting obscenities. I resisted, without wanting to provoke him, but I wasn't prepared to be dragged out of my chair by this young beast, so I held my ground. Drew laughed, in his hearty, amplified way. A widower for five days and he sure had his chuckle back. "I think you have a friend," he said.

Not that I know of, I thought.

"I think he wants you to go tuck him in."

The boy looked up at me, wondering, perhaps, just what kind of toy I was. Could I be kicked from the window and would I still love him? I didn't know the answer myself.

"Tuck you in? Well, that I can do," I said, and I took careful note of the level of wine still left in the bottle. I wasn't sure how deep Drew's stores were, and something in me wanted to fight for my share. I'd flown all the way out here and he'd better not hog all the intoxicants while I played mommy to his kid, for Christ's sake.

Over the next few days I helped Drew with the basics. I got the boys up in the morning, rolled them into their clothing, fed them strange objects from bright, colorful boxes, and ran with them to the school bus stop so I wouldn't be stuck with them all day. Drew went to work. An office, somewhere, with other people, presumably, and conveyor belts conveying crisp bricks of cash right into the mouths of his bosses. Some of this money must have come out the other end, and been gifted in a satchel back to Drew, because they—well, just he and the boys now—did okay. Nice house and two newish cars and furniture that didn't look like it also served as a face towel for the young. It was a fine setup all around. They were sure doing better than we were.

I told my husband it would be just a few days. I mean, I left that message on his voice mail. He quickly texted back a thumb, pointing up. To the girls I texted that I missed them, I really did, and that it was so sad out here, sad and hard, but Uncle Drew needed me right now and the boys, the boys. Oh my god you couldn't even imagine. The girls instantly fed all the right emojis back at me, covering all the possible ways that someone might feel about this.

When Drew came home we cooked dinner, at least for the first few days. The boys ate something Drew kept calling "cantebole." An Italian dish, I thought at first, and I was impressed. This is how they do it in the mountains. Were the boys ready for their cantebole, Drew would ask them. Did they want a big portion of cantebole tonight, or a small one; warm, or piping hot? It turned out that cantebole simply meant, literally, "can to bowl." Food that could slide, often in one sucking gelatinous cylinder, from a can right into a bowl. Drew had made up the phrase himself, and he seemed proud. I suppose that not all of us can claim an original contribution to the language. Cantebole looked like little pillows swimming in fake blood, and the blood bubbled and spattered when it came out of the microwave. I'm sure it wasn't repulsive, and sometimes I longed for a meal that simple. The boys would take their bowls over to the living room, where they sat on pillows and ate by themselves, wearing big, jug-like headphones over their helmets, watching their iPads, trying to spoon their food through their face masks.

"If you spill it, *what?*" Drew yelled at them during our first dinner together, maybe on my behalf, to show me how tough he was, how he hadn't forgotten his obligations as a parent.

When the boys didn't answer he yelled again. "What happens if you make a spill?"

"You'll clean it up," one of the boys said, and the two of them burst out laughing.

"Ha ha," said Drew. "I'm over here dying. You just killed me. Ha ha."

I thought that perhaps he should not joke about dying just after their mother, and then there was the issue of his soft, guilt-based parenting style. The permissiveness followed by the false threats. But I cast no stones. Too tiring, first of all. And anyway, sometimes the window is already broken, it's been broken for a long time, so why would you cast a stone into an empty, ruined house? Save your stones for a better target. One that's still standing.

Drew liked to drink at night, and he liked to tell stories. One out of two, I guess. I'd survive. I found that his stories required little of me except for a crazed grin now and then. If you occasionally express disbelief and admiration to people, just through your face, you won't be quizzed on what they are saying and they will gurgle on, engraving their message in the evening air all night long. If only it were a little simpler, though, and you could just flick a lighter and hold it up every now and then to keep the sounds coming.

I took over the kids' bedtime. Drew felt that he sometimes couldn't face the boys, didn't know what to say. Sarah had done a lot of this, and when he stepped in, it made him think of her, and he got sad. He'd lose track of what he was doing and the boys would notice and then they would get sad, too. I didn't really mind doing it. I needed a project, and it was like being a custodian for two hyper, slightly forlorn animals who'd forgotten precisely how to behave in the wild. I got the little guys on a tight schedule, and they knew not to try the helmet business with me, because I made up a story involving sleep and floods and helmets and drowning and lots and lots of dead people, and this seemed to momentarily convince them to keep their heads uncovered at night—strictly to survive. When the boys were brushed and bundled into their pajamas, their hair still wet from the bath, I tucked them in and dove between them on their big, shared bed.

"I ate a horse's face once," the littlest boy said one night.

"Oh? Did the horse cry, or was it already dead?"

"That's not what you're supposed to say. You're supposed to say *gross. Ew.*"

"Well, in some cultures, the horse's face is like candy. It's a rare treat."

"What's a culture?"

"It's a group of people who are stuck with each other."

"Like a family?"

"Yes, but bigger. Without a house. Spread all over the place."

"Is there a dad and mom?"

I snuffed out the conversation with some tickling. The two of them were ridiculously easy prey. I could gesture at them, a snatching motion with my hand, not even touching them, and they would weep with laughter, protecting their soft spots, which was pretty much every part of them. The tickling was foreshadowed, and I almost didn't even need to be in the room. I could hold up a single finger and they trembled. They were mine. I owned them. As I was doing it, triggering the most helpless giggles from these two little guys, I couldn't help thinking how much I'd love to be able to end an adult conversation this way. Just when things got fraught or tense or dull I'd slide my hand along an inner thigh or into an armpit, and poke into the sweetness to see what sort of explosive verbal helplessness came back. Except of course adults aren't ticklish. Profoundly not. Parts of their bodies have died, the whole interior—a kind of early death of the nerves. Immune to sensation to a large degree. Dead person walking, and etc. Being tickled, once you're older, is simply like being excavated, as if your flesh were soft and would give way, as if it could be spooned out of you with a long finger.

We got into a little bit of a routine after the kids went to sleep. Drew drank too much at night, then pretended, I think, to need my help getting to bed. He would act sort of out of it, almost asleep. Bereaved, tired, and drunk. He would murmur in some private dialogue with himself. The widower's soliloquy, I guess. I heard Sarah's name, but I tried not to listen too carefully—it was like eavesdropping on his thoughts, which I wanted no part of. I pretended that he was speaking a language I didn't know, and it sort of worked. I'd take his arm and escort him upstairs. Thank god he didn't really need to lean on me, because he was huge and leaden and I am only as big as I need to be—that's always been my size. We'd get upstairs and I'd help him strip down to his boxers and T-shirt. Beyond that I had no interest, or even tolerance, I don't think. There was not a human being on earth whose sleepwear concerned me, least of all Drew's. Nor were there any nude bodies beyond those freely available on the Internet that I felt I needed to see. Anywhere. And I must say that the human body, in this sort of man at this age, perhaps especially after the loss of a spouse, can cause some feelings. If I looked at him too closely I felt like I was at the morgue or the butcher or that the world had ended. Somehow I had started to associate Sarah's death with him. Because she had died I started to think that so had Drew, by association. Or literally. That he was effectively dead and whatever he'd been doing these last few days only amounted to final spasms and twitches. Throes, I guess they are called. Soon he'd stop seizing. Soon he'd go cold. I'd have to make a call and get him removed. I knew this wasn't true, of course, but I also worried that it was. I was torn between worry and knowledge, and worry was always more persuasive. Worry had the upper hand. It was best to just get Drew under the covers so that I didn't have to see. I could deal with his head, poking above the blankets. That was manageable.

"Sometimes I pay for hand jobs," he mumbled one night, as I was pulling down his shades.

I was hardly listening, and I didn't think he was even fully awake, but I was curious. "How much?" I asked.

He didn't answer, but he tossed and turned a little bit and issued a high-pitched cough.

"How much do hand jobs cost?" I asked again.

Drew rolled over and spoke into his pillow. "You have to pay for a massage, and then it's extra for that." Maybe he was being shy or maybe he was just barely awake. "Sarah knew. It wasn't like that. I mean, I never told her, but I know she knew. She was okay with it. We never discussed it. She didn't mind. I wanted to tell her."

"So you can't go in and say, no massage, just a hand job. I'm in a hurry?"

"No, you can't even say hand job. They will kick you out."

It sounded like he was talking from experience. I pictured him getting kicked out of a massage parlor, emerging into the afternoon light of a strip mall, shielding his eyes, deciding if he should maybe just get some ice cream. "So how much then?" I asked.

"Two hundred dollars."

"Interesting."

The next morning I got the boys to their bus stop early and they begged me to wait with them. Of course I would never have left them alone, but it was nice to be wanted, and I let them try to talk me into staying. Usually they'd just pull on my arms until I fell in the grass with them, and that was it, they'd made their case. I told them that they should both be lawyers, they were very persuasive young men. And I would say *just this once* as they sat on me and played with my hair, telling me that I was their favorite couch, the best couch ever.

The rule in the mornings was that the boys could wear their helmets to the bus stop, but when the bus came they had to take them off, and then I carried the helmets home, two stinking shells that clacked together and that I dreamed of hurling far into the woods, where I am sure they would serve as a cautionary tale to the animals, a dual beheading of some mythical beast. Except there weren't any woods. The land was too valuable in this neighborhood. Just lawn after lawn after lawn. For some reason, Drew had warned me not to use anyone else's trash can. Like, ever, or else I would have already ditched the helmets in one of them by now and then played dumb later. He was very solemn in his warning. If you put even the littlest piece of trash in someone else's can, they'd see you and they'd go nuts, apparently. It was worse than shitting on someone's floor, I guess. Every house had a massive trash can out front, nearly the size of my bedroom in college. You could easily put a body in one. You could stuff blankets and pillows down into the bottom and have, I bet, an incredibly cozy and private nap. No one would think to look for you in there. It was sort of the ultimate panic room. Hidden in plain sight. With mountains in the distance, too, if you drilled yourself a little peephole.

The boys held my hands and together we leaned over the curb and looked down the street to see if the bus was coming. No feet allowed in the street, I always said. At times like this the boys were fond of interviewing me. Did I know how to swim? Did I like cheese? Who was my favorite superhero? How old was I? Why wasn't I at my own house right now? Did I ride a school bus when I was a little girl? When was I leaving? Would I be gone when they got home from school today? How did I get to be an aunt? Is there a school for that? When did I meet their mom? Were we friends or enemies? Could I beat their dad in a fight?

"I have two girls at home, you know," I told them. "You guys have met them, but you were *little little little*."

I slipped into baby talk here, while holding my hand low to the ground to indicate how small they had been, and the boys suddenly looked uncomfortable.

"I'm sure you don't remember them," I said. "They are your cousins. They are very tall now. They are taller than I am!"

"Our cousins? We heard they tried to beat us up."

"Where did you hear that?"

"From our dad. He called them hitters. He said we were only babies and they tried to bounce us like basketballs. One of them kicked me in the face."

"By mistake," the little one added. "That's what Mom said."

I held the elder boy's face in my hands and studied it closely. What a soft and sweet and smooth little face. I squinted. I pretended to think. "Yes, hm," I said. "I believe I do still see a footprint."

He pulled away from me, giggling. "Liar!" he shrieked.

The little one wanted to look. "I want to see the footprint!" he shouted.

I thought back to the few times all of us had been together—morose, drunken, silent, family time, with the exception of Drew's explosive, alienating cheer, while the kids had squirted off to god knows where. All of this was possible, but if someone was truly kicked in the face, even a young boy, I'd like to think my daughter was provoked.

"Well, listen," I said to the boys. "If they had tried to beat you up I'm sure they would have succeeded, because they were bigger than you, and stronger than you. Still are. So no funny stuff. Have you ever heard of a teenager? Have you ever seen one? I'm not sure if they have them around here." I looked up and down the street. I pretended to be afraid.

"You're weird."

"I'm your aunt. That's how it is."

"Girls are smarter and faster and better at everything than boys," said the littler one.

"Oh? Who told you that."

"Our mom."

"Oh, yeah. Your mom. I really miss her a bunch. In fifth grade she wore a cape all year, and she wouldn't answer to her real name."

"But boys aren't bad, are they?" the eldest asked me.

"Oh, sweetie, no, they're not. Not even close. And you know what your mom meant when she said that, right?"

No, they didn't, neither of them. The looked up at me, waiting.

"That the two of you," I said, poking each of them gently in the chest, "in your own ways, are going to be special and great and fantastic at brand-new things, things no one has even heard of yet."

When their bus came the little one hugged me and the big one ran off without saying goodbye.

...

When I got back to the house, Drew had already left for work. On the table was a neat stack of cash. I counted it. Two hundred dollars exactly. I left it there.

It took me a little while before I felt like I could masturbate in that house, but soon I had a good system set up, and I grew more comfortable with my visit. If you're staying somewhere over an extended period of time, and you cannot masturbate, not ever, then you start to plot your exit. It's just untenable after a while. I have no trouble in hotel rooms, what few I've stayed in, but somehow it's different in a home other than your own. It feels more obviously complicated, although I'm not sure why. We take shits in other people's homes. That's arguably far worse than touching oneself delicately in the shower. I'd taken a shit right under Drew's nose the other day. We were making dinner, and suddenly I had to go, and I was gone for a while—ten minutes, maybe, more. I read several op-eds on my phone while sitting on the toilet. I definitely wasn't peeing that whole time. He knew for a fact that I'd taken a shit, or tried to, and I'm sure he didn't care. I guess I don't know for sure. But still, I'd been nervous about masturbation, even though it was part of my routine at home, and that had made me less inclined to do it. I can't succeed at it when I'm afraid or tense. But then I decided that if Drew wasn't home, and the boys were at school, with hours before anyone was expected to return, I could add this to my schedule, in between sorting and storing my sister's clothing, jewelry, and papers.

There was very little left to do with respect to Sarah. I organized her clothing according to type, then packed each group separately— sweaters, pants, socks. I boxed up her jewelry, leaving a few favorite pieces out for Drew, which he said he would keep in a dish on his dresser. I wasn't sure if Drew had a special dish in mind, so I just dumped the jewelry there, a tangle of metal and colored stones. Drew also wondered if Sarah's coats could be given away, and I took care of this, driving them down to a clothing donation center. I went through Sarah's computer and dragged her files to a folder Drew had set up in the cloud. It was called "Sarah." Would anyone ever open this folder? Would the boys grow up and one day decide to look through it, and would there even be computers by then? Instead of carefully going through her papers and everything else she filled her drawers with, I put most of it in boxes and tried to label things as accurately as I could. Holiday Cards. Pictures. Letters. There were fabric swatches and catalogs stuffed with yellow Post-its. Big plans. These went into a box called "Ideas." But soon her things were boxed away and that was that. I'd cruise through the house looking for objects that were explicitly hers, and eventually I found none. I'm not the first person to observe how little evidence people leave behind when they die. Or, I don't know, maybe I am. Sarah was just a few boxes, and the boxes were moved out of sight.

My husband called, wanting to know what was up. When was I coming home? The girls missed me, he said, which was poorly en-crypted code, and he should have known better. He didn't say "we" miss you. And by saying the girls missed me—since they were not exactly capable of believing that either of their parents were fully human—he meant that the technical side of their upkeep, which mostly meant the coordination of schedules with the intolerable parents of their friends, people he often refused to even name, suf-fered during my absence. I was needed to receive and relay signals, mostly, to rehearse concern with other parents over the frequently uncertain whereabouts of our children, who would soon be gone. A metal tower might have served the same function, and it wouldn't need to eat. What was true was that I sort of missed the girls, but if I was home their doors would be closed, and I wouldn't even be knocking. I'd stopped trying. I could miss them here, or I could miss them there. I wasn't sure it mattered.

I asked my husband about homework and bedtimes and food and screen time, in relation to our fiercely willful children, and he gave short, empty answers, assuming each question was a veiled accusation, designed to expose his inattention, which perhaps it was. I loved and trusted him, which turned out to mean that sometimes I also did not.

"So is Drew just a mess?" my husband asked. "Is he a disaster?"

"You know, he's okay. He's either in shock and holding it all in, or this is the extent of his reaction. I don't know him that well. It's sort of hard to say."

"I can't imagine," he said, which is often what we say when we obsessively imagine something all the time.

"The boys seem okay," I said, and he said, "Oh right, *the boys*. Holy crap. I forgot about them. The boys. Jesus. Are they just? Are they just so?" And he wasn't really able to finish the sentence. A silence bloomed on the phone. The boys. They were and they weren't, I thought. That's how I would answer that question. They were just the boys and that was all.

At dinner that night Drew explained that there would be a sum of money from the hospital. Accidental death, is what they called it. No one wanted a lawsuit, Drew told me—which I'm sure wasn't true. I'm sure there were lawyers living in the walls who pined with their pants down for any lawsuit, anywhere, ever. How much money would it take, the hospital apparently asked Drew. How much do you have, he answered. They named a number and he named a number, and those two numbers entered the sunless, dank bodies of a team of lawyers. Out came the shiny, fresh-smelling settlement, more than enough to keep the two young boys in bright new helmets long into their dotage. Mouth guards, helmets, visors, Doritos, and game consoles: a full, rich, satisfying life on this planet.

This was good, right? I asked. Of course it was no consolation whatsoever, and how could it be, but maybe having less financial pressure around the raising of the boys would help him somewhat, or help ensure a good life for the boys?

Drew shook his head. There was no financial pressure to begin with, he said. They were fine. The money didn't really mean anything. But it was connected to an idea he had. A kind of plan. And it involved me. He looked at me pretty carefully. It was something he wanted to run by me.

Drew would turn these funds over to me. Along with the two boys. That's what he wanted to talk about. There would be plenty of money to take care of them, to pay for clothing, food, and school. He didn't know what to do with them, what to say to them. He couldn't stand the thought of letting them go, and he couldn't stand the thought of keeping them. He put his head in his hands and I felt that it would not be a good idea to touch him right now.

There was no use pretending I hadn't seen this coming. He was such a hulking, sad figure. He thought his life would be easier without those two weird sweethearts running around bopping each other over the head.

"Just for a little while," he said.

When I called my husband, he met the request with silence. It was one of the ways he responded to things. A long, thoughtful silence. Sometimes he'd leave the room. Days could go by. The conversation wasn't over, you knew. It had just been suspended, time had stopped, and when he spoke again the world would start back up and life would continue. I admired this thoughtfulness, except when it reared up in situations that did not warrant long, pensive silences, like at restaurants when he was asked what he would like to order. Or now.

"Both children, both boys?" he asked, finally.

"Both of them."

"For how long?"

"It wasn't discussed."

"Which means forever."

"I don't think so."

"But you didn't ask."

"You're not here. You don't understand."

"I could say the exact same thing about you."

"Okay, no one is anywhere. No one understands. No one, no one, no one. Is your answer no?" I asked him.

"Why would you say that? That's not even remotely fair."

"Oh I guess it just reflects the joy and openness and enthusiasm you're showing about the idea."

I Skyped with the girls. They'd colored their hair. They were so lovely, so grown-up, so gone from me in every way. I told them what was going on, the idea that had come up. The boys might come back with me, live with us for a while. Go to school. Be their little brothers.

"Bring them here, bring them here!" they shrieked. "We will, like, totally put their diapers on!"

"They don't wear diapers anymore. They are pretty grown-up for their age."

They wanted this, they wanted this, they were sure that it would be fantastic. I couldn't help thinking that they thought they'd be getting a couple of pets. For a little while, maybe, or for certain hours of the day, that might almost be true. To a small degree. It was just those other hours, when the pet was a person, and the person needed things, and the person wanted things, and the person couldn't sleep, or the person was sad no matter what, just sad as a long-term unfixable way to be. That was what concerned me. The larger side effects of adding a human being to a situation. Any human being, of any age, blood relative or not.

"Talk to your father," I told them. "If this is something you want, and if you understand what this really means, really, without assuming that this will all be fun, and knowing that I am going to need a lot of help from both of you. Talk to your father."

"Dad?" They laughed. "Dad has never said no to us ever once in all of our lives. Has he?" They looked at each other in genuine puzzlement. Soon they were blowing kisses and begging to talk to the boys, or to just see them. But the boys, I said, were busy. They couldn't come to the phone right now. Maybe next time.

I started to show up in Drew's room before I went to bed. He'd pretend to be asleep, but he'd make the assignment easy for me, sometimes releasing himself from his underwear. Usually he was, if not hard, swollen enough for me to begin. It was like I was just taking over a craft project he'd already started. I sat at the edge of the bed and it never took very long. He wilted fast in my hand afterward. I wiped my hand on the sheet. Then I left. Cleanup wasn't part of the deal. That was his problem. He could pay his own sister for that, or some street whore, for all I cared.

In the morning there'd be money, and I'd tuck it into my bag. Soon my flight had been paid for and the missed days of work felt less impactful. I was getting into zero-sum territory, financially, and I had much more free time.

At the bus stop one morning, I mentioned to the boys that their dad would be bringing home their favorite pizza for dinner. The deep-dish kind, and, who knows, maybe there would be a surprise for dessert. This I didn't know, but I'd be going shopping, so I could take care of it.

"Our dad doesn't want us," said the big one.

"Oh that's not true."

"It's okay. He told us that." They both nodded up at me, as if they'd discussed this together and decided that it was fine.

"No, he did not. You are a big fibber." I smacked him lightly on his helmet.

"I know. But someone at school said that to us when we said we were leaving."

"Your dad loves you. My gosh. Are you kidding me?"

"We know."

The boys were holding hands.

"He really loves you," I went on. "And right now your dad and I think it might be better for you to come live with me, and your uncle and your cousins."

"Will our mom be there?" asked the little one.

"No, honey, she won't."

"Someone at the funeral tried to tell me where she is, but it was hard to picture."

"I know. I can't picture it either."

"Does it have a name?"

"It might. Should we make up a name for it?"

He made a face. "I don't like to make up things. I'm not a baby."

"Okay."

"I want to know the real name."

I found myself telling them that I would try to find out. I would look into it. I promised that I would do my best but that it might be very difficult.

"There is no real name," the big one told the little one. "She's gone forever." And the little one whispered that he knew that, he wasn't stupid.

I kissed them both and they ran off to the bus, and when they got on, they rushed to the back and pressed their faces against the glass, waving at me.

When I thought about how I was spending my time, I realized that I was masturbating two people. Myself and Drew. For the sheer sake of efficiency, just following the logic, I could reduce this work-load by 100 percent, saving time and effort, without forfeiting our mutual outcomes, simply by having intercourse with Drew. Suddenly I wouldn't have to masturbate anybody. I'd go from masturbating two separate people to masturbating nobody. A drastic reduction. But, in theory anyway, the amount of rendered orgasms would be the same, one for each of us, one per day. I was proud of this revelation but the shame was that I had no one to share it with. For some reason I thought of Sarah. This would have been something I could have shared with her. She of all people would have appreciated how efficient I was being. I would no longer have to masturbate her husband. I would no longer have to masturbate myself. It seemed like a clear win.

The transition to the new situation was not especially complicated. I certainly did not need to consult Drew. His opinion did not interest me. I readied myself before entering his room, so I could sit astride him and begin the procedure. Intercourse itself, if you dispense with various ceremonies, along with human speech, can be remarkably efficient. Probably, a long time ago, creatures had to perform intercourse in absolute silence, in the woods, in caves, or else they'd be detected and killed. We still have these skills, they are not entirely dormant in us, even if the threat is gone. Excess noise during intercourse is the sign of a decadent society. Drew still pretended to be asleep, although sometimes he put his hands on my hips, but even that seemed to broach an intimacy that I felt was not warranted. He cried sometimes afterward, and didn't try to hide it from me. But I wasn't there for that. I had the boys to think of, and I liked sleeping alone, where no one could touch me.

The plans were rolling into place. My husband texted me a picture, and it looked like he'd squeezed a bunk bed into the spare room and started to paint it. There were toys on the floor, old ones from when the girls were little. "Thank you," I wrote back. I sent him a red heart emoji, and I held down the button, so there'd be more of them than he could handle. He always came around. Even when he was far away, I could see his body pitching and turning, starting to bank, and then he would come around, back to me.

There was so much to do. Schools and doctors to call, appointments to make. Paperwork to sort out with Drew. He was very organized. He had a binder. He'd given it all a lot of thought. There was a bank account, and he gave me the card and the PIN. There was a caregiver's contract that conferred authority on me in an emergency. We would be in constant contact, he explained. He would Skype the boys every night. He wanted updates on every little thing. Pictures and videos and the whole deal.

"I don't know what to say," Drew said. And I knew that. I knew he didn't, and I expected nothing to be said. It was strange to see him in the daylight. At night he was just a shape, hardly even that. He cried out and he wept and he came, and he hid his face in the sheets. He did not speak and I never saw his eyes. He'd bought this palace and it was already haunted, he was already spooked. I wondered if he was always like that. Sarah had never said. But when I thought about it, I couldn't remember her mentioning Drew even once. It was always the boys, and what they were up to. The boys the boys the boys.

The trip was upon us, and the boys needed gear, so I took them shopping. I told them that they could pick out shirts and shoes and pants, even caps, along with socks and undies, but when I saw what they chose, I quietly put everything back and picked out a few things myself. They would never know the difference, and I'm sure they would have just as soon gone around naked. In the store they ran wild, their little helmets jiggling on their heads. When other shoppers glared at them in exaggerated shock I stared them down, ready for anything. Go ahead, I thought. Say something. Do something. *Think* something.

We went for french fries and milkshakes for lunch. I told them they were being so grown-up. So brave. They were such good young men. My little young men. We were all going to be okay, just great. We had a big adventure waiting for us in their new town.

"Daddy said he will visit," the big one said, and the little one nodded.

"Daddy will absolutely visit," I said. "He can visit whenever he wants to. And we will visit him, too. Everyone will visit everyone."

"Are there schools there? Are there other kids?"

"Yes and yes. And did I say yes?"

"What about those things you told us about. Teenagers. Do they have those there?"

"Your cousins are teenagers. They can't wait to see you. It will be like having two great big sisters. A big sister is the best thing in the world. They will always protect you. Your mom was my big sister. Just like you"—I pointed to the big one—"are a big brother to you"—and I pointed at the little one.

"Why?" asked the little one.

"Because your mom was born first. She came out into the world before me, and she looked around, she checked everything out, and then she whispered to me, wherever I was, that it was all clear. Everything was fine. I could come out."

"And did you? Did you come out?"

"I did. One year after your mom."

"Why did it take so long? Did you forget the way?"

"I was kind of slow. I was still sort of scared. But the whole time I was headed her way. I knew she was waiting for me and I was excited to see her. I just couldn't wait to see her face."

The boys looked at me and we all decided that it was probably time to go, because we still had to pack, and we had a plane trip tomorrow, and wasn't that going to be fun, but we'd better get ready and we'd better get a really really good night's sleep. At the curb to the parking lot the little one grabbed our hands and cried out for us to wait. No feet in the street, he said. Never, we all yelled. Never ever. He wanted to be the one to say all clear, so he held us back and looked one way, then the other. He took his time, and we waited for him to give the sign that it was okay to go, we could walk, it would be safe.

The Grow-Light Blues

Carl Hirsch didn't do holiday parties. At least, not correctly. All the so-called people, wind streaming from their faces. Fleshy machines spewing pollution, fucking up the environment. If he squinted, the celebrating bodies of his coworkers very nearly blistered into molecules, shining with color. Too often the whole of it—people, places, and things—looked to scatter. Everyone on the verge of turning to soup. So what if there was no precedent for a full-scale human melt, bodies reduced to liquid pouring from a window? You could still worry about it. Sometimes you had to.

Tonight's party was in one of those long, skinny city apartments you're supposed to verbally fellate with praise. It was like walking into a tiny, dismal doghouse, a real doghouse, and then kissing the furred ass of the dog who lived there, who was super annoyed to have you clogging up his tiny room. You were allowed to stay as long as you kept using your tongue.

Hopefully, this doghouse had sick drinks. And free money. And those soft bones in sauce they sometimes served at company parties. Even if he was only permitted to sniff them, because of his, uh, dietary regimen.

"The light, the space, my god!" Carl found himself saying to the small, perfectly dressed host, who stood on the landing.

The host greeted Carl with alarm.

Carl reached up, too late, to cover his face. He didn't want to be a burden—at least, not to just anyone. And yet, fuck this guy. Didn't Emily Post have a whole chapter on hiding all reaction to astonishing creatures who appeared at your door? Shutting your little face down so as not to reveal the horror and disgust you might really feel?

To the host, Carl said, grinning far too hard, "Just show me to my rooms and I'll get out of everyone's way. Jones is on his way up with my luggage. This is going to be such a fun year, roommate!"

The host didn't hear him, missed the joke. He was already looking over Carl's shoulder to where people were crowding up the narrow staircase, trying to push their way inside. Because heaven. Because drinks. Because loneliness and flesh pleasure. Because the invite said, "Levitate, my friends! Let us see the soles of your feet!" Because Mayflower, where they all worked, was pure shithouse. The future was ripe for sexual conquest, and they were busy greasing up their parts.

Carl knew he wasn't the type to get fondled when he passed out. Mostly it was because of his face, thanks to his job. Rough on the eyes, tough to the touch. Scratchproof, though, which was a bonus. Particularly if some long-shot apocalypse reared up and he had to go face-first into the bramble or some such. For now, partygoers pressing in behind him, he could do nothing but raise his arms and surf forward into the mob, hoping with all his might that the wave would carry him, safe and sound, back home to his bed.

In some ways, it was inevitable that Carl, a few nights later, would take a picture of his balls and send it to the Mayflower email list. After a hot bath, he propped up his phone in the dank zone and captured the crag and the woof, the topographical crimson scorch. He got the shot, pressed "share," and released the picture into the ether. It felt all right. A certain unburdening. Maybe even like post-coital clarity, chaste and lonely as it was. Afterward, he was tempted to stand at his apartment window and listen through the glass, into the pulse of the evening, as his message landed at key email terminals throughout the metropolis.

...

If you counted from the beginning, going back to the supposedly sunny morning when Carl was born, this was day ten thousand seven hundred and something of his tremendously joyful stretch of time, his project aboveground.

To hear his mother tell it, because certain mothers break into story when you enter their homes, the birds were in ecstasy the day he was born, squawking over the hospital. The air was so crisp and cool that day, his mother would add, that you felt hugged by the wind. Her phrase. When little Carl was born, the whole neighborhood, per his mother, held its breath. *Someone new is among us. Someone special.* It was a revisionist birth narrative, likely concocted when it struck Carl's mother, poor thing, that her son was just another piercingly boring need machine, underperforming and overwhelming, programmed to crave so much from her that she would soon forget her interests and reengineer her whole self in order to supply the mothering that would keep her child, at the very least, out of jail, out of a coffin, and out of the sex-change doctor's office. At which point she would subtly punish him with nearly imperceptible indifference and ambivalence. Parenting! As far as motives go, his mother had a pretty good one for her wholesale, self-serving fictionalization of Carl's birth, and he forgave her, not that she ever asked him to, for glorifying his unremarkable debut.

In his twenties, just before his mother died, when she was listless and storied out, staring through a different hospital window as if surveying the land for her own burial, Carl finally Googled the weather on the day of his birth. And, well, lookee there: rain, rain, rain, ash, fire, murder, murder, rain. A godless Tuesday. Unprecedented torrents flooding down from the north. Dirt and mud and broken trees and houses split in half. Sunshine, maybe, but not in his part of the world.

And birds? The Internet had little to say on the matter.

...

As it turned out, Carl's photo backfired. The folks at work who opened his attachment—the upper-level creatives at Mayflower as well as the engineers holed up in the silo in Albuquerque—mistook it for an image of Carl's pitiful neck. Or maybe a scalded bit of acreage under his arm. In other words, no one seemed to see anything uniquely scrotal in the photo. Just grim, if understandable, symptom documentation from a man who was perhaps Mayflower's most martyred employee. Slash medical subject. Slash guinea pig. Slash hero. Slash fool. Carl the Boiled, as he had started to think of himself. Taking one for the team.

At work the next day, expecting to be shunned and sort of figuratively barfed on, maybe swept into the farewell room, where underachievers got hand-stabbed by Kipler, the CEO, Carl instead collected a few drive-by hugs. He was heavily touched, right on the body, by people he'd hardly even met. A kind of unprecedented love was brought to bear all over his person.

"Oh, my gosh," Kora, from Nutrients, said, holding him at arm's length and staring wildly just above his head. She was always the one putting the needle in and sometimes forgetting to take it out.

"Carl? Honey?"

"I'm okay," Carl whispered, suddenly shy.

"I know!" Kora said. "You are! You will be! You are so brave. I can't believe you are being so open about what this is doing to you. It serves them right." She shook her fist.

Kora the Explorer. He wouldn't think of her that way anymore. He actually appreciated her kindness, if misdirected. If incorrect. Did it matter?

She squeezed his waist, and he felt himself pee a little. His bladder seemed to belong to someone else entirely.

Later in the morning, an older man ducked into Carl's cubicle, a man who seemed to have been designed, by experts, to embody sorrow and regret. He shook his head with deep, theatrical empathy. His name was maybe Murray. Maury? Perhaps it was Larry. He was a tech. He performed overnight adjustments to the computer displays that were slowly roasting Carl's face, in the service of the greater good. Money piles for Mayflower. Loss of bodily function for Carl.

"I'm just thinking about you and feeling for you," the man said to Carl, stooped in a kind of prayer bow. "And knowing that there's no way I can really know, I mean, I can't . . ." He paused. "What you're going through. None of us can."

"Everything we can't know," Carl said, shaking his head as cheerfully as he could. "Maybe it's time to cry uncle. Mysteries one, us nothing. We lose!"

The man dipped his head again, pressed his hands together.

"Anyway, it's what we signed up for, right?" Carl said, trying and failing to picture the exact moment when he'd agreed to take part in the experiment. Had it ever happened? He couldn't remember the last time he'd written his name, said yes, nodded his head, assented. Maybe by simply staying alive he implied his agreement and cooperation? Simply by walking the halls at Mayflower, and not crawling into a hole, he was saying, Yes, yes, please test your equipment on me. Especially the equipment that burns. I would be most pleased if you would.

How sweet of this man to visit and thank Carl for his service. The old Carl would have smiled and thanked him, but his thanking utensil, connected inexorably to his face, was broken. He had the paralyzed head of a mascot. What he needed now, in order to engage in human congress, were emoticons on Popsicle sticks that he could wave around, lest everyone start to think that he was dead on the inside, too.

Boiled Carl, alpha tester in this freak show, wasn't exactly sure how the whole UV feeding thing had even come about. Why would

Mayflower's cold commanders, motherfuckers extraordinaire, reveal their true road map to him, anyway?

He'd joined Mayflower's wearables team five years back and had been whiteboarding applications that tracked emotions, or tried to, so that the world's feelings could finally get accurately logged. And mined. And then probably ransomed back to the people who had the feelings in the first place. Using the data they collected, Carl's team had been able to match users' emotion narratives — the plotted vectors of what they felt over the course of days and weeks and years — with those of other users. Maybe even in their own apartment building. Certainly in their neighborhood. Unless they lived in the middle of nowhere. Or unless their feeling vectors were highly unusual. Carl's team proposed a kind of mood pairing. Who else is bummed out? Who doesn't give a shit? Who feels pretty good today, maybe borderline ecstatic, even though something bad happened in Angola? Who's lost the taste for staying out late, wants to be alone and would like a silent partner in solitude? Who eats his daily caloric value in one sitting at 3 a.m. and has a special reaction to that?

This wouldn't be just a dating service, even though, *ka-ching,* hello! Get paid, hashtag gritty times! They were pretty sure they were onto something. Carl thought that, with enough users shooting their feelings into the cloud, Mayflower would be sitting on a gold mine of data. It was the ultimate privacy grab, better even than a blood sample from every living person on the planet. Which the rumor sites also had Mayflower pursuing.

But management smelled too much choice. The whole thing stank of opt out. Self-knowledge was for the dead, they said. People don't like themselves enough to have to deal with other people with feelings so similar to their own. It makes them feel less special. A product shouldn't be trying to tell the truth so aggressively. That was a turnoff. Besides, the feeling sensors weren't where they should be, technology-wise, and only young people would want to wear the neck collars that Carl was proposing. Management pulled the kill switch. Management being Kipler, Kipler, Kipler, and Kipler, depending on his mood. Depending on his sweater.

Creative staged charrettes. Disruption was the watchword. Carl and his team were pressured to lift their legs and pee-shame the status quo. For a cash-yielding invention to work, for it to leak gold pudding and really destroy the economy, in Mayflower's favor, maybe even change the meaning of money, Kipler once said, it had to look inevitable, ridiculously obvious in hindsight. They all kept coming back to food. What a problem it was. And not just because there was so little of it left on the planet.

Carl was there when Kipler first brought the life hackers into the charrette. Brutal, loud, beautiful, aspirationally immortal. Just a bunch of ageless kid-looking creatures who were like Version 2.0 people. How old were they, really? Eleven? Kipler called them Mayflower's future. Early adopters of every health trend, enthusiasts of untested medical protocols. They micro-fasted, binged on superfoods, fussed over their own blood tests, which they posted cockily on the longevity message boards. Carl once saw them tearing down a hallway, something clear and greasy on their upper lips. They seemed deranged. Soon the life hackers were obsessed with a service called Jug. Every morning, a jug was delivered to your cubicle. It was all you needed for the day. Nutritionally bozo. Freakishly optimized, and they could load your meds into it, just to keep all your material input in one receptacle. Sometimes the jug held a thick lotion, more of a cream than a drink. Other times it was slippery and clear, with a foamy head. It depended on your bloodwork. As you graduated through jugs, the color and the quality of the liquid changed, responding to feedback. When you finished a jug, you spat your last sip back into the bottle, to be analyzed before the next day's potion was brewed. Or supposedly. The life hackers had brought their jugs to the charrette one day and swigged from them, burping a grassy steam.

The legend that developed is that Kipler smashed some jugs that day, swung one against his own head, grinning madly. Carl would love to have seen that. Some of the goo in those bottles looked as if it couldn't even spill. It would just hang in the air like a cloud. He pictured Kipler cream-soaked, coated in white foam.

What did happen is that Kipler said that the start-up that had invented Jug had missed the whole point. They were drawing your attention to your food, giving you a heavy accessory, isolating you socially, et cetera—he went on for like ten minutes of scathing criticism. Kipler destroyed the premise, the execution, the future of this product, and the life hackers, poor guys, seemed to wither at the table.

"Get rid of the jug," Kipler finally said. "Get rid of the liquid. Get rid of everything. What's left?"

No one answered.

Kipler smiled.

"Exactly," he said. "Nothing. There's nothing left."

He gestured into empty space, then pointed at the overhead fixture.

"We're all sitting here, soaking in light. We could have been eating this whole time."

Kipler was pretty quiet after that, and everybody was freaked out, looking up into the light, squinting.

Mayflower Systems regularly bought and destroyed small companies, mostly to crush progress. And maybe also simply to frighten the universe and increase world sadness? One of the patent portfolios that had come online at around that time involved grow lights. Using light as a delivery system for nutrients, not just for plants but for animals. A lightbulb went off, and a UV healing wand for sick animals became, at Mayflower, something utterly else and fucking wonderful. A nutrient-delivery system for the skin, for people skin. A goddamn human grow light, as Kipler put it, though he thought the word "human" sounded too technical. The way skin makes vitamin D from sunlight. Except this would be other vitamins, too, and micronutrients. And then, one day, the three amigos: fat, protein, and carbohydrates, who usually got inside us only through flesh eating and the like. The marketing hook was that meals were obsolete. Meals were a headache and a hassle. Meals were disgusting. Because of sauce. Because of stench. In the future, Kipler would yell, everyone would eat by accident, while doing other things. While working!

Who would volunteer? Who would saddle up and taste the greatness? Who was stupid? Who had nothing to lose? Who lacked a family to mourn him should things, uh, falter? Who wanted to be a hero? Who could withstand tremendous levels of pain without blacking out? Who could abide a chronic, deep itch under the skin that scratching merely exacerbated?

Those, in fact, were not the criteria. None of them. They bloodtested Creative and looked for subjects with gross nutritional deficits. In other words, people who ate like shit and had the blood numbers of a gremlin. The first goal was to see if the grow light could move the needle, boost a dude's vitamin A or whatnot. Actually satiate. And not, you know, hasten to expire. And then luminous efficacy would be stretched. Light-form carbohydrate spectrum, rays of protein. Yup. Radical color temps and other par value mods to the spectrum. The talk got geeky. If all went well, they'd pilot a dark strobe, something like a noise gate that regulated the feed? Just pulse darkness so as not to turn the poor subject into some kind of demon, twitching under a heat lamp.

Carl's bloodwork deemed him the most deviant, healthwise, and the applause he got, a king's greeting, which must have been cheers of relief, sort of decided the thing. It was Carl who'd be going under the light. All you can eat. Everyone hollered to give it up for Carl and then everyone sort of did, vocally. The entire room, as if they'd planned it, yelled, "Bon appétit, Carl!" Flashlights were clicked on, and these flannel-shirted semi-strangers gathered around him, shining their beams in his face, as a kind of joke, Carl guessed, but it was sickening a little.

Mayflower put Carl on a detox. Not Jug. Just some potions

cooked up in the cafeteria, sometimes administered to him in the men's room, when privacy was called for. Bone-broth Jell-O. Quite a lot of citrus. Cold coffee shot into his dark parts. A vitamin lotion smeared onto his newly shaved head, because hairless skin something something, one of the nutrient nurses explained. Your pores just gape open. Oxygen, she explained, was richer when emulsified into a cream.

Carl felt shaky, poisoned in a way he didn't quite mind, and when the day came he was ready.

The first time he ate the light, sitting at his desk starving his ass off, staring at his laptop screen, it felt like getting slapped. Rapidly. That was the nutrient penetration, they explained. Like shotgun pellets. To Carl, it felt as if someone had pinned him to the floor and was just pimp-slapping him into a puddle. Carl asked for goggles. His eyes hurt. His feet shrank and weakened. By the end of the first week his tongue clogged his mouth. Enough to foul his speech and make him sound like an animal. And he suffered from a bottomless, gnawing hunger. Maybe because he was getting only enough nutrition, at that point, to sustain a cricket.

It was hard, hard, hard to convert fat into light. The body, Carl's body, wanted good fats, bad fats, a salt lick, a fat friend. His cravings went berserk. He dreamed of fat, thought of eating parts of himself. The tech for the fat conversion was pretty crude. Understatement. Carl pictured Madame Blavatsky at a loom. How do you speed up fat, make it invisible, but also really fast, really powerful? You could do it, but badly, and this sort of light just balls-out hurt going in. Hurt and burned. Or the reverse. The flesh was chilled by it, for some reason, and there could be rot. Of the skin.

There were some glitches. Display burnout, necrosis. The paint on the cubicle wall behind Carl's head, which collected the light when he wasn't sitting there, bubbled up and peeled. There were side effects, including the dark hardening of Carl's face. They called it "blizzard face." A team was already at work on a grow-light recovery lotion to market as a solution to the problem they'd created.

Carl felt like an astronaut, a child, a corpse. He asked the obvious questions. Why not some other patch of skin? Something less, maybe, facial? But Kipler was adamant. The face was already getting bathed in light all day by people looking at their computers and phones. "All day! Take what's there and body-slam it!" he shouted. That was the entire point.

"We use the gestural habits that are already in place. What's already happening! There's nothing new to learn, nothing to do, nothing to think, nothing to feel. Victory! Do you not see that? Get out of my world if you don't see that. People don't want to think about eating. We are giving them a gift. The invention is hidden. It's nothing! Think nothing."

During an early charrette, after the experiment began, a tech ran in yelling about an update to the display, some UV dilation they'd pulled off to widen the protein band, muscling it into something called gray light. They'd crowded one more amino acid onto the spectrum, apparently.

"Carl," the tech said, bowing. "Your presence is humbly requested in Albuquerque. We've freaking iterated the shit out of this display. It's like pure food. We cooled the bitch right down. You're going to feast, my man. Bring your goggles."

And then, in a fight announcer's voice, the tech boomed, "Let's get ready for Pro-Tein!"

High fives all around.

Carl stood up and shadowboxed, ducking and weaving, but the effort left him dizzy and breathless. He sat back down.

When he returned from Albuquerque, he was hungrier than ever. He had a potbelly. A sore had formed on his chin. He'd enjoyed a small boost in his folate level. In iron. Magnesium. But he was still losing muscle mass, and he felt a tight bulge in one of his eyes. The medics kept waving him through, chortling about miracles. The project was considered a success. Carl was a great explorer. They pushed him in a wheelchair down hallways, just to keep his energy up. Sometimes he slept through a feed, waking up famished with a hot, tight face. Carl dreamed of the sort of hood used for falcons. Someone could push the shrouded man around and everybody would whisper, "That's Carl. Look at Carl. Oh, my god, there he is."

"I want what he's having," Carl would say to himself, in a voice he could no longer recognize.

When Carl finally sent his crotch shot out into the world, the testing had been going on for endless hungry, scorched weeks. The computer displays were fucking hot, and for a while, before the hardening, Carl rashed up. His skin tightened, his face itched, and something behind his face, the fascia, they called it, seemed to kind of break up. Which caused a kind of feature slide. He submitted to daily bloodwork. They gave him some drug called Shitazine, or that wasn't exactly what it was called, which turned him totally off mouth food. So they could do a full nutritional assay. On weekends, ravenous and puckered, he got a smoothie, jacked with protein, just to keep him off life support. Monday mornings they chelated him, or something that sounded like that, to zero out his nutritional stats, so that he could sizzle-fry in front of the panels all week and they could clock what was coming in.

If he thought about it, having survived the genital share, there wasn't a simple answer to why he'd sent the picture. But there wasn't a complicated answer, either. To Carl himself, it seemed both obvious and mysterious, inevitable and random. He could embrace nearly any interpretation. But since no one appeared to have seen it for what it was, trying to understand it suddenly felt bizarre. He was embarrassed that he'd done it and also disappointed that he hadn't done it well. He was ashamed and indifferent. Disturbed and content.

But most of all his body was empty and dry, and he was powerfully, powerfully hungry.

Carl was due at the lab on Thursdays, but this week they called him in early.

"You are technically malnourished," the doctor told him, smiling. "But here's the thing. So are most people, and they actually eat food. Being malnourished is not per se a concern of ours. You've lost a few pounds—well, more than that—but that could be attributed to stress at work. And, anyway, ideal body weight? Still not quite there. So okay. Pretty much. Muscle mass, sure. And your fingernails are brittle, which, of course. Well. What's important, what's kind of amazing, is that you're not starving. Your magnesium levels are ridiculous. I mean, just a joke, in terms of not eating anything. This isn't possible. What we're doing. It's not possible!"

"Okay," Carl said.

"I mean, you're hardly in ketosis here!" the doctor shouted, waving his clipboard.

Carl wanted to enjoy this news. Some carbs were flowing in. Whoopee. He was not technically dead. He looked at the two-way mirror, wondering who was back there. Kipler, no doubt, every single version of him. He had a lot riding on Carl. He needed this to work. Why was he hiding? Carl wondered. Afraid of a man whose face has died?

Then Carl did that thing he'd seen on TV where the suspect in the interrogation room gets up and confronts the two-way mirror. Pounds on it to call out the lurkers standing in judgment, deciding his future. Come on out, and all that. What are you afraid of? Except Carl did it sort of mildly. It was hard to walk. He tottered over to the glass, cupped his hands against it. He didn't want to break anything. Just a few taps on the glass. Hello? he thought. Hello? Did he really need to say it out loud? How much of this shit needed to be spelled out?

"Uh, what are you doing?" the doctor asked.

To answer that in detail, Carl would have had to wave a pretty complicated set of emoticons. Desperation, suspicion, apology, and, hovering over all the others, exhaustion. Just a yellow ball of tired face. Not yawning, though. Not that kind of tired.

"Tired face, tired face," Carl said to the doctor. "Just fucking tired face."

"There's nothing back there," the doctor said. "It's a closet. I'll show you."

Carl waved him away. He apologized. He was being paranoid, he explained. It's just that he was always so hungry, and it wasn't pain so much as tremendous pressure flushing through him. "It's like someone keeps pouring hot water inside me. Inside my whole body. I'm getting rinsed out by very hot water. Agony face. Face for I don't know how much longer I can do this."

The doctor looked at him but made no note.

"I'm just being foolish," Carl said. "You know me."

The doctor nodded. They hardly knew each other.

Carl ducked out and resumed his session at his desk. The light from his computer today was cool, almost soothing. Maybe they'd iterated a healing blue ray. Maybe this would all start feeling better. To kill time, he fired up a lost-person website and put in his own name. The tracking on these things was pretty poor. You could register, supposedly, and get better data. Live tracking was promised. Was it real? Could he pay the money and then see, in digital scribble, the path he'd been taking these past few months? Would the bird's-eye view reveal something new? Because he'd been through it on the ground, in person, and even he couldn't be sure.

The problem was that there were too many Carl Hirsches to choose from. Maybe thirty in Carl's region alone. You could pick only one at a time, then pay your money for the reveal. But behind each clickable Carl Hirsch was the same picture, the only extant picture of a Carl Hirsch anywhere, apparently.

The picture looked a good deal like Carl's own father, dead a long time now, who never lived in this area. Never even visited, as far as Carl knew. Was it really him? The picture was from that era when subjects did not look at the camera, so here was someone who looked very much like his dad, from so long ago, staring into the distance, at something behind Carl that he couldn't see. No matter how he jogged his head, he could not quite get those eyes to look at him.

The rest of the week went okay. The sympathy dried up, but all seemed well. Carl fried at his desk, sipped distilled water. His guards didn't seem to be minding him so carefully, and Kora hadn't come by to stick him with Shitazine, so he grabbed a scone at one point, and it burst into powder in his mouth. He fell to the ground coughing, a cloud of crumbs spraying everywhere, but no one at Mayflower particularly minded him. They knew his life was hell.

In the coatroom as Carl was leaving that Friday, Kipler pulled him aside. Out in the open, in front of the rush-hour crowd of employees, who pretended that their boss wasn't standing right there, huddled up with Blizzard Face himself.

"So what's with the crotch shot?"

"What?"

"Why did you send a picture of your testicles to so many strangers? People were revolted and confused. And over email. The least secure form of communication ever devised, including whatever the apes used."

"You knew?"

"A scrotum isn't some rare species, nor does any living person have a neck that fucked up. We know what your symptoms are. We caused them. I've probably seen forty unique pairs of balls. Just a round number. Not all of them up close, but I know what they look like."

"I'm sorry," Carl said.

"So are we. You're out. It breaks your nondisclosure. Honestly, even if it doesn't, it breaks something. Something is wrong. Your data. I don't know. I don't specialize in precise ways to say something so obvious. You're done."

"I agree," Carl said.

"Go have a sandwich, already. You're off the feed. We neutral-ized your panels a few days ago from a kill switch in Albuquerque."

"I was going to say," Carl said. "Something seemed like an improvement."

"The alpha unit wasn't friendly. We know that. Sorry for, you know. Mostly it was proof of concept. And guess what. Proof achieved. Through the so-called roof. Maybe your numbers weren't good, but they were numbers. You fed. Badly, and with little reten-tion. But you fed. We're moving to beta. The life hackers are going to strap in. This thing will make it to market. I'm sorry you can't take the ride with us."

"So am I fired?"

"Don't push your luck. The NDA still stands, for, like, three life-times. Your children's children, not that offspring are a likely out-come for you, can't even whisper it to each other. I'll be dead myself, but I'll leave instructions that your kids get slapped across the room and out a window if that happens. Slapped right the hell off the planet. So nary a whisper. Not that you're having kids. We find that it's easiest for you to keep quiet about all this if you, you know, don't even remember it. That way it's not a secret you're keeping. You don't even know about it yourself. Which is very nearly true. That's the argument from our side. Not even the argument, just the language. It never happened."

"Thanks," Carl said.

"I love you, man," Kipler said. He closed in on Carl, wrapped him in his arms. "What a bullet you took for us," he whispered. "A huge bullet. The biggest."

As the employees of Mayflower filed out of the building for the night, Carl held on to Kipler in the coatroom, squeezing him tightly, feeling the man's heartbeat throb against his face.

For a while, everything went quiet. Carl returned to mouth food with an animal focus, but he couldn't keep it down, and all the time he fretted about the UV panels. Showing up, who knows, in traffic lights. On televisions. At home, pulsing from his mirror. He stayed cautious of screens, skipped past them quickly.

The winter failed, and along came April, one of the twelve punishments. Carl had seen this month too often by now and had hardened against its pleasures.

April was a bastard name for a month so numb. Slush on the ground, a salty slurry in the air. Slush, most likely, in his insides, which he pictured as muddied guts down a hole.

Day after day, Carl tromped to work. He tromped home. His pants grew stiff with salt. He lost his security clearance and was migrated through Mayflower's cubicles once, twice. Finally, they exiled him, with the older, idea-free crowd, to a featureless room overlooking the vast, immaculate cafeteria. In Carl's new work corridor, the employees went uninstructed and drastically unpoliced. Did they really work there? They shared a single computer and a pristine in-box. To Carl, the workspace was a petting zoo, without visitors. People moved from table to window to door, moaning. He did his best not to touch anyone.

He soon lost his taste for food. Maybe he'd outgrown it, which possibly meant that his clock had finally run down, and okay, that was okay. A creature senses an ending. A window, a door, a hole opens, and he steps through. For now, he sipped the occasional yogurt drink and kept some bread nearby, but something had died in him, and he worried that eating, even a little, would feed it, would stoke the thing and bring it back to life. He felt safer with it gone.

Sometimes Carl woke up confused. He spent time trying to figure out how to reverse what had happened. What was the opposite of a human grow light? He tried the obvious: darkness, the deepest kind. He tried it and tried it and tried it. At home for days with the shades down, then—where the darkness was so much better, so exquisite and fine—out of town, along the sand roads, under the salt pines, in the dunes, or deep in the woods off the highway.

One night, the police picked him up, and they were not pleased.

What face could Carl show them but his own, burned and unmoving? What he told them, at length and through his charred mouth, was not true and it was not enough. They drove him home in silence, and when they dropped him off they saw him all the way to his door and inside, and after Carl locked up he listened for a long time, but never did hear them walk away.

At the age of forty-one, Carl left Mayflower and accepted an IT job in a school system near the water. Tech support turned out to be lightbulbs, wind blinds, a chimney. Chairs, phones, walls. The yard, too. Carl would maintain all of them.

The school kept Carl away from the children. He understood. Children's fears should be managed. Sometimes their eyes need to be covered. So much is better left unseen. There would be more and greater to fear when they were older. Best to save room. But Carl found a way to tend the landscape in the mornings, at a squinting distance from the school doors. From afar, he was a faceless man in a jumpsuit, leaning into his shovel, Carl the Small, the frantic waver. Every day, the kids, fired like missiles from the yellow school buses, waved at Carl, and he saluted them all, righty-o. Hello there, you guys! People should always greet one another that way. If he could store a message for creatures thousands of years in the future, it would be simple. Upon meeting one another in whatever passes, in your world, for a room, a hallway, a road, a field, do not play dead while you are still alive. Just try to say hello.

It turned out that there was a woman at the school who did not die from seeing Carl up close, again and again. They had lunch together, and lunch together, and lunch and a walk, and a weekend coffee, and lunch again, until something felt wrong when they didn't meet up, even if it was to do nothing much but take the woods path, or walk, once night had come on, right through town.

Her name was Maura, and she ran art and languages for the sixth graders. She asked what had happened to him, and he shook his head. He wanted to pull a long-story face. The hardened shell of him had withered by then, gone soft. It looked as if someone had died just outside his body and he was still wearing that person's skin. He shook his head, that was all, and this was fine with her. She said she understood. Which meant, to Carl, that in one way or another maybe Maura was keeping to her own nondisclosure agreement, one that she'd struck with herself or others, sometime in the past, far from here.

It was no romance, which relieved them both. Maura and Carl were plain about what they needed to feel pleasure. If their intimacy could feel turn-based and a little like a chore, just friends bestowing favors, like old women doing each other's hair, it was at least a manageable sorrow that he could endure. He could keep an eye on it and be sure that it didn't grow.

Maura was older than Carl. She was kinder, finer-looking, more at peace, as far as he knew, with having been born. What a gift, not to be constantly scouting for an exit! And if Carl felt private or mean he knew to leave the house and pour out his cruelty in a safe place, where Maura could not be hurt. Perhaps what was most animal in him had been cooked out by Kipler and his rig, burned or boiled or just reduced so that it hardly ever appeared. He hated to think so positively, because he felt as if it did a kind of violence to his brain, but perhaps something good had come of all that heat, all that light. An off-script use case to the human grow light that no doubt they'd never suspect over at Mayflower: you could use that fierce power to eliminate the wrong and rotten parts of yourself. Not a grow light but the reverse, which felt better to Carl than he would have liked to admit.

It was probably not the Lord who allowed Maura to conceive a child, even though she thanked Him. Carl tried thanking Him, too. His policy on the matter—as they tended her pregnancy all summer and into the fall, walking to school together on weekday mornings before silently parting for the day, then meeting again for the walk home—was that gratitude needed only to be released from one's person, spoken out loud. From there, it could find its proper destination on its own.

When his son was born, on a cold, cloudless October night, Carl could not help himself. Some very old words came back to him. What a tremendously ridiculous person he'd become, even though nothing that had happened to him had been ridiculous. The words he recalled were somehow suddenly available, wanting out. He whispered them, over and over, until the little creature, still unnamed, mouth bubbling on Maura's tummy, fell asleep for the very first time in his life: *Someone new is among us. Someone special.*

It hurt him to say this, because he was Carl. He knew the odds, the science, the facts. Or at least he used to. Was such a statement really as grossly untrue as it seemed? Just him being wishful, being scared? What, really, was so special about one more boy in the world?

Maybe the verdict on this could stay out for now. Just scattered into the distance, a verdict you could never really reach, even if you wanted to. Maybe, in whatever time he had left, Carl would work as hard as he could to keep the verdict on that question, along with every other question that pressed in, as far away from his family as humanly possible.

George and Elizabeth

When George's father died, he neglected to tell his therapist, which wouldn't have been such a big deal, except for those killer moods of hers. She knew how to punish him with a vicious show of boredom.

He'd been deep in a session with her, maintaining that when he was younger he had discovered that there was no difference, in bed, between men and women. Literally. At the biological level. If you could wrap a present, you could make one into the other. And therefore this issue of preference had weirdly become moot. You didn't have to check either box.

"Have you ever worked with clay?" he asked her. "Have you ever pushed pudding around in your bowl?"

George gestured to show what he meant. Spoon work, a bit of charade knitting.

Dr. Graco waved for him to get on with it.

It was finally, he explained, just a shame that there were no other categories he could sample.

"So you feel incapable of surprise at the sexual level?" she asked.

"I'm sure there are things out there I haven't tried, but in the end they belong to categories that have washed out for me. Just, you know, haircuts I've already had, beards, whatever. There's too much time left on the clock. I wish that I had paced myself."

"Paced yourself?"

"Yeah."

"Is it a race?"

"Yes. I just got my number. I should have pinned it to my shirt. Sorry about that."

"You don't take this seriously, do you?"

"Well . . . I pay you to take it seriously. Which gives me room to deflect and joke about it and put my insecurities on display, which you should know how to decode and use in your treatment. Another layer of evidence for your salt box."

"Do you often think about how I conduct your treatment, as you call it?"

George sighed.

"I thought about it once, and then I died," he said. "I bled out."

And boom, the session was over. He was in the waiting room putting on his coat before he remembered his news, what he'd been so determined to tell her, but he had to deal with the ovoid white noise machine which turned speech into mush, and the miserable young man waiting his turn who refused to ever acknowledge George when he burst out of his appointment. It was all a bit exhausting. Were the two of them really supposed to pretend that they weren't both paying Dr. Graco to inhale their misery and exhibit a professional silence about it? And couldn't they finally just unite in shame and even go sadly rut somewhere? Roll out their crusts against a building, even, or on the merry-go-round in Central Park?

Sex with sad people was something that could still deliver—in terms of sheer lethargy and awkwardness—but the demographics were stubborn. These people didn't exactly come out to play very often. It wasn't clear what birdcall you were supposed to use. You practically had to go around knocking on doors. And then the whole thing could verge on coercion.

The news of his father's death had come in yesterday from a laundromat. Or perhaps it was simply a place with loud machines and yelling in the background. Someone was on the other end of the phone asking if a Mr. George was next of kin.

At first George was confused. "To what?" he asked. The word "kin" made him picture the Hare Krishna display, human beings going hairless and sleek as they evolved. As if a bald, aquiline man couldn't swing a club and crush someone.

"All the tenants do a next of kin. I just need to know if that's you. Tenant name is . . . I can't really read this writing, to be honest. I didn't know this man. We have a lot of units."

George very slowly said his father's name.

"That's it. Check. And are you Mr. George?"

George said he was. Whenever someone tried to pronounce his true last name, it sounded unspeakably vulgar.

"I'm sorry to report your loss," the voice said.

Then don't, thought George. Keep it to yourself.

He guessed he knew he'd get a call like this one day, and he guessed he'd have to think about it for a while, because the initial impact felt mild, even irritating. He'd have to stick his head into the dirty, hot, self-satisfied state of California and try not to drown in smugness while he solved the problem of his father's body, which he hadn't particularly cared for when his father was alive. But what was most on his mind was this question of kin, and why they had not made another call first.

There was a sister, but she'd scored out of the family. It was hard to blame her. Better food, prettier people, sleeker interiors. George read about her now and then online. She'd achieved a kind of fame in the world of industrial materials. At some point she'd promoted her ridiculous middle name, Pattern, to pole position. Like Onan, maybe. Or Pelé. Her old name, Elizabeth, George figured, was holding her back, and in a way he couldn't blame her, given the sheep-ish Elizabeths he'd privately failed to grant human status in college. Sleepwalkers, enablers, preposterously loyal friends. Pattern was a family name belonging to their great-grandmother, who lived on a brutally cold little island, and who, according to their mother, had made a sport of surviving terminal illnesses. Now George's lovely sister Pattern, so many years later, was a person, a business, a philosophy, a crime. She did something in aerospace. Or to it. Had his brilliant sister once said, in a *Newsweek* profile, that she wanted to "help people forget everything they thought they knew about the earth"? One such bit of hypnosis had apparently resulted in immense profits for her, the kind of money you could get very paranoid about losing. She produced shimmering synthetic materi-als from terribly scarce natural resources — a kind of metal drapery that served as "towels" for drones — which meant Pattern was often photographed shaking hands with old people in robes on the tar-macs of the world, no doubt after administering shuddering hand jobs to them back on the airbus.

Well, that wasn't fair. Probably, George figured, her staff con-ducted proclivity research so that it could provide bespoke orgasms to these titans of industry, whose children Pattern was boiling down for parts, whose reefs, mines, and caves her company was thoroughly hosing.

At home Pattern was probably submissive to a much older spouse, whose approach to gender was seasonal. Or maybe his sis-ter wasn't married? It was difficult to remember, really. Perhaps because he had probably never known? Perhaps because Pattern did not exactly speak to any of the old family? Ever?

Now, with Mother in a Ball jar and Dad finally passed, George was the last man standing. Or sitting, really. Sort of slumped at home in the mouth of his old, disgusting couch. Trying to figure out his travel plans and how exactly he could get the bereavement discount for his flight. Like what if they tested him at the gate with their grief wand and found out, with digital certainty, that he super sort of didn't give a shit?

His most recent contact with his sister was an email from soldier1@ pattern.com, back when her rare visits home were brokered by her staff, who would wait for their boss in a black-ops Winnebago out on the street. Ten years ago now? His mother was dead already, or still alive? At the time George wondered if Pattern couldn't just send a mannequin to holiday meals in her place, its pockets stuffed with money. Maybe make it edible, the face carved from meat, to deepen the catharsis when they gnashed it apart with their teeth. Anyway, wouldn't his sister like to know that there was now one less person who might make a grab for her money? She could soften security at the compound, wherever she lived. Dad was dead. Probably she already knew. When you're that wealthy, changes in your biological signature, such as the sudden omission of a patriarch, show up instantly on your live update. You blink in the high-resolution mirror at your reflection, notice no change whatsoever, and then move on with your day. Maybe she'd have her personal physicians test her for grief later in the week, just to be sure.

The question now was how to fire off an email to his very important sister that would leapfrog her spam filter, which was probably a group of human people, arms linked, blocking unwanted communications to their elusive boss, who had possibly evolved into a smoke by now.

Simple was probably best. "Dear Pat," George wrote. "Mom and Dad have gone out and they are not coming back. It's just you and me now. Finally we have this world to ourselves. P.S. Write back!"

George went to California to pack his father's things, intending a full-force jettison into the dumpster. He'd only just started surveying the watery one-bedroom apartment, where he could not picture his father standing, sitting, sleeping, or eating, mostly because he had trouble picturing his father at all, when a neighbor woman, worrisomely tall, came to be standing uninvited in the living room. He'd left the door open and cracked the windows so the breeze could do its work. Let the elements scrub this place free of his father. He needed candles, wind, a shaman. And on the subject of need: after sudden travel into blistering sunshine, he needed salty food to blow off in his mouth. He needed sex, if only with himself. Oh, to be alone with his laptop so he could leak a little cream onto his belly. Now there was a trespasser in his father's home, suited up in business wear. It was enormously difficult to picture such people as babies. And yet one provided the courtesy anyway. An effort to relate. Their full maturation was even harder to summon. He was apparently to believe that, over time, these creatures, just nude little seals at first, would elongate and gain words. A layer of fur would cover them, with moist parts, and teeth, and huge pockets for gathering money. Was there a website where the corporate Ichabods of the world showed off their waterworks, gave each other rubdowns, and whispered pillow talk in an invented language? Perhaps a new category beckoned.

"Oh my god. You can't be George," the woman said.

George sort of shared her disbelief. He couldn't be. The metaphysics were troubling, if you let them get to you. But day after day, with crushing regularity, he failed to prove otherwise.

The woman approached, her nose high. Examine the specimen, she possibly thought. Maybe draw its blood.

"I can't believe it!"

He asked if he could help her. Maybe she wanted to buy something, a relic of the dead man. The realtor had said that everything had to go. Take this apartment down to the bones.

So far, George was just picking at the skin. He was looking through his father's takeout menus, skimming the man's Internet history. There were items of New Mexican pottery to destroy, shirts to try on.

Maybe he'd dress up like his father and take some selfies. Get the man online, if posthumously. If no one much liked him when he was alive, at least the old man could get some likes in the afterlife. Serious.

The woman remembered herself.

"I'm Trish, Jim's . . . you know."

"Uh-huh," George said.

"I won't even pretend to think he might have told you about me," Trish said. "It's not like we were married in any real official way. At least not yet."

Oh god. A half wife.

The last time he spoke to his father—months ago now—George remembered not listening while his father said he had met someone, and that she—what was it?—provided the kind of service you didn't really get paid for, or paid enough, because damn this country! And that this new girlfriend was from somewhere unique, and George knew to act impressed. Certainly his dad had seemed very proud, as if he'd met some dignitary from another planet.

So details had been shared, just not absorbed. Would she tell George now that his father had really loved him? Pined and whatever, wished for phone calls, had the boy's name on Google Alert?

"Of course, Trish," George said, and then he smacked his forehead, ever so lightly, to let her know just what he thought of his forgetfulness. She deserved as much. They embraced, at a distance, as if his father's body were stretched out between them. Then she stepped closer and really wrapped him up. He felt her breath go out of her as she collapsed against him.

George knew he was supposed to feel something. Emotional, sexual. Rage and sorrow and a little bit of predatory hunger. Even a deeper shade of indifference? History virtually demanded that the errant son, upon packing up his estranged and dead father's belongings, would seek closure with the new, younger wife. Half wife. Some sort of circuitry demanded to be completed. He had an obligation.

It felt pretty good to hold her. She softened, but didn't go boneless. He dropped his face into her neck. Lately he'd consorted with some hug-proof men and women. They hardened when he closed in. Their bones came out. Not this one. She knew what she was doing.

"Well, you sure don't smell like your father," she said, breaking the hug. "And you don't look like him. I mean not even close."

She laughed.

"Oh I must," said George. He honestly couldn't be sure.

"Nope. Trust me. I have seen that man up close. You are a very handsome young man."

"Thank you," said George.

"I think I want to see some ID! I might have to cry foul!"

They met later for dinner at a taco garage on the beach. Their food arrived inside what looked like an industrial metal disk.

George dug in and wished it didn't taste so ridiculously good.

"Oh my god," he gushed.

It was sort of the problem with California, the unembarrassed way it delivered pleasure. It backed you into a corner.

After dinner they walked on the beach and tried to talk about George's father without shitting directly inside the man's urn, which was probably still ember hot. George hadn't unboxed it yet.

"I loved him, I did. I'm sure of it," Trish said. "When all the anger finally went out of him there was something so sweet there."

George pictured his father deflated like a pool toy, crumpled in a garage.

"He called me by your mom's name a lot. By mistake. Rina. Irene. Boy did he do that a lot."

"Oh, that must have been hard," said George. Who was Irene? he wondered. Had he ever met her? His mother's name was Lydia.

"No, I get it. He had a life before me. We weren't babies. It's just that I suppose I want to be happy, too. Which is really a radical idea, if you think about it," Trish said.

George thought about it, but he was tired and losing focus. He preferred a solitary loneliness to the kind he felt around other people. And this woman, Trish. Was she family to him now? Why did it feel like they were on a date?

"It's just that my happiness, what I needed to do to get it, threatened your father," continued Trish.

"My father, threatened," George said. "But whatever could you mean?"

Trish laughed. "Oh I like you. You're nothing like him."

George took that in. It sounded fine, possibly true. He had no real way of knowing. He remembered his father's new radio, which he had watched him build when he was a kid, and whose dial he twisted into static for hours and hours. He could make his dad laugh by pretending the static came from his mouth, lip-synching it. He remembered how frightened his father had been in New York when he visited so many years later. George held his arm everywhere they went. It had irritated him terribly.

What else? His father made him tomato soup once. His father slapped him while he was brushing his teeth, sending a spray of toothpaste across the mirror.

George was probably supposed to splurge on memories now. He wasn't sure he had the energy. Maybe the thing was to let the memories hurl back and cripple him, months or years from now. They needed time, wherever they were hiding, to build force, so that when they returned to smother him, he might never recover.

After their walk, they stood in a cloud of charred smoke behind the restaurant. The ocean broke and swished somewhere over a dune. Trish arched her back and yawned.

"All of this death," she said.

"Horn-y," George shouted. He wasn't, but still. Maybe if they stopped talking for a while they'd break this mood.

Trish tried not to laugh.

"No, uh, funny you should say that. I was just thinking, it makes me want to . . ." She smiled.

How George wished that this was the beginning of a suicide pact, after a pleasant dinner at the beach with your dead father's mistress. Just walk out together into the waves. But something told him that he knew what was coming instead.

"I'm going to comfort myself tonight, with or without you," Trish said. "Do you feel like scrubbing in?"

George looked away. The time was, he would sleep with anyone, of any physical style. Any make, any model. Pretty much any year. If only he could do away with the transactional phase, when the barter chips came out, when the language of seduction was suddenly spoken, rather than sung, in such non-melodious tones. It was often a deal breaker. Often. Not always.

After they'd had sex, which required one of them to leave the room to focus on the project alone, they washed up and had a drink. It felt good to sip some so-called legacy whiskey from his father's Pueblo coffee mugs. Now that they'd stared into each other's cold depravity, they could relax.

Trish circled around to the inevitable.

"So what's up with Pattern?"

Here we go.

"What's she like? Are you guys in touch? Your father never would speak of her."

Probably due to the nondisclosure agreement she must have had him sign, George figured.

"You know," he said, pausing, as if his answer was more than ordinarily true, "she's really nice, really kind. I think she's misunderstood."

"Did I misunderstand it when her company, in eighteen months, caused more erosion to the Great Barrier Reef than had since been recorded in all of history?"

"She apologized for that."

"I thought you were going to say she didn't do it. Or that it didn't happen that way."

"No, she did do it, with great intention, I think. I bet at low tide she would have stood on the reef herself and smashed it into crumbs for whatever fungal fuel they were mining. But, you know, she apologized. In a way, that's much better than never having done it. She has authority now. Gravity. She's human."

"What was she before?"

Before? George thought. Before that she was his sister. She baby-sat for him. He once saw her get beaten up by another girl. She went to a special smart-people high school that had classes on Saturdays. Before that she was just this older person in his home. She had her own friends. She kept her door closed. Someone should have told him she was going to disappear. He would have tried to get to know her.

In the morning Trish recited the narrative she had concocted for them. Their closeness honored a legacy. Nothing was betrayed by their physical intimacy. They'd both lost someone. It was now their job to make fire in the shape of—here George lost track of her theory—George's dad.

Trish looked like she wanted to be challenged. Instead George nodded and agreed and tried to hold her. He said he thought that a fire like that would be a fine idea. Even though they'd treated each other like specimens the night before, two lab technicians straining to achieve a result, their hug was oddly platonic today. He pictured the two of them out in the snow, pouring a gasoline silhouette of his dead father. Igniting it. Effigy or burn pile?

"We didn't know each other before," said Trish. "Now we do. We're in each other's lives. This is real. And it's good. You're not just going to go home and forget me. It won't be possible."

George would sign off on pretty much any press release about what had happened last night, and what they now meant to each other, so long as it featured him catching his plane at 9:30 a.m. and never seeing her again.

As he was leaving, Trish grabbed him.

"I would say 'one for the road,' but I don't really believe in that.

Just that whole way of thinking and speaking. It sounds sorrowful and final and I don't want that to be our thing. That's not us. I don't like the word 'road' and I definitely don't like the word 'one.' Two is much better. Two is where it's at."

She held up two fingers and tried to get George to kiss them.

George smiled at her, pleaded exhaustion. It was sweet of her to offer, he said, and normally he would, but.

"You know, research shows," Trish said, not giving up, "that really it's a great energy boost, to love and be loved. To climax. To cause to climax. To cuddle and talk and to listen and speak. You're here! You're standing right here with me now!"

"I'm sorry," said George. "I guess it's all just starting to hit me. Dad. Being gone. I don't think I'd bring the right spirit right now. You would deserve better."

It didn't feel good or right to play this card, but as he said it he found it was more true than he'd intended.

Trish was beautiful, but given the growing privacy of his sexual practice, such factors no longer seemed to matter. He would probably love to have sex with her, if she could somehow find a way of vanishing, and if the two of them could also find a way to forget that they had tried that already, last night, and the experience had been deeply medical and isolating. It was just too soon to hope for a sufficiently powerful denial to erase all that and let them, once again, look at each other like strangers, full of lust and hope.

Is that a bad thing, George asked his therapist, after returning home and telling her the basics.

"And please don't ask me what I think," he continued. "The reason people ask a question is because they would like an answer. Reflecting my question back to me, I swear, is going to make me hurl myself out of the window."

Together they looked at the small, dirty window. There were bars on it. The office was on the ground floor.

"I'd hate to be a cause of your death," said the therapist, unblinking.

"Well, I just wonder what you think."

"Okay, but I don't think you need to lecture me in order to get me to answer a question. You seem to think I need to be educated about how to respond to you. There are also many other reasons people ask questions, aside from wanting answers. You're an imbecile if you think otherwise."

"Okay, you're right, I'm sorry."

"Well, then, I think it must be lonely. I do. To find yourself attracted to a woman who also seems, as you say, attracted to you — if that's true — and to think you'd be more content to fantasize about her than to experience her physically. So it sounds lonely to me. But we should also notice that this is a loneliness you've chosen, based on your sexual desires. Your sexuality seems to thrive on loneliness. And I can't help but sense that some part of you is proud of that. Your story seems vaguely boastful."

"Plus her being my father's widow."

Dr. Graco frowned.

"What was that?" she asked.

"You know, her also having been involved with my father, before he died. I guess I left that part out."

Dr. Graco took a moment to write in her notebook. She wrote quickly, and with a kind of disdain, as if she didn't like to have to make contact with the page. A fear of contaminants, maybe. A disgust with language.

It had sometimes occurred to him that therapists used this quiet writing time, after you've said something striking, or, more likely, boring, to make notes to themselves about other matters. Grocery lists, plans. One never got to see what was written down, and there was simply no possible way that all of it was strictly relevant. How much of it was sheer stalling, running out the clock? How much of it just got the narcissist in the chair across from you to shut up for a while?

She wrote through one page and had turned to another before looking up.

"I am sorry to hear about your father."

"I should have told you. I apologize."

"He died . . . recently?"

"Two weeks ago. That's why I was away. My missed appointment. Which I paid for, but. I was gone. I'm not sure if you."

"I see. Do you mean it when you say you should have told me?"

"Well, I found the prospect of telling you exhausting, I guess. I was annoyed that I had to do it. To be honest, I wished you could just, through osmosis, have the information, in the same way you can see what I'm wearing and we don't need to discuss it. It's just a self-evident fact. You could just look at me and know that my father is dead."

She resumed writing, but he did not want to wait for her.

"That's not a criticism of you, by the way. I don't think you were supposed to guess. I mean I don't think I think that. Maybe. You know, to just be sensitive and perceptive enough to know. I am sometimes disappointed about your powers, I guess. That's true, I should admit that. I just wish I had, like, a helper, who could run ahead of me to deliver the facts, freeing me up from supplying all of this context when I talk to people. Otherwise I'm just suddenly this guy who's like, my father died, blah blah. I'm just that guy."

"But you weren't. Because you didn't tell me. You were not that guy."

"Right, I guess."

"So then who were you?"

"What?"

"You didn't want to be the guy who told me your father had died, so by not telling me, what guy did you end up being instead?"

For some reason, George saw himself and Pattern, as kids, waiting on a beach for their lunch to digest, so they could go swimming. Pattern was dutifully counting down from two thousand. It was a useless memory, irrelevant here. He remembered when he shopped and cooked for his mother, when she wasn't feeling well, and then really wasn't feeling well. He cleaned and took care of her. His father had already planted his flag in California. He was that guy, but for such a short time. Two weeks? He'd been very many people since then. Who was he when he didn't tell Dr. Graco that his father died? Nobody. No one remarkable. He'd been someone too scared or too bored, he didn't know which, to discuss something important.

"That just made me think of something," he said finally. "The word 'guy.' I don't know. Have you heard of Guy Fox?"

"I assume you don't mean the historic figure, Guy Fawkes?"

"No. F-o-x. Porn star, but that's not really a good label for what he does. It's not clear you can even call it porn anymore. It's so sort of remote and kind of random, and definitely not obviously sexual. Or even at all. I mean almost, just, boredom. Anyway, it's a new sort of thing. He provides eye contact. People pay a lot. He'll just watch you, on video. You can stream him to your TV, and he'll watch you. People pay him to watch while they have sex, of course, or masturbate, but now supposedly people just hire him to watch them while they hang out alone in their houses. Whenever they look up, he's looking at them. They are paying to have eye contact whenever they want. They want someone out there seeing them. And he's just amazing. Apparently there's nothing quite like getting seen by him. It's an addiction."

"Ah, I see. Well, I'm afraid we have to stop."

Afraid, afraid, afraid. Don't be afraid, George thought. Embrace it.

For once he wished she'd say, "I'm delighted our session is over, George, now get the hell out of my office, you monster."

Bowing to a certain protocol of the bereaved, George acquired a baby dog: hairless, pink, and frightening. His therapist had put him onto it after he kept insisting he was fine. She explained that people who lose a parent, especially one they weren't close to, tend to grieve their lack of grief. Like they want to really feel something, and don't, and so they grieve that. That absence. She said that one solution to this circular, masturbatory grief, is to take care of something. To be responsible for another living creature.

Except George and the animal had turned out to be a poor match. That's how he put it to the dog catcher, or whatever the man was called when he sent the wet thing back, and then hired cleaners to sanitize his home. The animal was more like a quiet young child, waiting for a ride, determined not to exploit any hospitality whatsoever in George's home. It rarely sprawled out, never seemed to relax. It sat upright in the corner, sometimes trotting to the window, where it glanced up and down the street, patiently confirming that it had been abandoned. Would it recognize rescue when it came? Sometimes you just had to wait this life out, it seemed to be thinking, and get a better deal next time. God knows where the creature slept. Or if.

Did the animal not get tired? Did it not require something? George would occasionally hose off the curry from the unmolested meat in his takeout container, and scrape it into the dog bowl, only to clean it up, untouched, days later. The animal viewed these meals with calm detachment. How alienating it was, to live with a creature so ungoverned by appetites. This thing could go hungry. It had a long game. What kind of level playing field was that? George felt entirely outmatched.

One night George tried to force the issue. He wanted more from it, and it wanted absolutely nothing from George, so perhaps, as the superior species, with broader perspective in the field, George needed to step up and trigger change. Be a leader. Rule by example. Maybe he had been playing things too passive? He pulled the thing onto his lap. He stroked its wet, stubbled skin, put on one of those TV shows that pets are supposed to like. No guns, just soft people swallowing each other.

The dog survived the affection. It trembled under George's hands. Some love is strictly clinical. Maybe this was like one of those deep-tissue massages that release difficult feelings? George forced his hand along the dog's awful back, wondering why anyone would willingly touch another living thing. What a disaster of feelings it stirred up, feelings that seemed to have no purpose other than to suffocate him. Finally the dog turned in George's lap, as if standing on ice, and carefully licked its master's face. Just once, and briefly. A studied, scientific lick, using the tongue to gain important information. Then it bounced down to its corner again, where it sat and waited.

Months after his father's death there was still no word from Pattern. After he'd returned from California, and cleansed himself in the flat, gray atmosphere of New York, George had sent her another email, along the lines of, "Hey Pat, I'm back. I've got Dad's dust. Let me know if you want to come say goodbye to it. There are still some slots free. Visiting hours are whenever and whenever and whenever. — G."

He never heard back, and figured he wasn't going to—on the Internet now Pattern was referred to as a fugitive wanted by Europol, for crimes against the environment—but one night, getting into bed, his phone made an odd sound. Not its typical ring. It took him a minute to track the noise to his phone, and at first he thought it must be broken, making some death noise before it finally shut down.

He picked it up and heard a long, administrative pause.

"Please hold for Pattern," a voice said.

He waited and listened. Finally a woman said hello.

"Hello?" said George. "Pattern?"

"Who's this?" It wasn't Pattern. This person sounded like a bitchy tween, entitled and shrill.

"You called me," explained George.

"Who's on the line," said the teenager, "or I'm hanging up."

George was baffled. Did a conversation with his sister really require such a cloak-and-dagger ground game? He hung up the phone.

The phone rang again an hour later, and it was Pattern herself.

"Jesus, George, what the hell? You hung up on my staff?"

"First of all, hello," he said. "Secondly, let's take a look at the transcript and I'll show you exactly what happened. Your team could use some human behavior training. But forget all that. What on earth is new, big sister?"

She wanted to see him, she said, and she'd found a way for that to be possible. They had things to discuss.

"No shit," said George. He couldn't believe he was actually talking to her.

"Wait, so where are you?" she asked. "I don't have my thing with me."

"What thing?"

"I mean I don't know where you are."

"And your thing would have told you? Have you been tracking me?"

"Oh c'mon, you asshole."

"I'm in New York."

She laughed.

"What?"

"No, it's just funny. I mean it's funny that you still call it that."

"What would I call it?"

"No, nothing, forget it. I'm sorry. I'm just on a different, it's, I'm thinking of something else. Forget it."

"O-kay. You are so fucking weird and awkward. I'm not really sure I even want to see you."

"Georgie!"

"Kidding, you freak. Can you, like, send a jet for me? Or a pod? Or what exactly is it that you guys even make now? Can you break my face into dust and make it reappear somewhere?"

"Ha ha. I'll send a car for you. Tomorrow night. Seven o'clock."

...

George met Pattern in the sky bar of a strange building, which somehow you could not see from the street. Everyone had thought the developers had purchased the air rights and then very tastefully decided not to use them. Strike a blow for restraint. The elevator said otherwise. This thing was a goddamn tower. How had they done that? The optics for that sort of thing, Pattern explained to him, had been around for fifteen years or more. Brutally old-fashioned technology. Practically caveman. She thought it looked cheesy at this point.

"A stealth scraper," said George, wanting to sound appreciative.

"Hardly. It's literally smoke and mirrors," Pattern said. "I am not kidding. And it's kind of gross. But whatever. I love this bar. These cocktails are just violent. There's a frozen pane of pork in this one. Ridiculously thin. They call it pork glass."

"Yum," said George, absently.

The funny thing about the bar, which was only just dawning on George, was that it was entirely free of people. And deadly silent. Out the window was a view of the city he'd never seen. Whenever he looked up he had the sensation that he was somewhere else. In Europe. In the past. On a film set. Asleep. Every now and then a young woman crept out from behind a curtain to touch Pattern on the wrist, moving her finger back and forth. Pattern would smell her wrist, make a face, and say something unintelligible.

But here she was, his very own sister. It was like looking at his mother and his father and himself, but refined, the damaged cells burned off. The best parts of them, contained in this one person.

"First of all, George," Pattern said. "Dad's girlfriend? Really?"

"Trish?"

"What a total pig you are. Does this woman need to be abused and neglected by two generations of our family?"

"How could you know anything about that?"

"Oh cut it out. It astonishes me when I meet people who still think they have secrets. It's so quaint! You understand that even with your doors closed and lights out . . . Please tell me you understand. I couldn't bear it if you were that naive. My own brother."

"I understand, I think."

"That man you pay to watch you while you're cleaning the house? On your laptop screen?"

"Guy Fox."

"Oh, George, you are a funny young man."

"That's actually a fairly mainstream habit, to have a watcher."

"Right, George, it's happening all over the Middle East, too. A worldwide craze. In Poland they do it live. It's called a Peeping Tom. But who cares. Baby brother is a very strange bird.

"So," she said, scooting closer to him and giving him a luxurious hug. "Mom and Dad never told you, huh?"

"Told me what?"

"They really never told you?"

"I'm listening."

"I'm just not sure it's for me to say. Mom and Dad talked about it kind of a lot, I mean we all did. I just figured they'd told you."

"What already, Jesus. There's no one else left to tell me."

"You were adopted. That's actually not the right word. Dad got in trouble at work and his boss forced him to take you home and raise you. You were born out of a donkey's ass. Am I remembering correctly? That doesn't sound right. From the ass of an ass."

He tried to smile.

"I'm just kidding, George, Jesus. What is wrong with people?"

"Oh my god, right?" said George. "Why can't people entertain more stupid jokes at their own expense? Je-sus. It's so frustrating! When, like, my worldview isn't supported by all the little people beneath me? And I can't demean people and get an easy laugh? It's so not fair!"

"Oh fuck off, George."

They smiled. It felt really good. This was just tremendously nice.

"You don't understand," he said, trying harder than usual to be serious. "Mom punted so long ago I can't even remember her smell. And Dad was just a stranger, you know? He was so formal, so polite. I always felt like I was meeting him for the first time."

He tried to sound like his father, like any father: "Hello, George, how are you? How was your flight? Well, that's grand. What's your life like these days?"

Pattern stared at him.

"Honestly," said George. "I can't stand making small talk with people who have seen me naked. Or who fed me. Or spanked me. I mean once you spank someone, you owe them a nickname. Was that just me or were Mom and Dad, like, completely opposed to nicknames? Or even just honey or sweetie or any of that."

"Jesus, George, what do you want from people? You have some kind of intimacy fantasy. Do you think other people go around hugging each other and holding hands, mainlining secrets and confessions into each other's veins?"

"I have accepted the fact of strangers," said George. "After some struggle. But it's harder when they are in your own family."

"Violin music for you," said Pattern, and she snapped her fingers.

He looked up, perked his ears, expecting to hear music.

"Wow," she marveled. "You think I'm very powerful, don't you?"

"Honestly, I don't know. I have no idea. Are you in trouble? Everything I read is so scary."

"I am in a little bit of trouble, yes. But don't worry. It's nothing. And you. You seem so sad to me," Pattern said. "Such a sad, sad young man." She stroked his face, and it felt ridiculously, treacherously comforting.

George waved this off, insisted that he wasn't. He just wanted to know about her. He really did. Who knows where she'd vanish to after this, and he genuinely wanted to know what her life was like, where she lived. Was she married? Had she gotten married in secret or something?

"I don't get to act interested and really mean it," George explained. "I mean ever, so please tell me who you are. It's kind of a selfish question, because I can't figure some things out about myself, so maybe if I hear about you, something will click."

"Me? I tend to date the house husband type. Self-effacing, generous, asexual. Which is something I'm really attracted to, I should say. Men with low T, who go to bed in a full rack of pajamas. That's my thing. I don't go for the super-carnal hetero men; they seem like zoo animals. Those guys who know what they want, and have weird and highly developed skills as lovers, invariably have the worst possible taste—we're supposed to congratulate them for knowing that they like to lick butter right off the stick. What a nightmare, to be subject to someone else's expertise. The guys I tend to date, at first, are out to prove that they endorse equality, that my career matters, that my interests are primary—they make really extravagant displays of selflessness, burying all of their own needs. I go along with it, and over time I watch them deflate and lose all reason to live, by which point I have steadily lost all of my attraction for them. I imagine something like that is mirrored in the animal kingdom, but honestly that's not my specialty. I should have an air gun in my home so I could put these guys out of their misery. Or a time-lapse video documenting the slow and steady loss of self-respect they go through. It's a turnoff, but, you know, it's my turnoff. Part of what initially arouses me is the feeling that I am about to mate with someone who will soon be ineffectual and powerless. I've come to rely on the arc. It's part of my process."

"You think these guys don't mean it that they believe in equality?"

"No, I think they do, and that it has a kind of cost. They just distort themselves so much trying to do the right thing that there's nothing left."

"And you enjoy that?"

"Well, they enjoy that. They're driven to it. I'm just a bystander to their quest. And I enjoy that. It's old school, but I like to watch."

"So you are basically fun times to date."

"I pull my weight, romantically. I'm not stingy. I supply locations. I supply funding. Transportation. I'm kind of an executive producer. I can green-light stuff."

"Nobody cums unless you say so, right?"

"That's not real power," she said, as if such a thing was actually under her control. She frowned. "That's bookkeeping. Not my thing at all. Anyway, I think the romantic phase of my life is probably over now. My options won't be the same. Freedom."

"Jail time?" asked George.

"It's not exactly jail for someone like me. But it's fine if you imagined it that way. That would be nice."

George hated to do it. They were having such a good time, and she must get this a lot, but he was her last living blood relative and didn't he merit some consideration over all the hangers-on who no doubt lived pretty well by buzzing around in her orbit?

"All right, so, I mean, you're rich, right? Like, insanely so?"

Pattern nodded carefully.

"You could, like, buy anything?"

"My money is tied up in money," Pattern said. "It's hard to explain. You get to a point where a big sadness and fatigue takes over."

"Not me," said George. "I don't. Anyway, I mean, it wouldn't even make a dent for you to, you know, solve my life financially. Just fucking solve it. Right?"

Pattern smiled at him, a little too gently, he thought. It seemed like a bad-news smile.

"You know the studies, right?"

Dear god Jesus. "What studies?"

"About what happens when people are given a lot of money. People like you, with the brain and appetites of an eleven-year-old."

"Tell me." He'd let the rest of the comment go.

"It's not good."

"Well I don't exactly want it to be *good*. I want it to be fun."

"I don't think it's very fun, either, I'm afraid."

"Don't be afraid, Pattern. Leave that to me. I will be very afraid, I will be afraid for two, and never have to worry about money again. Depraved, sordid, painful. I'll go for those. Let me worry about how it will feel."

Pattern laughed into her drink.

"Sweet, sweet Georgie," she said.

It was getting late, and the whispering interruptions had increased, Pattern's harried staff scurrying around them, no doubt plotting the extraction. An older gentleman in a tuxedo came out to their couch and held up a piece of paper for Pattern, at eye level, which, to George, sitting right next to her, looked perfectly blank.

Pattern studied it, squinting, and sighed. She shifted in her seat.

"Armageddon," said George. "Time to wash my drones with my drone towel!"

Pattern didn't smile.

"I hate to say it, little George, but I think I'm going to have to break this up."

He didn't like this world, standing up, having to leave. Everything had seemed fine back on the couch.

"Here," Pattern said, giving him a card. "Send your bills to William."

"Ha ha."

"What?"

"Your joke. That you obviously don't even know you just made."

She was checking her phone, not listening.

On the street they hugged for a little while and tried to say goodbye. A blue light glowed from the back seat of Pattern's car. George had no idea who she was, what she really did, or when he would ever see her again.

"Do you think I can be in your life?" George asked. "I'm not sure why but it feels scary to ask you that."

He tried to laugh.

"Oh, you are, George," said Pattern. "Here you are. In my life right now. Closer to me than anyone else on the planet."

"You know what I mean. How can I reach you?" He didn't particularly want to say goodbye to her.

"I always know where you are, Georgie. I do. Trust me."

"But I don't know that. I don't really feel that. It doesn't feel like you're even out there. When you're not here it's like you never were here at all."

"No, no," she whispered. "I don't believe that. That's not true."

"Is something going to happen to you? I don't know what to believe."

"Well," she said. "Something already has. Something has happened to all of us, right?"

"Please don't make a joke or be clever, Elizabeth. I can't stand it. There's nobody left but you. What if I don't see you again? What will I do?"

"Oh Georgie, I am right here. I am right here with you now."

George kept quiet about his sister in therapy. He talked about everything else. But sometimes he'd catch Dr. Graco studying him, and he'd think that perhaps she knew. She didn't need to be told. She might not grasp the specific details, the bare facts—who and when and what and all those things that did not matter—but it seemed to George that she could see, or was starting to, that someone out there was seeing him, watching him. That someone really knew him and that, whatever else you could say about him, it was clear that he was no longer really alone.

At home George listened, and hoped, and waited, but his phone never made the strange tone again. He found nothing on his sister in the news, though he looked. Whoever had been calling for her blood had gone quiet. And George couldn't decide if their silence meant that they'd lost interest, or that they had her, they got her, and Pattern was gone.

One night it was late and he'd let his uncertainty overpower him. It had been a year since he'd seen her. Where was she? How could she just disappear? He'd been saving up his idea for a moment just like this one, so he sat down at his desk and wrote his sister an email.

Elizabeth—

Is it just me now, or are you still out there? Don't write back. I cannot imagine how busy you must be! There is a lot that I cannot imagine. But that's okay, right? You're out there looking, I know. I am waving at you, wherever you are. I am down here saying hello. Do you see me? Send a sign, if so. Send a person, send a thing, send some weather. Or better yet, send yourself. There's no substitute. I will be looking out, I swear. I will see you coming.

Your brother,
George

A Suicide of Trees

Before my father went missing, he taught me to give the weaker man a chance. The advice occurred when I was a child, after a baseball affair on the gentle border of soft Ohio, right where Widow Mountain is being rebuilt by our young inmates. As usual, there were children in competition that day much smaller than myself. I was compelled by park rules to utilize the gear designated for my age group, which I had long ago outgrown, such as small hand-slips and swatters—thus, I felt, unfairly restricting me from succeeding at a festival that seemed precisely designed by the sports council to bring my family shame.

So I called it upon myself to ask Paul Mattingly, the bald servant, to loot our vehicle for my own customized gear, which I then politely applied to myself for my next opportunity in front of the judges, who were supported by pillows in the low-lying viewing arena. It was just before this crucial moment that I noticed Jane Rogerson leading my swollen father—he was pink and glistening, as if something had stung him on the inside of his body—over to the fence—the only thing standing between me and the people who were going to watch my comeback. I was getting ready and taking big swings and doing lunges to keep my legs from going cold. My father standing small in the summer dust raised up his hand to initiate a semaphore. Held it open, twisted it, pulled it down. This meant go to him now, or else get caught up in the blows and belts and slaps of his helper Rogerson, which she dispensed with the authority of a baker punching down dough. He summoned me over to him and talked me out of the whole affair. He talked the helmet off me and somehow got the bat out of my hands and the extra-large cleat off of my batting foot and talked me over to our vehicle where I was given children's coffee and consoled by my mother, who even in close quarters could express an intense interest in the distant horizon, just beyond wherever I might be sitting. I watched from the passenger window as my batting turn was forfeited and the zero was hoisted up next to my small name on the scoreboard, snapped into position with the crispness of an egg cracking. A sharply bleating siren, accompanied by a flare that sizzled over the field, indicated that I had been disqualified, and several area televisions began to moan. Later in the evening, my father talked me into bed after Jane had given me a brief, forceful bath with her terrible sponge. When I was tucked in, he entered my room and sat on my bed and asked Jane Rogerson to leave us. Be reminded, please, that this story depicts a boy much younger than myself, who has little or no bearing on the individual that I have become. I will not entertain the pity of people I do not know.

"You are a strong boy and you are beautiful and you are my son," my father said to me. "But you must remember that this is not true of anyone else, nor will it be, nor can it be."

We were involved in what might be called a darkened room. There was his mustache to regard, for me, and that was all. Indeed it was often all that I saw when my father came at me in the dark. For discussions and such. The blond crop that styled his words to be so fatherly.

And then he taught me what it was to be much stronger than others, which is a lesson I am still proud of. The mustache seemed to retreat, but how quickly did it borrow my air and slam right onto me, scratching my face and digging at my eye! My breath failed at the sight of it, my father's yellow mouth-fur like an animal spun from a pitching machine to pin me on my bed. He asserted some great weight onto my neck until I was stilled. No, I could not think of any way to move and he clenched my arms in his hands and I thought he might drive his shoulder into my chest cage.

The house was calm, the blinds drawn. I had never before waited so long to breathe. He was breathing fine, loud, hard. There was air coming onto me that I could not have, you see. One was in bed covered in his father. A certain impatience bloomed in me. The man was using his largeness to effect a stillness in his son. And in his air the sounds came up and burst open—his, my own, the room's, I do not know.

"What are the circumstances, then? Exactly what might the case be here?"

Oh dear I could not move the air into me.

"Who gets to decide what happens next? Do you think it might be you or do you think it might be me?"

My feet were cold and they stuck out and I had scratches on my leg I could not get to. My father was so close to me I could not see him. There were birds of light cresting into my blackout. No mustache, no body, no bed, no house.

"Me or you," the words. "Me or you."

My father is gone now, but maybe yours is too. Is yours dead or has he vanished? If you do not know, we are in the same old boat, and the boat is made of rotten mush. But as much as I would be pleased to relate to you, to suggest that our lives are virtually the same, right down to the disfigurement between our legs, however laughable that sounds, I warrant that you have not also lost a second person, a lodger from your very own home, to be precise, who vanished or died in or around the same day and time as your father. And that you may or may not be a suspect in the situation. A person of interest. Or even a person at all.

...

These days we practice our supper at a large oak affair. There is Jane Rogerson, Paul Mattingly, my mother, and myself. The leaves of the dining board have been snapped under to soften not just the loss of my father, but also the lodger, who'd been leasing rooms from us these last endless years. Our two men are disappeared or dead, we do not know, and we can hardly tell the difference anymore. They vanished around the same time, and our smaller minds believe the events may be related. The candles and the newspaper rack and the candy bowl—in which my father dipped his little finger before making a speech—are gone, and the curtains are now bound up with wire. We keep them open because no one is much bothered by the glare, although Paul says he gets distracted by the many gray birds that now circle the house, their beaks bearded in dark foam.

The only sounds at supper are the huffing sobs of Rogerson, my father's lady-in-waiting. I watch this woman carefully when she weeps, not least because of the glaring sexuality discharged by those who frequently cry. She will not meet my stare. Her body comes in a small parcel and she likes to deny herself in pale sweaters knitted so minimally that one could pass an entire hand through the holes to stroke the person beneath.

At first my mother took Rogerson's sadness as a sign of hunger, and urged me to pass her more fish, which is no problem in terms of supplies. We never run out. But I have tired of scraping out her portions later into the day laborers' food mailbox and now we only serve her enough to color her plate.

At my mother's request, I have requisitioned my father's room for scenarios. We have a Thursday night theater that features a quite credible imitation of my father by Paul, who is twice the size of our lost man. Paul stoops and shuffles through the room, one hand clutching his collar together, the other hand held out for money. Even my mother giggles at the accuracy of it, or she coughs and seems to choke, and always recovers with a smile. Paul can certainly render a man. A plate of sweet pastry is kept nearby.

On Mondays I sometimes query Jane Rogerson in my father's

room. She enters nervously just after her nap and does not survey her surroundings, which vexes me a great deal. She has lost a mourner's share of weight and her face has taken on the deep creases of an old man's bottom. If she knows something, it will be hard to determine, for there is more to Rogerson than a woman who once nearly sponged the life out of me at bath times, a treatment so fantastically rough that I often bled from the road burn on my back. Some might warrant that she sponged my missing father too, yet with a more delicate hand, in a mature style, a transaction that occurred off-hours, with a soundtrack of deep moaning. One can easily overhear certain insinuations about their bathing ritual. If I spent more furtive time in the servants' quarters, I could hear many sorts of things from Paul Mattingly and his guests. I am usually strong enough to decline such easy acquisitions of knowledge.

I have performed minuscule rearrangements to my father's bedroom items to catch Rogerson off guard. If she inhabited this room during the late hours, for instance, when a sexuality might be attempted, she could be startled if my father's array of his "forest jewels," the acorns and pinecones and woodland scruff he collected and staged so meticulously, no longer sprinkles over his bureau. She has little to say. Her speech returns mostly to moments of my childhood, a topic I feel can have no bearing on the investigation. She entreats me to recall scenarios that apparently featured just the two of us, strolling overland to some knoll or other that would host our required picnic, me with my elastic-waisted pants down around my ankles to better regulate my faulty gait. When I concentrate my mind on the matter, however, I can remember nothing of the sort, just small, red people on boats being splashed in a terrible syrup. It is the one memory I have confidence in.

Sometimes I sit beneath the window that gives out onto the scene of my father's disappearance. Somewhere, ghosted into the glass, is the blueprint of what happened here. A father, my own, swifted off: by someone else's power, by a higher power, by the powers that be. Mostly I look out at the burned yard, I sip from a bowl of soup, I surround myself with my father's trade magazines: *Population Now, The Limits of Rooms*. I will not be approached for conversation, unless it is the detective, who enjoys broad legal access to my person, and who has spectacularly failed to turn his interrogation of me into the kind of courtship one so often reads about in literature between accuser and accused: a fiery, sexual battle of wills between fiercely intelligent if facially destroyed men who, though they differ in moral composition—one man kills children, the other man does not—overlap so deeply in other respects that they are like brothers who share a single, knotted torso.

In the many scenarios of my father's disappearance, all of which have been whiteboarded in the living room and summarily dismissed, wanton speculation is succumbed to like a delicious drug, and I am ashamed at our collective lack of intelligence, imagination, and vision. Our heads may as well be crushed. We may as well lease ourselves for experimentation down at the night school.

My father, goes a theory put forward by Paul Mattingly, is caught in a crowd of day laborers—known to cluster at the head of our driveway—and is swept into the back of a truck, mistaken, perhaps, for a subdivision carpenter, someone grimly determined to support his family. The men in the truck are cheerful and talkative and they motor up a smooth road into the hillside. When the rain begins, a tarp is tented over the cab of the truck, ballooning in time with the anxious breath of the passengers. This is when my father becomes nervous and asks to be released. He uses simple phrasing. He does not disguise his voice. His captors are impressed by his calmness, but kill him anyway.

My dissent from this view is not so important. It is not that I think Paul Mattingly is a simpleton, at least not precisely. He is a nice man to play fort with, and I am glad he is able to help my mother. But one cannot be too cagey. The belongings of our lodger, whose disappearance features a lower grief index—if it rates at all—are now in the possession of Paul Mattingly, who apprentices himself after the great collectors. With so little to do around the house, now that my father is not here to spearhead some garden project—our sole video footage of the lost man finds him squatting on his camp foldout, barking orders through a megaphone as unidentifiable children shuttle mulch to the juniper shrubs—Mattingly has been known to round up the items of various men who are missing and to store these items in glass cases. Creating his bias, so to speak. The certain feeling that he might be rooting for someone, therefore blunting his instrument of assessment.

Additionally, Mattingly's narrative nowhere mentions our lodger running like buster through the woods, quite possibly on fire, screaming for his life. I saw this myself. Asleep or awake, I saw it very clearly.

In mythology, when a stranger from a distant land catches fire, it can signal that he is from the underworld, and that the kindness of his hosts—their ministrations with warm soup, the private massage offered by the eldest daughter, the gift of hand-drawn currency folded in muslin—has caused him to swell with shame, and then to combust. This suggests that our domestic tranquility has built-in protection from peril—intruders will burn if they seek to harm us—and it gives some comfort. Our lodger, however, came from Cleveland Village, the north end, and if we were unduly kind to him I'll admit that it was not under my watch. In other words, our lodger caught fire for reasons mythology cannot quite explain. A different sort of logic applies to his immolation.

All throughout the late summer, when the detective visits he is distracted, he is sad, he is happy, he is handsome and witty, he repulses me. I assure him that I have nothing to hide, but can anyone ever say this with any honesty? Who can legitimately speak in such a way? I have so much to hide that I may one day break into pieces.

Today, while I am theorizing with him, he checks his watch repeatedly, but clearly does not see what he desires there. What a sorrow it is when our disappointments come from something we wear on our own bodies. I cannot say that I feel for him, because my feelings have been littered elsewhere. They are gone from me. But I see his predicament. I see it and I honor it.

It is important to me that he knows what I know, to a certain extent, anyway. Beyond that certain extent, I'm not sure he could handle his own mind. I wouldn't want that responsibility.

I give him to understand the moment that informed the disappearance: my father, an assistant at the Institute, whose job it was to test the occupancy rate of its rooms and offices and elevators, recruiting bright young humans to fill those spaces until the floor joists started to creak. His morning tasks to occur in or around the home. The garden, the path, the hedge, the mailbox. A sliver of lunch before the bicycle ride to work. Daily my father had to navigate the cluster of day laborers clogging our driveway, who enjoyed a lightly sexual heckling of my father as he tried to get his bike moving from an uphill standstill with his little legs. Many times I watched the day laborers grab at my father's crotch as he tried to cycle his way free, while my father grimaced or smiled, I was never sure which. All of this produced the sound of a father going away. One should issue a record album of such sounds, the acoustics of departure, even forced departure, undertaken while muscle-bound workers fan your groin. A man like that can be heard for miles. How could we possibly lose track of him?

His supervisor Lauren Markinson asserts that he showcased an appearance no more disheveled than usual when he submitted his revised population figures during his final day in our lives, and my mother alleges an evening encounter with him, although the latter is easily refuted, given that Mattingly is the only sire my mother is allowed, whether or not my mother knows this. Young men in my situation, who are now no longer young, must early on make a reality calculation on behalf of their mothers, to keep them just shy of the amount of information that would ruin them.

One cannot help entertaining the theory that my father, given his professional inclinations, worked a population reduction upon his own home, clearing the way for his only son, myself, to thrive, the way old-growth trees are known to suck poison from deep in the earth in order to weaken themselves, just as the baby saplings around them require more room to grow. A suicide of trees, I believe it is called. It is a fancy name for a father throwing himself under a bus, allowing his son to thrive. It is part of a larger genre of misassigned heroism, but I am pleased to let my father enjoy the credit. And now I am filling the cavity left by two men, my father and the lodger, swelling into the newly vacant rooms. Space is for taking, and my father knew this.

After all, what's mine is mine, and also some of what isn't.

My father would also say that metaphors are for the dead, or winning is for losers, or that the expression "good day" is an oxymoron.

Until now, the question around here, posited by friends, family, strangers, and the police, has been punishingly literal: Who took my father? We have failed to ask, at least out loud: Might he still be on the property, buried alive, barely breathing? Or might it not have been his time? Could we admit that in some instances it is just more polite to quietly disappear? Did he leave of his own accord? And the lodger? Did they leave together, hand in hand? How many abductions are self-engineered, simply out of kindness?

But it is not my job to posit the questions, only to field them, however much I'd like to be stationed behind the detective's face so I could better attack myself and take charge of the drama that should have resulted by now.

When my father was alive, I had to wake and look into a mirror that rigged me into an old man, a limper, with a face that looked newly leaked of air, as if I had been sleeping on one of those airplanes that never land, ejecting its occasionally dead passengers over the Atlantic. My father's living body on the property was a caution to me: like a crystal ball smeared with the blood of a neighbor's pet. If there was a really good question, it might be: Why should a younger man be forced to look upon his own crippled future, in the form of an older man? What purpose could that kind of dark forecasting ever possibly serve?

In other words, in these tired times, why have a father at all?

Pursuant to his investigation of my missing father, not to mention the lodger, the detective shows me pictures: trucks, men, trees. In folklore, when an authority figure visits your house, even to interrogate you about a so-called crime, you are obligated to return his gifts in kind, so I have offered sweet coffee, a duck prosciutto, and Jane Rogerson's braided fry bread with shards of dark sugar, but the detective has declined. He does not seem suspicious of me so much as arthritically afflicted, and while I inspect his materials he paces the great room as if he's dodging crippled birds on the floor. He shows me photographs of gray shapes that resemble planets attacked long ago, and I study these, not sure if I should shake or nod my head. I hadn't realized that landscapes could be guilty of something, but locations, the detective reminds me, foster guilt, they contain and stage crime and are therefore far more useful than mug shots of men and women, which have apparently lost professional credibility. I am meant to address the images he shows me, trap though that might be, and say "whatever comes into my mind." This is presumably the exhausted pink man's technique for locating my lost father, and possibly also our lost lodger, and I will certainly indulge him. If you can find a disappeared man this way then I am pleased. It is always fascinating to discover the truth-divining techniques used by sweaty, small, nervous men, who even while succeeding appear to be in agony. Pinched, suffering faces, fat bellies, and bad skin. They mean so well, they try so hard, feeble though they are! I imagine what he really wants to do is climb inside my head and thrust away into the hidden folds of my brain, until some evidence leaks forth onto my face. It is not entirely unpleasant for me to contemplate such an assault.

Of the detective's evidence, the pictures of trucks are what I enjoy, since they have apparently been stolen and returned, sometimes with blood and grass in the bumper, sometimes with a tooth in the wheel well, sometimes with three different kinds of semen dried into the cup holder. It does suggest quite a party for my father, if he died this way. A festive demise. Most of the trucks are lovely vehicles abducted for the secret uses of people we know little about. I admit to the detective across the coffee table the central mystery that overwhelms us all. We do not know the people who drive the roads. We do not. There are so many of them, and we will never speak to them or hear their stories. We will not see them make love or die, we will not reach our hands down their throats to massage their lungs.

When people steal trucks, the detective tells me, they seem keen to perform the most illegal acts, which can tend to require a certain degree of what is called off-road travel, a jagged lurching into restricted areas where the law cannot easily survey. Here they smash people, they tear them, they bury them. And then the truck thieves seem compelled to leave a morsel of human waste, doing so out of a sense of duty to history or statistics, a desire to belong to the elite population of people who defecate at a crime scene.

Some witnesses say the truck that may have taken my father—the one that sped past our house the morning he went missing—was dark navy, although my imagination tends to apply a red stain to things. All I frequently remember of a person is his mouth. My father's lips frequently looked boiled down into a sticky wound. I sometimes watched him as he slept next to my canoe-bodied mother, and there was his mouth, glowing like candy, which always made me think that dirt and hair would be more likely to stick to it: dirt and hair and debris, and maybe some unidentifiable shining thing, stuck to my father's face like a jewel.

I breathe into my coffee mug and imagine my father riding in these trucks, bouncing in his seat like a hand puppet, on his way to being spectacularly killed. If it is true, then bravo for him. I am well pleased. I want to tell the detective how proud I am of my father. It offers some satisfaction. There is an age for a young man when he realizes his father will no longer excel or succeed at anything, that he will pursue decline in various degrees, perfecting his small stabs at failure until he seems like a machine designed to demonstrate mistakes, rather than a man. It is nice when an exception to the rule arises, even if it comes at a cost.

The men and women who study body mass and space, bearing loads, clustering, and oxygen quotas, have, according to my father's publications, proposed an apportioning system, called Melissa, that distributes additional air to children when a room exceeds a certain occupancy rate. The term "Melissa" must stand for something technical that can now be acronymized into the name of a child, most likely dead now, maybe one of those taken by van and dumped in the sea, with only an audio recording remaining of the splash she made when she went down.

But what does Melissa mean for the rest of us? That the children, once our buildings buckle and spill over with a sweetness of people, will be trampling over our dead bodies before too long, that they'll be breathing their own sugary air when we are blue and cold on the floor, that these devices will be tripped accidentally and the children will walk forth with a great new power.

In other words, it's clear that a person requires an exit strategy that can be executed without oxygen, and I recall the one issued by our own Thomas Jefferson, who said that the best exit strategy of all is simply never to arrive in the first place.

Which leaves me here at 4523 Westmoore Ave. to puzzle out the mystery. My mother and the others come and go, and I would mistake them for shadows were it not for the sweet vegetal reek of people who sleep and cry too much, that legendary scent often said to rise off the backs of people who have lost their leader.

Perhaps the lodger was not involved in orchestrating my father's disappearance. I would be glad if he were innocent. Perhaps Mattingly, the hairless house assistant, is no liar. It is so trying to accuse a stranger of some terrible thing when one feels predisposed to blaming someone nearer at hand. But nor is it kind to accuse a man of his own disappearance. A trap seems waiting for this sort of behavior. One should possibly instead be issuing a gentle "Bravo." Perhaps one will soon do so. Who cannot admire a man, even a father, who otherwise brooked so little admiration, to so cleanly vanish?

The detective brings my attention to the lodger, tapping a folio in his lap of what is apparently a collection of lodger data. What was his routine? the detective would like to know. How would I characterize the varieties of his ingress and egress? Always the same door? Did he glance at my father or touch my father or make mention of my father either in the company of my father or not? And, in turn, did my father return the attention or spurn it? Did he chase after the lodger, did he grab him or hold him or did the two of them ever succumb to kisses in the evening?

If we examine the routine of our lodger, I suggest to the detective, we find little to worry about. On Fridays, for instance, our lodger was frequented by certain of his mathematics peers, hobbyists all. The gentlemen of these were tidy and quiet. In the oaken entranceway, where the finials appeared to imprison our visitors, his guests often stooped to sniff from clear bags of crumbs, a health-chew so rich in calories that one needed only to suck the nutrients from a fistful of the stuff and later spit the dried shards onto the garden, a compost of the mouth that spiked our flowers with deep blasts of energy. The visitors carried knapsacks and reserved their humor for the German tongue. At times, a language was uttered as if one might be avoiding a mass of bread in the mouth, after which followed always the sharp barks of laughter coughed into their fists, their eyes gleaming and tearing. One of the men liked to grip his own neck brace as if he would topple over without it.

The women who befell our lodger in the afternoons were not so many as the gentlemen, but they stayed longer and made great noises, slamming the walls with their big hands, barking math formulas into a long cone they passed between them that required many refills of dark water. They wore large trousers and let their hair go to their waists and appeared somewhat stronger and vaster than the men. My mother, the gracious hostess, shook their hands and trilled what little German she knew in their direction, squirting about them with the excitement of a hotel dog. These women handled my mother rather too freely, I believe. They passed her around between them and adopted a mechanical halt to their speech, an aloof-sounding language that was only spoken while they held my mother, until I had to intervene and usher them from the house. My mother's sweet gasps for breath left her convulsing mildly afterward for hours, unsure whether she had been attacked or made love to, a mother who confused suffering with valor as she heaved and panted in the garden in between restorative sips of her cloudy mint drink. It would take days of private swaddling and sessions beneath the panel-light to calm her.

I tell the detective I am poor at math and a weak listener. Other people's words can invite me into a deeply passive tranquility. Can their message possibly matter to me? I am given to wonder. Is their speech in some way medically necessary to my being? The lodger and his visitors performed operations on the chalkboard I could never decipher. I sat on the viewing couch some afternoons at their theater of operations and watched them frenzy over their figures and formulas, as if they were scooping extra air out of the room and lathering it on themselves. They did not seem to mind my presence, though I might have been sent out for something they called "crisps"—a word they seemed to use for anything that could be eaten—after which the door was frequently bolted and their laughter erupted like a flushed toilet. When I stayed on the viewing couch, a heckler invariably shouted up from his seat next to me to vex the man or woman with the chalk, whoever was laboring at the board to the scrutiny of everyone assembled. There was a considerable deal of backseat solving when they practiced their math together. More than once I saw a man brutally felled by the crisp backhand of a woman who could solve the problem faster.

I am eager to place blame, and to place it here, since it fits the differential that the intellectual elite killed the king. I believe, along with Emily Dickinson, that smart people have little to do, in the end, but make love to their children and assault those in power. But although the mathematicians were aggressive and mean and aloof, although they were sexual to a nearly unbearable degree, and they undressed me and killed me with their eyes each time I soiled the room with my presence, they were not kidnappers or killers.

As a grown man, my body has shrunk down and corrected to the society I keep, as if some corset in the air has kept me from becoming a disgusting giant. Since my father's big poof, I am mostly couch-bound, heaped in blankets, awash in my own greenhouse effect. There will be no photos of me, but you might picture a boiled-faced man, long ago threshed by children with sticks. My age, when sounded out slowly, is also a word in Spanish, meaning "the fat behind the knee." My height is not important, because I do not stand up much, unless the detective is visiting and he entreats me to survey the yard and the field beyond to search for clues. Then I slide on my garden boots, and off we go.

What I took him to see first was the burned outline of a person in the grass, way out on the back property. Like the chalk outline of a dead body, but made with fire. Had the person been on fire before he fell, thus burning the grass in his very own shape? That was the likely explanation. The detective photographed the singed grass before new grass and weeds grew in, and thank goodness, because now there might be burned ends of certain grasses here and there on our back property, but nothing coherent enough to suggest that a man, very possibly on fire, fell here and probably died here, although where he went after that no one seems to know.

Invariably we return to the garage, where wooden slats, smeared with a grease, lean in the corner. We'll call this grease an inedible substance that might help machines operate more quietly. This grease has simply been rubbed just about everywhere, creating such a lovely shine on the older things of our home, a glistening creaminess on the wheelbarrow, the garbage tins, the withered football, the tenoning jig. There is an excess of it coating the baby flamethrower, propped in the corner. I tell the detective that the flamethrower belonged to my father, who used it to scorch our bamboo field each autumn. Always preferable to hacking at the stumps with a scythe. I do not tell him that a gasket can be removed to extend the flume, when giving chase, for instance.

And the wooden slats? They are new. No one can account for so many oddly shaped wooden slats now filling the garage. And they can be pieced together, after much puzzlement, to form a most terrible structure.

But, on the other hand, what items of our world cannot?

Upon our first visit to the garage, I told the detective about the wooden slats, but I did not demonstrate what could be built with them. Why build monsters for strangers? He puzzled over the grease that soon covered his hand.

"You say this is a new substance?" he asked. The utterance of the question seemed to exhaust him.

"I do not remember it before," I replied. "You can taste it if you want to. I could have Paul bring us a spoon." I looked around for a sign of Paul, willing my face into a searching gesture, even while inexplicably picturing Paul demonstrating intercourse to an audience of scientists in a field.

The detective sniffed his hand and held it to the sun. His face winched and he gagged, and then he laughed a little bit and seemed also, perhaps, to be crying.

He wanted to preserve some of the grease for a laboratory test, so I held open the wide-mouthed Ziploc bag he produced. I had to massage his long thin hand through the bag in order to extract the grease. I milked each finger, I felt his bones through plastic and flesh, I squeezed them down until the grease pinched off into a pasty smear at the bottom of the bag. I want to say that it felt strange—like a piece of pork—but it didn't feel strange enough; it felt exactly and terribly just like a man's hand should feel: there just aren't any words.

As we hiked back up the rottenstone path, I considered the common use of grease. A body is greased so that it might better slide into a crawl space. And grease on a body can delay, for at least a short while, the effects of a high-intensity flame. These uses I kept to myself, since the detective had given in to his sadness. I walked just ahead of him so he could do his weeping in some bit of privacy, although he turned out to be the sort of man whose weeping was devoid of pathos or gravity or even any clear emotion. It sounded merely as if he was catching his breath after jogging, and I wished we had a toolshed for precisely those moments when a stranger spoils the afternoon with his expressions of feeling.

When the detective first started his inquiry, I had hoped we would join together in our wonder, our bafflement, our aching curiosity, to probe the mystery of these lost two men, collaborating so intensely that we would be reluctant to resolve the case. Why? Because certainly that would mean a farewell so devastating we might claw our own faces off. This would be the project of a lifetime, even as wives and friends came and went, as houses eroded around us and we migrated to a trailer on the back property, where one of us peed from the steps while the other continued taking notes. During long days of research, the detective and I might discover, deep in the lodger's web browser history, for instance, a series of site visits that would link him to my father, providing a motive so compelling that his murder of my father would seem entirely forgivable and inevitable. Our book would be called *A Very Understandable Murder*, and while editing the proofs we'd have several scratch fights and someone's glasses would be smashed, but we'd emerge even closer than before, particularly after I produced a wrenchingly personal chapter admitting that, though I cared for my father, I would have killed him myself had I been the lodger. And the detective and I, now old companions who occasionally bathed and groomed each other in the evening, might choose to delay the resolution of our work, each of us keenly saddened by the prospect of such resounding success, because where, in the end, would crushing accomplishment leave us, but tired and alone and full of anxiety for the future?

I do not like to speak of others. It is tiring to shine my light on people, who might shrivel under its glare and suddenly become reduced to meat and bone, a few stray teeth and a pile of hair. But remarks made in reference to the lodger are in some sense going to be remarks made about my vanished father, and are therefore permissible and useful.

We shared a certain prejudice for exercise that permits me to discuss his terribly fascinating body, which, even under the glare of my flashlight while he slept, revealed little to me. For instance, I jogged daily with the lodger down Multer to the Beeves cul-de-sac and then up Forstinge and across the Bus Road and back to the house.

At the outset of our jogs the lodger declined to limber himself. He stood at the driveway and studied the section of the newspaper devoted to numbers while I conducted my preparations. I believe in bending deeply on an inhale until my inner light goes brown, as though the buttocks of a giant are swallowing me. When I fold my body at the waist, the world around me darkens like an oily painting and I begin to see myself as people in the distant future might see me: crushed, glistening, scarcely human.

Once aground we invariably observed the universal jogger's silence, grim men at their exercise, charging in tandem from the house, until the lodger turned down Korial at the Forstinge precipice, electing a route he referred to with a string of numerals, a decision that roused in me an instant fatigue and anxiety, tempered by an ever-so-slight, and unspecified, sexual response. And off I ran after him.

Sometimes I chanced upon the lodger attempting the jog alone, usually in the cold early mornings when we were just discovering how much of our garden had been eaten by the woodland deer, who roved up every night to strip our land of its beard. I'd step into the brick-lined ivy patch to survey the waste and see the lodger trotting nervously along the roadway, studying his feet as if he was rehearsing tactical steps. In the evenings the lodger stood for long periods at the toilet, hands akimbo, before the water was stirred slightly by his weak drops of pee. Around the house, I did not like his hands, for he could barely hold his food and he trembled when he ate. In folklore, a trembling guest usually indicates that a demon is harbored inside his chest struggling to gnaw his way free, and that the guest is just a shell the demon has used to invade the house. I sometimes horse-stamped behind the lodger on the stairs so I could see his startled face in profile, one of the biggest faces there was. Saint Francis of Assisi, who loved all creatures, admitted that he loathed large-faced men, even as he prayed to God for more tolerance.

...

How odd that we can be geniuses and morons at once. Given everything we know in this world—some of it, or even most of it, oppressive and meaningless and distracting—we don't always know who is alive and who is dead. There are creatures, at large in the world, whose status eludes us. In other words, where are they, and do they breathe? Is there finally any other question we might ask?

I believe in respect for the dead. When it is warranted. When it is earned. Do you disagree? So let me not criticize he who is perhaps perished. The perished should enjoy only our praise and highest regard, unless the perished have maneuvered in the wrong, pursuing error, which leads to disgrace, regardless of the perished's status among the living. I am fond of the perished, and do not wish to condemn them. Unless they are condemnable, and then the perished are worth at least several critical remarks. The perished are good people, usually. But when they are not, we would like to kill the perished a second time, or we would like to magically revive the perished and then sit on the perished with our bare bottoms so their last breaths come from deep in our asses. And maybe even then we would boil the perished until only their bones remained. From the bones comes a very fine powder. Very fine. You can nearly make something extraordinary with it, extraordinary and new. In this instance, let me be entirely fair, or even more than fair, just in case, so that someone who may now be dead will not be rendered before you and then reduced to dust: the lodger's physique was stunning, wrapped in a skin so white one could almost call it clear. He was one of those young fellows whose white cap of hair made him seem all the more youthful, like a child in a silver fright wig. He was, too, apparently a brilliant mathematician, although he always made it clear that he loathed the professionalization of math, the corruption, the rampant mediocrity, the sort of sexual obviousness of the whole enterprise.

I will certainly miss the mathematicians. In the early days of their visits, when my father still loomed bodily over the property, I would watch from my window as they stopped to chat and laugh with the day laborers, sometimes pointing at our house, and my breath bounced from the glass back over my face, shrouding me in a steam that, while deeply foul and rank, had a sweetness that was unmistakably my own. It is a climate I would like to share with the detective, a homemade climate that, if only he could walk in it regularly, might afford him a far deeper sense of just what kind of people have managed to stay alive and accounted for here. Even if it's just air, it's our very own brew, and it's been steeping around us for as long as we can remember.

There has been no talk of acquiring a new lodger. His room has been ribboned in yellow tape by the police, which my mother dusts so that the tape does not lose its shine. His board is paid through the year. No kin have emerged to siphon a refund from us. His blackened shoes are hardening in place outside his door. It is not clear to me why Paul has refused their inclusion in his missing persons collection, but now the shoes have stiffened into the floor, as though a leathery growth has arisen from the oak parquet, and even if I trip against them on the way to my room at night, the shoes do not yield their position.

It's been three months and still no progress on the investigation. The detective is finished, he says. No more. He admits to a retreat of fascination on the part of his employers, a change in the subject. He brandishes his notebook and waves it over us, proving something about the inadequacy of its contents. A language of withdrawal is being used in his workplace, he says. Speech and behavior will no longer be brought to bear. The investigation is going dark.

"There are no suspects, then?" I ask.

"Sometimes the suspect and the victim are, shall we say . . ." A smile takes over his face and he coughs and appears to choke. He bends over and waves me away, but I am not going near him.

In the quiet speech I reserve for myself when stern talks are in order, when I have strayed from my own aims and softened in my resolve, I give the detective to know that, after all, he needs no title, and no official sanction, to visit us and puzzle over the family subtraction. It might be years and years later, when his visits here are classified merely as those of a hobbyist. He might simply be a long-retired gentleman who continues the courtesy of looking in on our diminished family, since he was once paid to wonder about what happened here, to leverage his advanced intellect onto the problem of the two missing men. Only politely will we, out of duty, remark on my father, sometimes fondly gazing at the photo that shows him anxiously clutching his high school diploma. Should not every family, missing men or not, enjoy its own detective, a professional to chase down and systematically address each puzzle that arises?

I further give him to understand, whispering now, that even if the official institutions are fetishizing progress and resolution, there is no need for our local group—beholden to absolutely no one or thing but our own refined style of courtesy—to suffer such a glaring failure of concern.

The detective remains folded over himself, coughing weakly, and I might be inclined to wonder if my syntax itself is acting as a diminisher. I think of the giant, in the Whitman poem, who spoke so forcefully that everyone around him was crushed small, so so small. The people in his life could only recover and grow back to full size if he remained absolutely silent, but the giant had trouble with this. As much as he loved his people, he could not keep from talking, however it wounded them.

It is only as the detective cheats his body toward the door, like a lump of meat moving under a rug, that my periphery is clouded with figures I know all too well: Rogerson, Mattingly, and my mother, who holds in her hand a tub of what I have come to know as a rather extraordinary ointment. The aroma that suddenly sharpens in my nose is unmistakable: here are people who will not let a man stand down.

As they close in around him, I turn back to my window, which no doubt will be recording all there is to see, the shadows moving and thumping—a struggle so soft and magically gentle that one must fairly wonder about complicity, the way animals with rope will actually bind themselves to a post, the way, in the athletic footage, a man will crumple microseconds before he is tackled. Who among us, after all, does not dream of being elected for a smothering?

Our final criteria for men, including the detective, should be this: How do they look once felled? All of us should be knocked to the floor and finally judged asprawl. The detective is down. I do not think he will rise again.

In his pocket I find a Ziploc bag, unopened, featuring a clouded bolus of paste. The grease that never went to the lab. On his notepad I discover text for the items that he is meant to purchase at the grocery store, etched in a script adorned by his curly enforcements, his to-do lists. The technique of his doodling hand is not as precise as I might have guessed, particularly for a man trained in unknown whereabouts, a whereabouts specialist. I would have hoped for an architectural style, a man who drew buildings or at least boxes and geometrical shapes linked with suggestive vectors. Systems and such, the blueprints to an interrogation room. Perhaps some numerical formulas. The suggestion that he has mastered his world and might soon launch a powerful campaign. Instead he is a balloonist, a man whose handwriting diminishes the meaning of everything he writes, infantilizing the people and trivializing the objects. This is handwriting that will take many days to undo, language that now must be unraveled and forced to lie flat, in a single line, meaning nothing once again.

We will take the words out of his book, as if they'd been written in a single miles-long piece of thread, and we will stretch the thread taut, until no more words gargle up, until uttering them out loud is simply to breathe. However long it takes.

I crouch down closer, against the last outgoing heat of him, where the air is still adjusting to the loss, closing in on the space he once occupied, and I see the hairy particulars of one man's escape. Sometimes you can smell a hole even if you can't see it. It is, I must admit, a hole I'd rather fancy entering myself, and I can imagine the flush of applause such a departure would excite, the signature admiration my descendants would feel for me if I crawled from life in plain sight and left nothing but questions. Questions and envy. Is it what my father felt when he left us? Pride and joy and fear and delight?

Nathaniel Hawthorne said that each question we ask is a costume for fear. We spend a lifetime getting out of costume, removing layer after layer, but most of us, he says, run out of time. We die too soon, still wearing the mask, the cloak, the cape, the paint on our faces. What can we do for our friends but help them along in this endless, complicated disrobing?

I beckon to my mother, to Rogerson, to Mattingly, and together we crouch down against the cold shape of our friend and get to work, removing from him everything that has ever stood in the way of showing who he really is—the disguises, the clothing, the skin, the inner shield. Piece by piece we take that man apart.

3

Critique

In the year of I Can't Breathe, a hospital occurred on the island.
The building was fashioned, rather quaintly, of matter. Bricks,
windows, smoke. The hospital used flesh traditionally—draped
over the anguished little need machines we call people. Space was
pushed through rooms, to keep them from collapsing, or so it
seemed. In truth, no one understood how such a spectacle could
remain stable. Religion and science broadcast a distant wisdom, no
different from birdcalls, and actual birds policed a space the size of
the whole world.

The air was breathable. The scale, despite appearances, was one
to one.

One commends the level of detail in this realistic hospital. Even
the most advanced scrutiny did not reveal rigging. Blood tended to
be housed inside puppets, who, in a surprising touch, were repre-
sented by actual people, pulled into the space and dosed with purpose. Traces of bone were found in the air, a dust misting over the
island. The use of bone in such a way felt far too obvious, almost
embarrassing. In other words, this spectacle was supposed to seem
like it was taking place right now, in our own world. A full set of
chemical tests were not conducted, but one felt, after witnessing
the hospital and the elaborately created area around it, a strenuous
petition to exist, as forceful as any area anywhere, ever.

Part of the suspense, in participating in this hospital and its surroundings, involved the mystery of who would do what and what would happen. The hospital neither increased nor decreased one's curiosity. If mood alteration was at work, or indeed any manipulation of emotion, it was being done environmentally.

The buildings behind the hospital, in an interesting touch, were real. In the distance beyond the island loomed another island, attached to a skyline of actual buildings, many of which must have taken years to erect, and beyond that, a vague landscape was inferred, a possible continent, as if this was all taking place in a kind of world. Even different weather erupted in these other areas. A tremendous amount of care was taken to create details in the very far distance beyond the hospital, as if the materials elsewhere, in a space that was days away on foot—not that we could ever travel there—were just as important as the materials right in front of us. One heard reports of people perishing hundreds of miles away. Real people were born and lived out their lives never hearing of the hospital. Even the waterway bordering the island was fabricated with real water. Such a democratic approach to detail is troubling. It amounts to a celebration of technique, suggesting a creator slightly too satisfied by method, showcasing a skill, as if the making of something mattered more than that thing's purpose.

Is not real water a dull choice here? Water, perhaps the most overused substance of our time. And so much of it. Actual water even at the greatest of depths, surrounding the island, running under it. It is not clear who is meant to appreciate such effects, or why, more importantly, a valuable resource is made so glaringly inaccessible. One senses a kind of hostility in the gesture. A taunt.

Even after we have gotten the point, the point keeps getting made.

The hospital staged a series of exhibits, punctuated by intervals called the workday, evening time, the shadow, and a fourth category of time that would seem to have never been named. Night and day occurred on schedule, but something felt wrong, as if the whole notion of time had simply been given too little attention in the first place, unless its very design was meant to cause deep ambivalence and dismay.

At the hospital, for instance, the day might feel too long, the night too short, or the night was too long, followed by a series of short, secondary nights and then a sudden flash of day, which seemed to never end. People expired at a steady rate, regardless of the time, but for some reason, one could not hear little popping noises each time someone died. It would have been so easy to implement such an effect, a little popping noise when someone died, so that to live and to sleep and walk the earth would be to listen to a steady stream of popping noises, marking death in the vicinity.

Sometimes at the hospital, just when night would seem to have expired, night continued to deepen instead, achieving levels of darkness heretofore thought impossible, with the hospital presumably hidden inside this purely dark fold, operating as usual, even while night kept bursting deeper, with people now expiring at an accelerated rate, faster than they were being born. An accurate measurement of the true passage of time could not be obtained. The fourth interval was determined to go unnamed. The people, too, if that's what they really were—a definitive test was impossible—would be unnamed. That whole part of the world could feel likewise unnamed. On a map the area would be blurry, never quite coming into focus.

It is hard to escape the feeling that this is a weakness of the project, no matter how profoundly ambitious it is to create a world, build things in it, and then allow life to bloom. It is a clear weakness to create an erratic, confusing experience out of time, to give each creature an apparently unique perception of time, and then to make time itself inconsistent, poorly designed, and finally simply too hard to believe. An unfortunate weakness in an otherwise intriguing project.

Moving inside, the hospital featured people bent over each other in postures of carnage. These exhibits did not expire, which makes it awkward to comment on them now. One must believe that nothing of interest will ever happen again in order to declare anything of substance now. The trick behind work like this is how foolish it makes you feel for trying to observe anything about it. To be invited to the exhibit, you had first to fall ill, then be carried there in an ambulance. Or you needed to apply for a job and then actually perform it, which guaranteed a bias that prevented lucid reflection on the hospital itself. To join the exhibit was to recuse yourself from a rational state. This would explain the long lines, the carefully constructed illness narratives, the displays of frailty. It is perhaps no accident that leaving one's home is also called "joining the exhibit."

Attention to detail on the island was staggering. An actual landscaping firm had been hired to produce what was probably considered actual landscaping. Grass and pavers, shrubbery patterned after a shield. From high above, the topography achieved a devastating insignia, most awful to behold, but no one was privileged to this view. As with many buildings, something unbearable was inferred. You didn't need to see or even know about it. It was inferred, and that was certain.

The streets surrounding the hospital, themselves authentic in materials, were given actual names, and the names were ratified through constant use. Advanced surveillance revealed significant adoption of the streets, with a troubling degree of realism. Pedestrians questioned there showed no sign that they were aware of being part of the exhibit. In some ways, these pedestrians were perhaps the exhibit's most striking feature, a clear sign of the new kind of work being done today. Certainly a trend can be observed in which the civilian members of an exhibit insist that they have arrived under their own power, pursuing tasks they are sure they thought of themselves. Very few of these civilians seem aware of their true purpose. Dissection revealed otherwise, of course. Dissection revealed a clear program carried out at what can only be called the cellular level.

Testing revealed that the inhabitants of the island came from all over the world. They had been born into different families, grown with food, sometimes managed by handlers, other times left alone. Some of them actually existed. No real pattern in their origins could be detected.

The doors to the hospital operate just as one imagines real doors should. Inside, a series of smaller exhibits takes shape as you approach them, then vanishes from view when you turn your back. This effect—objects vanishing if you are not looking at them—is ingenuous, and so easy to take for granted.

In one piece, set inside an authentic-looking room, a man in a doctor's costume approaches the sickbed. This is not a painting. The man seems made of a soft, fleshy substance. You have this feeling, looking at him, of wanting to touch him, but not romantically. Actual vocal noises emerge from this piece. Heaps of cloth surround the sickbed, faces buried inside. These are ostensibly the loved ones of the patient, collapsed in postures, one must guess, of grief. The cloth would appear to be real cloth. It's uncanny. Even the bed seems fabricated of actual material: steel, plastic, and cotton. One is impressed by the trouble such fealty must have taken. The hospital makes a mockery of convincingness. The hospital achieves believability so easily, with such facility, it seems to suggest that believability is a terrible criterion for our daily lives, one we would do well discarding, and yet everywhere throughout the hospital believability seems to be what matters most. Perhaps the hospital satirizes the idea of being alive. Certainly there is a critique, in this piece, of waking up, of bothering to live.

So much of the piece is well made, not in the classical sense, but in the brutal, violent sense. It looks as if it was made by skilled craftspeople at gunpoint. The hospital looks like it was built at gunpoint. The people inside the hospital look as if they were born at gunpoint. The hospital looks as though it was positioned on the island at gunpoint. Even the island, when one examines its undercarriage, when one swims its circumference, seems to have been assembled, piece by piece, at gunpoint, dropped from the sky at gunpoint, made to decay just as real things decay, at gunpoint. One looks at such a hospital at gunpoint, then one walks away at gun-point, travels home and goes to bed at gunpoint, only to wake up years later with the same awful gun held to one's head.

The hospital is deliberately made to outlast us, to still be stand-ing when we're gone. There is a clear critique of the ephemerality of people, the way they reliably perish. The hospital would seem to gloat; not in the personified sense. Can a piece like this be faulted for its desire to feel more lifelike than we do? One pleasing feature of the piece is that you can reach into the space surrounding the bed. You cannot touch the bed itself, for some reason. The bed is off-limits. But you can handle the space around the bed, digging your fingers into the cloth where the patient's loved ones are hiding their faces. With practice and focus, you can feel the faces inside the cloth, and they seem to actually respond to your touch. One has one's hand kissed. One feels tears against one's palm.

Years later, as the piece ages, the room and the bed and the cloth are gone. We do not see them removed, they never appear to decay. But they do not survive the passage of time. What remains of the piece are the lifelike bodies—living bodies, one surmises—hovering in space. The floor is gone. What remains of the hospital is too little to remark on. It would seem that the entire hospital has been removed with surgical precision. The area where the hospital was is brighter than what surrounds it, as if a piece of furniture has been moved across a wood floor, exposing an unlived area just wait-ing to catch up to the rest of the world.

In the piece, the man who once wore the doctor's costume but is now incomplete ("naked" would seem to be the wrong word, since he lacks finer detail) approaches the patient who, years ago, because of his bedclothes, was not visible whatsoever. Now we can see him and the effect is terrible. The patient's loved ones, no lon-ger hidden in cloth, but not naked either—unborn is how they also seem, their mouths unfinished, their hair not quite resolved—exist in a tangle on the side of the patient's bed. The hospital and its host island are gone. The nearby island, tethered to a possible continent, is gone, and the extreme distance yields nothing to the observer. All that remains are the few people in what was once a room but is now nothing, even as these people begin to fade and soon leave just pale shapes, themselves dissolving slowly into nothing that can be named.

The hospital recalls a time when the entire world was referred to as Potter's Island. A certain era is evoked when we lived on the graveyard. The hospital suggests that it is a myth that there are zones of earth in which bodies are not buried. It is a myth that some areas of the world are graveyards while some are not. One might accidentally, and infrequently, walk across a plot of earth in which, upon which, people have not been smeared away, hidden in soil once their time finished, but the chances are small. The chances may be nonexistent. The dead are beneath us, but the air contains the dead as well.

One strains not to be too judgmental of such work. While the project is ambitious, it is deeply imperfect. It celebrates the sorrow of knowing nothing. It revels in bafflement. It asks us to admit that we might not really be living. It seems to invite us to die without understanding even the most basic principles.

Perhaps we might be more sympathetic to the creator. Water is so hard to get right. It is difficult to do shorelines. The horizon is next to impossible. Horizons have never been done well. They cannot be forced, but so often they are forced, and then they are disgraceful. Hospitals are tricky, but not just hospitals. The people in them. The people outside them. People, in or out of buildings, on the ground, floating, at rest. People conjoined, people alone. Such a disgrace when they are not done right and they have never been done right. They are done badly, all the time, and then soon that is simply the way people are always done—with bodies and eyes, with feelings, so finally conventional, so deeply unimaginative— and something disgraceful becomes the norm. The norm is the hospital. The norm is people on their beds, having trouble breathing. Not breathing, in truth, is the norm. If a true norm must be spoken of, it would have to be not breathing, not moving, no longer living. Taking into consideration all the people who have ever lived. The norm would be to be dead. One must admit that being dead has become the norm.

A vacant hospital might have been easier for this artist, set in a vacant lot, itself situated in an empty space free of obstacles, a space so pure that no one could enter it. Perhaps no one could even know about it. A smaller, contained project, through which this creator could test out ideas more safely. Vacant vehicles to flow in and out of the empty hospital, across transparent roads, discharging vacancy, creating no impact whatsoever on the surroundings, which has never been achieved. That might have been a better apprentice work. Or simply the hospital itself, without a lot, without a site, absent a landscape. A real hospital for today, satisfying all of today's true needs, if that's not too much to ask. A hospital twisting in space. Less complicated. But space is hard. Rarely has depth been done well, for instance. Ever? Often it seems so melodramatic. One cannot recall a time when space has been done well. Sometimes evening is believable. Sometimes. Should one—one must ask—stop desiring what has never been achieved? Is this hospital, in its near miss of authenticity, meant to remind us how finally unreal everything will always feel, or is such an effect simply too old-fashioned to commend?

One thing this piece does impeccably well is to use wind to create feeling. On the island a wind, created in the usual way, travels around objects, cooling them, but that's not all. The wind is not created with any special technique. It is as technologically simple as it ever was, but this creator has a special feel for the use of wind. This creator is, without question, a genius in the use of wind in spaces both outdoors and in, a wind that follows one home from the hospital, across the realistic waterway, back to the adjacent island, itself so deeply real one feels an enduring confusion, a confusion one must now conclude is wind caused. This creator has fashioned a wind that does not leave you alone, even as you enter your home, which was created especially for this project, and even as you crawl into your highly vivid, full-scale bed made of real materials, this wind follows you, encircling you, holding you rather coldly as you wait, perhaps forever, for more understanding. Even if one will never arrive at this fuller understanding, this wind makes one certain that such an understanding is out there, however finally unavailable to people like us.

Lotion

A child was sick in Kansas. He had fever. His father prodded him awake, dressed him, led him outside in the dark morning for chores. The child slumped and the father raised him upright, propped him on the machine. When the father turned away the child fell, seemed to die. The father drove the child to water and sank him at the head, lowering his body into the cold lake, but the child sputtered and cried. Back at the house, in the front yard, the father warmed the child's body in the sunshine, shook him to rouse him. The father slapped the child, as he'd seen done to other children who would not respond, and the child sat up and cried, looking at his father with fear. The child's sister came and struck her father, climbed on his back. She was too small and could not stop her father and yet he stepped away. He was afraid now.

The doctor came in the evening and measured the child's temperature, tested his limbs for heat, for bloat, drew a vial of blood. There was a fever, but no infection, no mistakes heard in the child's cavity. The boy was tired and should rest. Yet something other was afoul. Had the child, the doctor asked, been down a well or in a cave by the lake, or had the child tasted something dead. What is this, the doctor asked, scraping something from the child's body. The doctor wiped the child's mouth with a rag, then sniffed the rag. He questioned the child and the child grew soft and loose in his arms. There was no indication of poison's nine signs but there was the listlessness of the child, its cold body. There was the unidentifiable paste the doctor had removed from the child, a whitish glue, a tacky gum. Had something been scraped on the child or pierced him or had the child been operating any of the yard machines without his mask, breathing too much of their smokes and fumes? The father did not think so but he agreed with the doctor that they would treat the child as though he'd been harmed from the outside. They took him to his room and they waited each day for the child to rise as ever, to commence his day's chores, but the child kept to his bed and took no food and allowed himself only enough water to soothe his mouth. He would not read and he no longer sang in the morning, before his family had woken. When his family visited his room, the child did not look at them. He no longer spoke. At times, from downstairs, they thought they could hear him speaking, in the voice of an older man, calm and mature, but when they arrived in his room the child was silent and perfectly still, staring at the wall, hardly breathing.

The doctor had heard of this, or something like this, and he thought he might know of someone. He made a call to a colleague in Chicago who had returned some children from spells and coldness, and the colleague telephoned a contact of his own, along a chain of professionals threading into ever more mysterious illnesses. A week later, a specialist from North Dakota arrived at the child's house in the early morning. He rubbed a cream on the child. The child thrashed when the cream touched him, clutched at his own throat as if to choke himself. The specialist asked that no one watch. By nightfall the child sat up. He got dressed in his best clothes and tidied his room. He sang one of his old songs, but coldly, a march he learned at the nursery. He spoke it like a foreign language. He combed his hair wet, posed at the mirror. He appeared cured, but when he spoke, to his father and the onlookers — the doctor had asked his colleagues to come view the techniques of the specialist — his message was not kind. First the child told them that they would die. He told them where and when. Sometimes he mentioned how, and he smiled, his boyish mouth pale, his teeth yellow from the illness. The child touched each of them at the face when he sentenced them. There seemed to be no possibility that he was wrong. They stayed perfectly quiet, receiving their dates, blinking with the new information. To his sister the child announced a date of death many years distant, more than a hundred years away, and her face was small and serious as she tried to count out her dying age in her head, so far in the future. She seemed to know she could not live that long and she laughed, hoping her brother was joking. Her brother, unsteady on his feet, spoke in whispers, moving through his room. It took all of his strength to speak. Some spots of blood were seen at his eyes. The specialist flinched each time the child spoke, as if he'd be harmed. He put more cream on the child and the child staggered back, falling to his bed, only to rise up again, speaking in the calmest voice of matters none of them cared to hear.

The child was dead the next morning, his body small and cold. The specialist went home. In his lab he extracted water from the cream until it thickened into a salve. He booted the cream in a charger. He ran softeners along the underside to raw out the hardness. From his cabinet he selected finer ingredients, to support knowing, thinking, remembering. He used a cooling herb for a skin, then peeled it back leaving only a membrane. The water that he would add back to the salve, to cream it, could only be water extracted from the human being. Then the product passed through a purifier and, to be sure, the specialist tested it on himself, using the cream over his torso, documenting his own fevered speech, days of it, on the machine.

Over the years the specialist visited similar patients in the western states, in the heat-blackened towns. He worked the neighborhoods of Chicago. Children stricken with fever. Children too cold to think or move. Adults who'd gone quiet. He spread salve on the children from a metal tin and before they passed away the patients grew calm and sometimes spoke. Sometimes they wrote. Messages of demise, usually, predictions of peril. Medically induced prophecy. A prophecy cream is how it came to be understood. It was requested and dreaded. As they spoke the children postured at wellness, arranging their rooms just so, tidying their possessions. In flat, slow voices, they spelled out sorrow, pointing out the doomed persons in the room. Then they died.

The specialist explained to the families that he needed to study these cases in order to possibly save some other boy or girl, some man or woman whose lights had burned out. The specialist pressed the speeches onto filament, parsed them for meaning, and set the deathbed claims on a pinned grid. He compiled a truth map, finding it faulty. The auguries of the children obeyed a pattern outside reality, surpassing sense. People lived beyond their predicted dates, or perished sooner. The cream-induced prophecies were not accurate. The cream yielded mainly mistaken claims.

The specialist ceased his practice of applying cream to the ill. He desiccated the cream again, removing the human water. Then he spread the resulting salve on people who were well. He used it over and around his own body, on his clothes, in the rooms he visited. He tried and failed to atomize the salve into a mist. With volunteers at his lab, the specialist initiated a revised cream at their necks, in varying dosages, a cream debased by earth sugars. Then the specialist migrated across the body of the volunteer. He spread a weaker cream over one leg, the other, a hand, a fist. He had parents hold down their own children while he spread the cream on their backs. A cream was used inside clothing, slurried into cones through which the volunteers, in weak voices, commenced to sing.

Each application of each revised cream produced fits of speech. A literature ushered from the mouths of the volunteers. Prophetic, cream induced, forgotten later by the speakers, sometimes denounced. In content the language extractions were plain, banal, riddled with fear, without clear meaning. The specialist transcribed them all, logged them into English text, released them back into the world under different names, different titles. Documents from the salve. Provoked by cream.

Late in life the specialist gave up his practice. Many years after he died, the specialist's daughter, now a young doctor herself, discovered samples of the darkened cream in his lab, maturing in a cabinet, a crust of sand along its surface, along with a notebook recording his results. She broke the cream down, ripped toxins from its core, added back salves. She kept the skeleton of the cream and built over it a new body. Her father's patents for each medical bolus he produced were rogue, indicating a larger plan, to which the salve was only a small feature, a lubricant. Each portion of salve, released from its tin and rolled thin into ropes, was meant, according to a diagram she found, to join together, serving as a kind of circulatory system for a machine that did not exist yet, or for a machine, she later came to think, that was hiding in plain sight, a machine we could not see properly because we wore it. She could not picture what machine this salve would enable, what contraption it might grease, other than a human body, an animal body. She sensed a criminal component, a kind of weapon latent in the salve. At each site of fever, each home of a child who spoke ill and died, an unknown paste was found, sometimes inside the child's body, predating any illness in the area. Implicating her father as the bringer of fever, only to test his prophecy cream. Her father would have seemed to be designing a weapon all along, using plant and chemical products together in a balm to bring a violence on the body. A body in fever will not keep its secret, was one of the notes she found. And other such claims. The specialist's daughter found references to grave site applications. A cream rubbed on stone. On trees. A cream—this one an early iteration of her father's product—spread over roads. Applied to the wheels of cars, which rolled through a territory. He called it, at times, a privacy cream. Batches of it were manufactured at Thompson, each tin numbered, the numbers etched free, indicating the properties of mind the cream would give or remove. Sometimes indicating nothing.

The rest is history, just not the kind that comforts. By the time of the specialist's daughter's death, creams of understanding were no longer new. Lotions smart and otherwise. Fortifying pastes across the torso, or in skins hovering at face level. Surrogate torsos made of lotion. A cosmetic fore-face that hung in liquid suspension in front of the real face, which turned as old and muddy as a coin. Bodies of cream worn like clothing. And so decorated. Foreign-language creams at the throat, to make speech plain. A cream at the back of the neck to release secrets. A salve for the mute and a salve for the tongue. A swishing lotion for inside the mouth, to protect the speaker from cream-induced prophecy. An unwitting release of secrets, compelled forth by perfect application, unbeknownst, of a cream. Applied in the woods. In the home. At work. Underground. On people, things, and space.

Omen

It was April 29 and the streetlights were flickering in and out.
And yet—little miracle—power was still on at Fowler's house.
Barely. He still had water. Heat. The clock on his stove was blinking, so at some point in the night he'd lost electricity. Briefly. His
house might go dark again. It was out of his hands.

The flood had come on hard yesterday, the answer to a season
of mountain rain. They'd seen it coming, and all the clay-faces had
been crying about it on the news. Whimper whimper out of their
omen holes. Everybody run for the hills. But you couldn't force
people from their homes. Yet. You could scare them to higher
ground, another town, a school gymnasium outside the flood zone.
You could conjure the odds of survival, showing the footage of past
disasters, a child's sock in a ditch, the imprint of a little person in
the grass. Most people would scatter.

Most people. Excepting his truly. Fowler the Last. There would
be no heirs. He'd waited out the evacuation because certain projects
flourished in an empty neighborhood. Houses hollow. No people
around to see. Most of what was really urgent to do necessitated a
near-total absence of the living. Hell yes, he was relieved, but there
was a sack of undesired emotion inside him. Instincts boiled up,
even in idiots. His blood was on notice. His body could be scared
and so what. Death to all feeling soon, right? RIP and whatever,

because darkness forevermore. He wasn't in charge of his feelings. It was kind of a relief. Just see where the secret engine pulled him, and don't show your goddamn cards.

From his doorway Fowler could see a distant light burning in the hills. Given what he knew about the terrain, a light of that sort didn't compute. There were mud barriers up there, rock dams, and lookout blinds, sometimes with little huts attached. There was what was called a sluice. He'd been to a few of the huts. He knew the hills pretty well. You could enter a hut, go to sleep. No one bothered you. You could think of it as your own home when you wanted to.

But there were no power lines at that elevation. Not even animals, really. The word "hideout" had obvious problems. Connotations. You pictured a shoot-out. You pictured an old dirty bed with handcuffs on the floor, a shit stain on the wall. But he used the word privately as a kind of code. He knew what it meant. He could call it whatever he liked.

He found it hard not to worry. A light pulsing in the hills as if someone had just plugged in the eye of God. Was there a work crew dug in up there, and did that mean there'd been a significant mudslide, bringing a hut down with it? With some daylight he'd have perspective. Shapes would come out and show themselves.

He held something of value in the hills, is why he cared. That was a safe way to think about it. Holdings. A lien. A claim. Nothing on paper, of course. Never that. You had to keep yourself from even thinking of these things in any detail. In case of what? Men, women, and children, first of all. Spies of varying skill sets, which was more or less the entire human race. People who were not whole. Certain citizens, just a mush of sadness on the inside, ached and pined and agonized unless they could lick your insides for whatever you knew. They had to sniff you over like you were a dog bowl and tear off a piece of your special core and just rub it all over themselves. Your own true water. Not that there were people who could stethoscope your thoughts. He wasn't stupid. But the operating wisdom now, in the year of all hell breaks loose, was that you didn't know who could hear you, see you, know you. Weren't you the ultimate fool if you thought you had a secret that was yours alone?

At sunrise Fowler stepped outside his house, closed the door gently so as not to disturb his wife. It would be pretty hard to wake her, he laughed to himself, because she wasn't home. Hadn't been for a good while. How funny that he kept doing that, tiptoeing around, being so careful, so quiet, because she always said his steps were too heavy. She could hear him breathing in the next room. She told him he coughed too loudly, and once she said that when he coughed like that, with such a rumble, she felt threatened.

Threatened like, what, he was going to hurt her?

She wasn't sure. She said she didn't control her own reactions. How was she supposed to just pretend it didn't scare her? Did he want her to do that? She could try to do that. Would that make him happy, she asked, if when he did something she found frightening, she kept quiet and calm and acted like it did not upset her?

He didn't want to smash her head in. Nothing like that. He would know if he regularly had thoughts like that. He wasn't really that way. She wasn't here, anyway. He couldn't get to her if he tried.

Fowler wandered the waterlogged neighborhood, mud spilling over his Bogs. What a strange vacancy all around him, like everyone just had to get off the planet.

He wanted to be able to look up into the sky and see a stream of people, just slashes and dark marks, shooting off and away from here. A proper evacuation. A full-on abandonment of the world. That wasn't something you often got to see. The word "evacuation" should be held in reserve for such an event.

From Burdock Road to the Deering radial there were uprooted trees drifting by like canoes. The people who had left yesterday had left badly. Doors to some houses were still open, lights shining inside, which, if he didn't have something else to take care of right now, he could be a good neighbor about. He bet there were cats. People often left a cat behind. During calamity, Fowler could pick a house, and go on in, and run into a cat or two. See who wore the crown then, who owned the planet. He didn't really know who kept cats. You had to be a regular in someone's house before you knew if they kept a cat.

He got the occasional invite, but mostly he knew these houses from the outside. Sometimes the cats never appeared when someone strange was over. The cats had an idea of their own safety and they practiced it carefully. People less so, which, well. A different attitude toward safety. Someone comes to your house, and you happen to be in the other room, you come out. You don't crawl under your couch. Mostly because of being polite. That would be a good chart to look at. Just all of the creatures and how they supervised their own safety. Strategies against harm, real or imagined. Accurate or inaccurate view of a threat. Good choices, bad choices. Success rates. How was the species doing overall, in relation to its enemies? So many charts he'd like to examine.

Anyway, if this all kept up for a few days—rain in the hills, loosening slabs of earth—he'd start to know who kept cats, and had left them. He'd hear them.

It was funny. To have waited so long for this opportunity, a time when no one was around and he could do as he pleased, go straight to the designated location, which he would not name to himself, and grab those items of interest, which he would neither name nor picture.

But the going was hard outside in the water. And something seemed wrong. Which, well, of course.

Waders. He had them at home. Walking through dark water, you had no real idea what you kept running up against, what was under your feet, what bumped your legs. Half of your world was blind. In reverse, that would really be something. A sheer darkness above the belly. Moving through a cold, thick mass, unable to breathe or see, your legs kicking freely below as if dangling in space. That'd be a ride he'd pay for.

Maybe he should return home, have lunch, and think through his plan again. He pictured himself at the table, his waders folded over a chair in the mudroom. Half a person with the bones removed. If only he'd already taken care of his errand, crossed it off his list. Screw it, screw it, screw it. There was so little time.

Slowly he aimed himself toward the girl's house.

It was at the block party a year ago when his plan started to grow a sort of awful hair, and leak, and sort of slobber on him no matter what he did or where he went. Regarding the girl. The girl, the girl, the girl. Who created this inadequate language that rubbed all of the detail off a thing and still ruled supreme as the primary currency people hurled at each other to make themselves known and whatnot?

A block party last year. Of all things. There was a fire engine parked on the street, and there were food tables, and the neighborhood association had rented a dunk tank.

Every so often, a great big splash sent water hurtling over the crowd, and a fat, shirtless man climbed out of the dunk tank, laughing.

Fowler came around to talking with some of the men gathered in the street. First he waited in line for a sausage roll. The one they gave him was sweaty and soft in his mouth. Something like a bone seemed to run the length of it.

"You caught yourself a beauty, there," one of the men said to him.

Fowler looked down at it. In these situations, you could eat, and people understood you wouldn't be answering right away.

Men were easy, in that as long as you showed you'd heard them, you could go a very long time without saying anything back. It was a mercy.

He knew that it was a little bit of an accident that he was a man. It would have been an accident of a different kind had he been a woman. It was a small accident, really, that he was a person in the first place. A chart of all those little accidents, along with drawings of his bones, adding up to who he was—that'd be worth looking at.

In his little group, the men were talking about hunting, even though only one of them seemed to do it. The others got by on saying how much they would like to do it, or intended to try it, once certain conditions were met. A season was beginning, the hunter was saying, or a season was ending, and then something else about traps. Where you put them, when you checked them, and how you baited them.

"Really, now," the hunter said, "I just load the fuckers up with candy."

The men all chuckled.

Fowler looked at them, one by one, and very nearly saw through their faces into something more. Punishing insights. Understandings. But it clouded over. He lived in an unpromising time; that was just a fact. A time of terrible ignorance. Too little information about what mattered the most. There wasn't, as yet, a good tool to get a clear picture of exactly what others were thinking. This ability was probably on its way for people, a hundred years out, maybe. One hundred and fifty. Things would open up, in all sorts of ways. A method of getting in there and really knowing something. But Fowler would be dead before such technology came along.

He wondered if, on his deathbed, he'd want to be told what was really in store. Deathbed. That was a joke. There'd be no bed. Fowler could picture himself, all too convincingly, running through trees, scrambling up a hillside, taking bullets to the torso. They'd itch going in, he figured. Itch and burn. He hadn't been shot before, but it didn't tax the imagination to picture it. It came to him sometimes almost like a memory.

The hunter went on about traps. You had to clean them after

each use, and the process sometimes needed a hose, or even this thing, and he tried to make a drawing of it with his hands. He said one thing he saw in a trap was something he'd not forget. An animal eating candy with a jaw-clamp of knives sunk into its haunch. Almost happy. Going through the candy pretty slowly, sort of relaxed.

You heard a version of this story as a kid. Animals caught in traps chewed off a leg to escape. Fowler had to wonder. Obviously it hurt a little bit. That wasn't something anybody would really want. But if you did have to do it, and you found yourself, as an animal, chewing into your own flesh, tearing it away, trying to gnaw through the bone, which was when the project got serious, was there ever a moment, even just for a second, when you felt like you'd been born to the job? A kind of pure calling? The slow destruction of oneself with one's mouth? You'd be smart leaving room around categories like that, he thought. Not to believe that you know what there is to be known. You don't.

They were standing in a circle, eating. Some of the men held little glass jars of beer. Fowler kept away from that. He took in all the liquid he needed at night.

The kids were out today, because everybody said that the block party was really for them. You did this kind of thing for the kids. And then you also took part in it for the kids. You went to work for the kids. You cooked dinner for the kids. You cleaned up for the kids. When you had kids, according to the people who blasted Fowler with their views, what you did you did for them. Even when you had more kids, you did it for the kids you already had, and when you struck one of them in the face, everyone should know whose good it was for. Whereas if you didn't have kids, like Fowler and his wife—despite a verbal project that circled the possibility, but had long since faltered—what you did you apparently did for yourself. Or maybe for no one. To hear the parents talk, without kids you were nothing, a quarter person, a kind of costume that could be hung on a hook. You powered down in the evening and your body deflated in the corner. Someone could kick you down the street like a trash bag.

Some young people at the block party were making a disturbance. Fowler caught sight of the girl pretty quickly. The girl—this wasn't really how he would come to think of her. It was just that the usual words were not ideal. They didn't fully seem to function. There was too much slippage, like an electric short that kept them from sticking. He would learn her name, and wish he hadn't. In Fowler's view the name didn't suit her. It was like a small lie that needed to be owned up to. He would come to an arrangement with himself not to use it. He would go to her house, watch her sleep, but this first time, out in the wild, was different, and he'd never see her that way again.

The girl had on what looked like men's pants and a sort of circus sweater. The pants were high-waters and the sweater, too, but on her arms, like maybe she'd gone swimming and her clothes seized up, tried to vanish off her body. A creature who fell asleep for a very long time and woke up too large for her clothing. Her hair was piled in some kind of bundle as if her crafter had dropped it on her head from the sky. Because she was not ordinary. She had not been made in the normal way.

She was singing or she was shouting, and maybe what was making all of her friends laugh is that they weren't sure which one. In a group of creatures, regardless of the species, there is sometimes one who seems to control the blood of the others.

Fowler tucked deeper into his sausage roll and saw all the men looking at her, not hiding it, their faces made of rubber and their eyes scratched from their heads, like in a picture.

As the girls walked by, the men turned small and strange. No one breathed. They just waited for the girls to get clear and then you could feel them catching up on their breath.

They again gave each other glances. Just a significant exchange of silence, trying not to break into pieces.

"Well, thank god I don't shit in my own backyard," one of them finally said, shaking his head.

"Hell, I don't shit in my own toilet," someone replied, and they all laughed.

Fowler would see her asleep in a month. You didn't keep records for things like that, because of course. He would stop in, take a look, gather some items, and truck them up to the hut, where a certain kind of situation was taking shape. A residence, a place, a grave. Today her face seemed filled with air. He squinted so she could be blurry.

A bit more chatter, everybody silently agreeing that they wanted to destroy what they'd seen, that they could remove the small parts of their bodies and make a pile there in the street. For someone to find later. Someone smart, a sort of scientist, who could look at it, throw his hand into it, and have a close enough idea of just what had happened in this place.

Then the men tensed up. "Shut up, shut up," someone said, "here they all come."

It was the wives, bombing at them from the other side of the street. They closed in pretty fast and acted like they'd missed all the fun.

"What are you all laughing about?" One of the wives turned to Fowler.

The Shebster wife, the Coramper one. He didn't remember. Those sounded like fake names to him, like they had all lied about who they really were. He wanted to keep eating. A tough bit of cartilage was lodged in his mouth. He was almost done chewing. He'd do anything not to look at the girl. You had to follow a ration.

This wife was really on him.

"Tell us what these guys said or we will torture you," she shrieked.

Fowler saw where this woman would be buried and he saw the weather for it, her children crying at her grave. If he really strained he could see the children themselves get old and bloat with fluid until they burst.

She touched him and he stopped eating. "Are you ticklish?" The men all watched.

Fowler was occupied with the larger question of how many ways the girl could look, doing different things, even long after she'd died. As bones, as powder, at night, having all of the different feelings, and if any of those ways would change what he felt should happen—that she and Fowler should combine themselves in a remote location. Even the girl's father, whom Fowler had seen, and once spoken to, had, buried in his face, something that drew Fowler in.

So it wasn't the girl in particular, was it? Maybe the father would do, or the mother, or, if it were possible, ancestors going back further, if you could arise out of where you lived and drift into the past, to make selections. Because the attraction—even though that was the wrong word, really—was just the cells, and the blood. A precise arrangement of them, regardless, really, of the carrier, rendering her face and body just so. Maybe the girl herself didn't matter, even if she seemed to hold a more concentrated level, as if a strong dose of it had funneled down into her for the time being. He couldn't ignore that. He'd be lying to himself. What would he want from her as an old woman? It was a problem.

The tools didn't really exist for him to scrape what he needed into a bottle.

"Marjorie," the woman called over to Fowler's wife. "Hey, Marjorie, I caught myself a big one!" She'd grabbed Fowler now and he started to sway, eating his sausage again, trying to smile in just the right way for the guys.

The other wives looked down and laughed. The laughing had changed. It didn't make him feel good to hear someone say his wife's name. It never had. Early on, when they were first just getting to know each other and he hoped to show her some of the paths in the foothills, before they had embarrassed each other with nudity, he wondered if that meant they should not be married. Her name wasn't entirely her fault.

Marjorie was nearby, in a circle of people, and she didn't seem to immediately notice she was being called out. When he saw her he could tell she didn't want to look up—she had on her *do not disturb* face. She'd be gone in three months, leaving with no argument, the two of them nearly shaking hands. He wanted to keep these people from bothering her. But she looked over at them anyway.

"What do you say?" the wife asked, pointing her finger right into Fowler's body. "Is this one ticklish? Your husband! Is he?"

Marjorie shrugged, and it was like they all suddenly felt the same thing, with this woman's finger pressing into Fowler, as if she knew what she was looking for, when really she had her hand in something she should not be touching. The group quickly fell quiet. Maybe each of them, in their own way, was picturing themselves being launched off the street, as Fowler was, and propelled high up into the air, then rapidly hurtling through space. Their faces spreading in the wind as it rushed by them, and all of them looking down at their whole neighborhood, where everything had turned so small. Killable, dismissible, unreal. There wasn't really such a good word for how it all looked from up there where he was.

Now Fowler was out in the neighborhood, just where the block party was a year ago, and everyone was gone, evacuated. He could do what he liked. The streets were empty. Yesterday some vehicles had lifted in the muck and floated off. The biggest things, in the right weather, were suddenly weightless, beautiful. Should not people, on occasion, float past one another, weightless and rolling? The problem with the laws of physics was repetition, dullness. There was a kind of deep insult buried in the way the world was designed.

Pretty much everything was hidden by a rumbling flow of mud. Some houses were seeing damage.

Mud, they all knew by now, because you heard it on the news every time the rain started, slid down from Moyer Creek, which nearly ringed the town from above. Nearly. From space the creek might look like a broken circle, a circle with a tear in it, where some beast had maybe broken through. But today you couldn't really look into the hills and think the mud was coming from just one place anymore. Someone long ago had named the area a basin. Not a scientific term. In the neighborhood they called it a bucket because it did fill right up.

Stupid to put houses in it. Stupid to put people there. True of any place if you took the long view. Pretty much any location anywhere featured its own notable extinction. Sudden death. But people did not exactly get to see a list, for example, of all the people who had died in the place they were thinking of living. Plus how they died, going back a good enough ways to give them the picture they really were entitled to have. Probably it would be unbearable to know. Who died here. And here. And here. How they died. When they died. Probably no one would care to know. But still, freedom of information. If you felt yourself to be strong enough, you should be allowed to know.

There was probably an ocean here long ago. And before that, what, maybe hot plains, they said, too hot even to stand on. Jungle, too. Sharp beds of coal. A meadow of knives, Fowler had read somewhere.

Fowler had to figure that, throughout history, one animal had hunted another in this very spot. What were the larger observations one could make, in terms of who escaped, who was caught, who was eaten? You could think that you walked down the street in your town, but you didn't. You participated in something else entirely.

A chart depicting every creature who passed this way, going back to the beginning. Did they know they were in danger? Did they intend harm to others?

...

When he got to the girl's house, it didn't take him long. Her bedroom was off the kitchen, and not upstairs with the other bedrooms. Nobody was home, but Fowler couldn't help calling out. He instantly regretted it. What if there was a recording instrument? They'd have captured his voice. Except, nonsense. That was nonsense and he knew it. In the entryway, dripping mud, he debated between boots or socks. Which sort of footprints were called for? A pair of clogs in the shoe rack solved the problem. Belonging to the girl's father, no doubt, owing to their size. Perhaps for gardening, or cooking. He pushed his mud-caked feet into them, then clomped to the girl's bedroom, the same way her father must have done many, many times.

It had taken a little bit of hiding to be able to stick around yesterday, when the patrols came through on bullhorns. Men at the door pounding away. Everyone barking in animal voices. You shouldn't have to take cover in your own house. But the county had learned its lesson from last time, when no one got out, no one was scared enough, no one wanted to be troubled.

It was last year's flood that had them all crazy. The bunch of little people they'd lost to it, just around the corner from here. The Larsen boys and their friend whose name Fowler always forgot. Everyone acted like their own children had died. You had to be prepared to discuss the matter, and be silent about it, too, when that was called for. So no one was fooling around this time. They were going to scoot off and play it safe.

Not him, though. A couple of items could get scratched off his to-do list if he sat this one out and had the place to himself. He'd squatted under a window for most of the day, crawling here and there for supplies, and clocked a good bit of the mayhem going on outside.

...

Today at the girl's house Fowler found a backpack to stash the stuff in. If the girl cared for the backpack, which he figured she must, since it was on her bed, then that was one more thing she'd be pleased to see.

If he got her up to the hut, if that was something that would ever really happen. After he'd solved some of the logistics. Acquisition. Transport. If the hut was even there anymore. So far, when he pictured it, he could not summon any shapes out of the darkness. The visualization was proving difficult. One's imagination often failed.

Fowler walked home, the backpack raised over his head. He was careful not to get anything dirty, impossible as that was. If anyone came along, it'd be a sorrow, but he could sink the backpack into the mud. Objects like that seemed to reappear in the girl's room over time, in different colors and shapes, so he could always fetch them again, but, well.

At home, Fowler peeled off his mud-stiffened clothing and dropped himself into the hot bath. He warmed a soup for lunch, then dialed into the news. A water-volume report was coming up later in the hour. Numbers on the flood so far. How much of it there still was to come down. To rise up. That would be a good number to know.

The news never reported on the mountain roads. Too few people lived up there. Possibly no one. A crushed hut wouldn't make the news.

The girl's diary listed her top ten favorite things. Some of them were people. Her mother and dad. But they weren't invited. They had spent enough time with their daughter. Time's up. Other items could be crossed off the list. If a hut came down, and its contents spilled, what would they find? A girl's pillow. A basket of stuffed animals. In the backpack today was a poster he'd had to fold. When it went up in the hut, with a thumbtack, it would have creases. There were four little guys in the poster. They had grown-up hair. No names. They looked stunned, like they'd opened the wrong door. One of them held a raccoon.

A set of markers and a pad. A blanket with a picture pattern of some people Fowler couldn't place. Certainly they were famous. More stuff from that top dresser drawer. He would just reach in and see what came back out. What you did on a dig was you collected artifacts and kept your own ideas out of it. Your own ideas almost always led to trouble.

He could just as well take a sliver of wood from the floor in her room. A divot of Sheetrock from inside her closet. All throughout the house, her yard. He could scrape enough pieces. Where did it stop, and why not her father, her mother, her friends? All of them brought, in pieces or whole, to the hut, which could never hold it all. It was getting too crowded already, but there was no way to know where it ended.

What you're trying to do is make yourself whole. Which it's stupid to think another person's bones can't help you with.

In the same way it didn't pay to say the girl's name, it didn't pay to think about her. It didn't pay to go into her house. It didn't pay to know where she went to school and what her schedule was each day of the week, when school let out and practice began. Band or sport. Musical instrument or study group. Nothing paid. You got an answer and nothing broke open.

Two creatures, built of cells, fueled on blood. A system of bones at the core. If they died in the same area, or were buried together, and then, hundreds of years later, were found by archaeologists, the archaeologists might easily think that they had stumbled across the remains of a single creature. There would be a way to reassemble these bones, of him and the girl, for instance, if they had died or were buried together in the same area, into one beast on their wire frame. There would be redundant bones, two of each, but a bigger and a smaller, and it would be just as easy to tell a story about this creature, to create an exhibit, to show it to children, or whatever they called their young, who could stand and look at it in awe.

The carcass of a single creature. It was just that the bones of this creature had gone into scatter, and they needed to be gathered up. Put back together.

At around dinnertime, a trooper came to the door.

The sun was going down. An unpleasant spectacle. It wasn't a given that the sunset would be something universally considered beautiful. At the outset of things, when that feature was put into place, he didn't think it was a given. It could just as easily have become something that routinely horrified the citizens of the world. Made them crazy. Made them ill.

There were two troopers when Fowler opened up. One right there on his doorstep, the other leaning against a Jeep down in the street. Water to his knees.

"Evening rounds," said the trooper. "Safety check. Passing through. Saw that your lights were on." The trooper squinted past him into the house.

"Okay," said Fowler. "All's well here. We're doing fine."

Lots of lights on all over the neighborhood. Was the trooper going to every house?

They stood talking on the steps.

A bad spot of weather, they agreed. Too much rain collected in a place that couldn't hold it. So down it came. Pretty fast, actually. The trooper had once used his speed gun on a flash flood, he told Fowler. Clocked it faster than a car. And if the ground was too warm, and too goddamn loose, then forget it. Too much of the mountain peels away and you can't stop it.

Fowler agreed. He had often stood with another person, discussing recent phenomena, and found agreement on everything that could not be done. It was shameful to bond over powerlessness. Shameful. Here he was engaged in it again.

"Anyone else home?" asked the trooper. "Wife?"

"No, sir," said Fowler. "She's up in Rooneville."

"No kids?"

"Not yet." Fowler crossed his fingers and held them up. I wish I may I wish I might.

Just words in his head he would not share.

"Okay, well," said the trooper. "I'm supposed to do my best to talk you folks out of your houses. That's my best. I've done it."

"Oh yeah, other people stuck it out?" Fowler asked, looking up the street. He'd seen no one today. Heard nothing.

Witnesses, was the worry. Except what had he really done? Just the one home invasion, although that was a strong way to name it, with no one being home. Wasn't every bit of motion, anywhere, an invasion? You invade a room, you invade the street, you invade your own bed.

"A few folks. Here and there. Holed right up like you, no doubt. But look, we could get you to dry ground, no charge. Pack a bag real quick. Better safe than sorry."

"Right. Or both."

"What's that?"

"Safe *and* sorry."

Well, he should not have said that.

"Sorry about what?" asked the trooper.

He couldn't find an answer. This man sure could talk and now here Fowler was, answering.

"Just a lot of suffering," Fowler said finally. "For the people who suffer. I'm sorry about it."

The trooper gave Fowler a pretty long look.

"Anyway, good thing you're up here on this rise."

"Good luck for us," agreed Fowler. "Plus the stilts."

"What's that?"

"Got the house up on stilts. Even last time with, what was it, six feet of it coming right through town, we kept it pretty dry in here."

"Good for you," said the trooper. He looked around. "You've got a nice little situation. You all take care."

"We had the work done when we bought the house. Never could have gotten a mortgage without it."

Stupid to keep talking. When someone leaves the conversation, you let them go. Never keep talking. Just let them go. If he ever had to write a manual for how to be a person, that would be in there, right at the top. Just look for the silence and be the first to practice it.

The trooper turned back. "So, no children in the house, huh?"

That seemed to be a funny way to ask. Fowler looked at the trooper and tried to make the question go away with his face.

"No," he said. Simple was best. It also happened to be true, which made him more uneasy. That's where they got you, when you said the truth but did so falsely, nervously.

Fowler saw himself doing unspeakable things. That didn't mean he'd do them. He'd come to terms with that difference a long time ago.

"I had to ask," explained the trooper, waving as he left.

Had to ask. Fowler knew the feeling. He thought of all the things that he had to ask, too, and that he never would ask. The things he wouldn't say. The things he wouldn't think. Statements waiting inside him, if only the right listening device were deployed. Mostly you walked the world in a kind of lockdown. Mostly.

He couldn't sleep so well that night. Rain and mud and rain again, and then thunder shook the house. Weather like this could peel back a mountain. A hut had no foundation. It sat on rocks. When the soil softened and the rocks shifted, then the hut was merely another grave, unearthed, sliding off, with no bodies in it yet.

No one questioned an empty grave. It was often just mistaken for a hole. No one noticed that empty graves were everywhere, inside houses and out, on mountains and right in town. Areas being readied for the dead. All areas. You more or less could not occupy an area, anywhere, that was not once, or would not soon be, a fairly ample grave.

Fowler had to feel it didn't matter. He was in his grave already. He and the girl. Their graves were on the move. The question was how best to fix them in place. Get the thing formalized.

When he finally got out of bed, in pure darkness, he confirmed that his power was down. Streetlights, too. Nothing in the hills. No light. Too little sound. Water and heat and everything, finished for a while. How he had kept power this long was a mystery.

How big the outage was, along with its long-term forecast, would remain unknown for a bit. He had a radio that took batteries, but the men who spoke on the overnight broadcast had little to say. Farmers and thinkers and worriers. Sensibilities from another time. Imaginary creatures with old sad voices whose message, perhaps, had never been clear. If they ever had information he could use, he'd found, they withheld it from him, in ways that could seem intentional. A promise of what they might be discussing, which they never did in fact discuss.

He had a flashlight. He had a telephone landline that used to work, though he hadn't checked it in a while. Phone calls were not his specialty, though he was capable of receiving them. Should one come along, he'd be ready.

Probably he had candles and matches if he wanted to go and look. This was the sort of thing you did when you had a partner in the darkness, a blackout friend, Marjorie used to say. Light up some candles and make a home out of it. Marjorie had always been pretty good about keeping a kit. She'd get him to fill the tub with water, to help the toilet along when the pump was off. You'd want to move that water out of your home. Keep a little bucket by the tub. Sometimes the bustle and panic was for nothing, and sometimes he was grateful that she'd thought of it.

For a minute he wondered if she was out of power wherever she was, too, but then figured that it wouldn't be too likely. Not that he knew for sure. Rooneville was just a town name he'd given the trooper. There were lots of good town names, each of them as likely as the other. Each the name of some place you went to die. You could give them out and they seemed to work. She was asleep somewhere, he would bet, unless she'd gone and leapt a time zone, which wasn't really like her. She was safe and warm. He could hear her voice anytime he wanted to. She would wake up soon and make tea.

Probably what he would do was sit up and wait for morning. The time right now was unclear. It could be midnight or it could be 4 a.m. Something might have happened and he would not know it. Something big. He hoped it was closer to day. Waiting wasn't his specialty. From his kitchen window he could look to where the sun would be, expecting advance notice of some kind, but right now there was nothing out there, no lights in the hills, none in the sky. The power outage would seem complete. From far away was the whole planet dark? Maybe, if things seemed stuck out there, in terms of the sun, some kind of rupture, he'd move his chair to where he wouldn't even have to get up. He could sit there looking for it, be the first to see it, a front-row seat for when the world turned back on.

Some people, apparently, suffered a disturbance where they were afraid the sun wasn't going to come up. It was a fear and it had a name. His wife had read about it. She said these people had to be consoled at night, but you couldn't console them. There was a kind of therapy for it, but she didn't remember what it was. Supposedly it didn't much help. They were as certain as you could be about anything. They fought you off and yelled.

Fowler pictured these people in a dark house, holding each other, trembling. When the sun finally came up they stood and shook themselves, relieved. They'd be embarrassed, apologizing to everyone. What a lot of fuss over nothing. They kept looking out the window to make sure the sun was still there. Weeping and hugging each other, shaking their heads, feeling foolish, foolish. Then the day, of course, advanced, took a left turn, deepened, the afternoon came on strong, and they felt a pull again, a terrible suspicion. They went outside, staring and pointing. They watched and wept, holding each other as tightly as they could, as the sun went down again, for what genuinely felt like the last time on earth.

A fear like that doesn't just come out of nowhere. Some people always know, ahead of all the others, what to be watching out for. One day, sooner or later, those people wouldn't be wrong.

And where would he be? he wondered. Would he be complete? Would he have done whatever it took, no matter what, to make himself whole?

Stay Down and Take It

James is home early saying that goddamnit we really seriously need to pack. Hup hup, time to go. It's the weather, again, and it bores me so. We live where the water loves to visit. Just a little bit of rain off the coast, that's all, and it will try to flood into our home. It loves to soak our rug and rise up the walls, and once it loved to seep into our electronics, inside the TV cabinet, and destroy our precious entertainment center, which keeps us, or me anyway, from raiding the medicine cabinet at night for other pleasures. Otherwise, well, we have brilliant sunsets and the kind of grass that is absurdly tall, taller than you or me. I don't know how it doesn't just fall over. You'd think it had a long slender bone in it, in each blade. Some original, beautiful creature that needed no limbs or head, because it had no enemies. Who knows.

James bustles around the house, grabbing what he can. He says to pack light and to pack smart. I like this military side of him. I almost feel charmed. The evacuation is mandatory this time, something nasty and mean and serious is barreling down on us, and I almost wish we had a pretty siren in our little community for occasions like this one. A siren adds a feeling of gravity—to an evacuation, to a catastrophe. Just a feeling that something important is happening, which one so often does not get to feel. James says that he'll grab our "go" bag, which I didn't even know we had. Does it have pears in it, and medical marijuana, and Percocets, and frozen

Snickers bars? Something tells me it's more of a batteries and rope and candles and matches kind of bag. James is huffy and swollen and red as he loads the car. This is a little bit much for him. Still, it's nice to see him excited, in charge, alive. It's been hard to watch a man his age slowly lose his purpose, as he's been doing, shuffling around the kitchen trying to perfect his long-simmering sauces, which only get poured out on the back lawn when he's done, since how much gravy-drenched flesh can the two of us reasonably consume?

There is just one road out of here, and everyone we know is on it, moaning silently, I imagine, gently rending their summer linens at this unwelcome disruption. It gets tiring waving at them all—stressed-out wrinkled accidents of the human form, with white hair, or no hair, or nubby yellow sun visors. Grimacing, hunched over their steering wheels, as if they are being chased by men with guns. We know these people by their cars, which are long and dark and quiet, just like ours. We could all just call each other, share information and prop up each other's nervous systems with voice-based medication, but people are saving their cell phone batteries. We've been through this drill before. Who knows where we'll all be tonight. James also prefers me not to talk on the phone when he's driving. He does his best to tolerate it, bless him, but he tenses up so terribly that I fear he will break open and spill everywhere, even while he insists, sometimes angrily, that he really doesn't mind. Really really really, with spit fluffing out of his mouth and a look of pure murder in his eyes. I feel that he is daring me to make a call, but when I consider the risk, I sort of daren't. After all, I am also a passenger in the vehicle that he is driving, and I must consider my own safety as well.

"This is the hardest part," says James. "Just getting out of here."

Well put, and doesn't that just apply to any old situation: a meeting, a party, a relationship, a life? Always that sticky problem of the exit and how to squeeze through it.

When I don't respond, James says, "Do you agree?" It's what he often wants and needs. Assent. I tend to pay out as much as I can, with my mouth and otherwise, but always one must monitor the personal cost, careful not to add to the deficit, which can swell up and trigger a low-grade rage. Not my prettiest style. I never knew that I would be called on so relentlessly to agree with someone. Mother never said. Ask not, I guess, and I sort of haven't.

I touch his leg. "Oh I do. I was just thinking, in fact, how right you are. This is the difficult part. This right here." I would so love to point at the two of us, the fact of us, here in this car, on this road, on this day with a storm coming, in this particular life, just to say that *this* is the difficult part. Because, well. But the precise gesture eludes me. Hands can only signify so much. Usually they should just rest in one's lap, sneaking beneath the garment now and then for a wee scratch at the tuft. This is possibly why one is supposed to use one's words. I think. Plus, James is focusing all of his energy on the road ahead, which is really just an endless line of cars pointing west, away from the storm, away from home. We will be here a while. We might as well table any immediate feelings.

"This is about the only time I hate this island," James says. "When it keeps us prisoner."

"Yup," I say. "Me too."

It's not really an island that we live on, or it wasn't until some developers got clever. Because people love an island. I guess *we* love an island. I'm told they used explosives. They bombed a little spit of land that connected two bigger blobs of coastal blah, then built a baby road over the obliterated spit, the road we are now stuck on. So, poof, our little town became an island, and the houses suddenly cost more. The wind was arguably sharper and cooler after that, the light more intense, more knowing and intimate. More light-like. According to the marketing, anyway. Oh it was instantly spectacular, and all it took was some dynamite stuffed into the gaping pores of an old, rotted peninsula. Blowing your way to beauty might have been a nice slogan. One's whole attitude to life was said to deepen, thoughts and feelings growing ever more rarefied and special. Island life. Too bad we can't all die here, too, just to sustain our purity, but the island has a rule. You can die here, sure, and many of us have, spectacularly and otherwise, usually otherwise, but you must be buried across the sound, where the regular dumb folk reside and perish, and where the ground will open up for any old dead person, no questions asked. Even a living one, maybe, although who can say? Of course cremation is, as the saying goes, a workaround. A fine one. You *can* come home again—in a jar—and some of us have, but the victory seems small. I look at certain old friends, rendered to dust in their tureens, placed on various island mantels, and it is hard to feel just what it is they've won.

"What's strange," I say, as we idle in traffic, "is that the sun is out. It's such a fine day. So weirdly beautiful."

James cranes his neck to look out the window, trying maybe to be fair, and he has that expression, as if he's evaluated all of the evidence but still, he's very sorry to say, he just cannot bring himself to agree. It would violate his delicate moral compass to cede any ground here. "I'm not sure that's so *strange*," he says, as if there's a superior adjective he's reluctant to share. "Quiet before the *you know,* and all. Plus I see some . . ." And he points into nowhere, where there is maybe nothing, and I'm sure I don't even need to look.

Oh, he's probably right. What do I know when it comes to *strange*? Gosh knows I'm no expert in the uncanny.

"Yes, well, should we have music, or just listen to each other's bodies complain?"

"You think I'm complaining?" says James. "Because I'm not. This is a little bit stressful. I'm trying to get us out of here."

"I understand," I say. And I do. It needn't be said aloud, but I was referring to the sounds we make, each of us, which are whorishly amplified in the car, and not exactly my preferred music. Sounds of hunger, sounds of anxiety, sounds that have no explanation whatsoever—just the body at work, leaking and churning, groaning at a frequency no one was ever meant to hear. Live with someone long enough and you learn all of their gruesome lyrics, memorize all of the squishy instrumentals that gurgle out of them, note by note.

I click on the news and for a little while it's just the sound of the storm elsewhere, where it's ripened into a roar. We are to believe that the storm has paused in the lee of a mountain up north, where it's gathering strength, pawing at the dust like a bull. They have a microphone penetrated deep inside this poor storm, I guess, and I'd give anything to sound like that. So sweet and angry and brand-new, a kind of subvocal monster simply cooing at the pain and pleasure of life. It's perfectly beautiful and soothing, on such a nice day, until people start talking over it, explaining where this storm is from and where it might go, what it could do along the way, and then saying just how this storm makes them feel. Feelings! Every one of them would seem to be stirred up by this storm, by every kind of person. When it's over, I'm exhausted and confused. I examine myself for feelings, carefully checking in the usual hiding places, and there are simply none to be found.

We aren't kids anymore. We are old. Older. Nearly dead, really. My husband, James, is nearly dead, at least. He shows it. When he went to the doctor recently he hid the results from me, and I didn't really ask, because we have to ration our concern. We can't waste it on false alarms, and even if it's a genuine alarm we must, I have come to believe, enact a protocol w/r/t what we feel. James shows his feelings so liberally that they come at a discount, and their value diminishes. When he says he loves me, usually in a threatening way, it always seems to beg for reciprocation. I guess he cries wolf. More or less sobs it. One could argue that whatever James says is merely the word "wolf" in one language or another. If he loves me, it is because that might open the portal for more cuddles and touches. That's all. He needs to be swaddled and I just happen to often be in the same room. If I ever dare to walk past him without touching his hand, or his head, or stopping to outright kiss him, he pouts all day and looks up at me with mournful eyes. A husband, these days, is a bag of need with a dank wet hole in its bottom. The sheer opposite of a go bag. I comply with James's wishes when I can, but the day is long and I have other projects.

I guess I want James to die. Not actively. Not with malice. But in a dim and distant way I gently root for James's absence so I can see to the other side of the years I have left, get to what happens next. For a good while, James was what happened next for me. As a person he was a sort of page-turner. I moved through parts of him and made discoveries, large and small, and he led me to places and ideas I'd not seen or heard before. This looked and felt like life. And then, and then—even though I don't think it happened suddenly—the story died in my old, tired husband. It ended. I knew everything there was to know: what the nights would be like, how the morning would feel. What he would say. What he wouldn't. How I would think and feel around him. How I wouldn't. Knowledge is a lot of things, but it definitely is not power. Dread is the better term, I think, though I do understand how that ultimately fails as a slogan.

The hotels inland are full so we follow the endless line of cars to the shelter. We are shown to two cots in the center of a high school gymnasium. There must be five hundred beds here, scattered out in a grid. At midnight the sleep sounds must be symphonic, particularly with the soft lowing arising from the pornless apertures of the elderly. The scoreboard is on in the gym, but it seems that no one has scored yet. Zero to zero. I'd like to feel that there is meaning in this, but I am tired and hungry. "Voilà," says the volunteer, who has a walkie-talkie on his belt that squawks out little birdcalls. He is a handsome young man and he seems unreasonably proud to be playing this role today. I picture him unplugged, powered down like a mannequin, maybe sitting in a small chair in a room with sports banners on the wall. James and I stare at the cots as gratefully as we can, and for a moment I wonder if we are meant to tip the volunteer, because he stands there expectantly as wild children rocket past our feet.

"Just let us know if there's anything we can do for you," he says.

Anything? What a kind offer. A softer mattress, I think, and bone-chilling privacy, and a beef stew made with red wine. Some sexual attention would also be fine, if not from you specifically, because I fear you are too polite. Maybe you have a friend? After drives like that I often crave a release. But only a particular style of lovemaking will do. I have evolved a fairly specific set of requirements. If you don't mind reading over these detailed instructions, briefing your friend, and then sending him to meet me in the janitor's closet, that would be fine.

We tell him thank you, no, and we wait for him to run off before we start whispering our panic all over each other.

"Yeah, no," says James, looking around, fake smiling, as if people were trying to read his lips. "No fucking way."

"Maybe for a night?" I offer. I would like to be flexible. I would like to bend myself around this situation, which is certainly not ideal and is almost laughably experimental. One imagines doctors behind dark glass somewhere, rubbing themselves into a scientific frenzy over the predicament they've designed for us—two aging soft-bodies forced into an open-air sleeping environment. Maybe we are tired enough, and armed with enough pharmaceutical support, to render ourselves comatose on these trim little cots until it's safe to go home. But wouldn't people fuss with our inert bodies? Wouldn't they see that we were so heavily tranquilized as to be unresponsive and then proceed to conduct whatever procedures they liked upon us? I only surrender myself to all my sweet medicines when I can lock a door, because I hate the thought of being fiddled with when I've brought on elective paralysis and can't exactly fiddle back.

"The storm hasn't even touched down on the island yet. We are talking days, maybe," says James, rubbing his face. He rubs it with real purpose, pulling the skin into impossible shapes, before letting it not exactly snap back onto his head, taking its time to retract like the gnarled skin of a scrotum, and I fear for him a little bit, as if his hand will drag too far and pull his face free. I can't really watch. If he must dismantle himself, piece by piece, I wish he would do it in private. Together we look around, as we might if we'd just entered a party. There's no one here we know. It's just a crowd of ragged travelers, forced from their homes, with far too many children running free. The children seem to believe that they have been released into a kind of cage match. Kill or be killed, and that sort of thing. The cots, mostly empty, are simply launching pads for child divers, exploring their airborne possibilities. They leap from bed to bed, rolling into piles on the floor, whooping. A style of topless nudity prevails, regardless, it seems, of age. Certainly there is beauty on display, but it's ruined by all of this noise. One might reasonably think that there should be a separate evacuation receptacle for children. A room of their bloody own. Answering their special needs. Relieving the rest of us from the, well, the special energy that children so often desire to display. Lord bless their fresh, pink hearts.

I text Lettie, because there's no way she and Richard would put up with this sort of bullshit. Are they here? In what quadrant? Could they issue a specific cry, maybe holler my name?

Airbnb! she texts back. *Headed to Morley's for clams and bloodies. Where r u?*

Oh Jesus, right. People made *plans*. People thought ahead. I think it's best not to mention this to James, because that's something I could have been doing while he drove, securing our safe, private, *cozy* lodging and making dinner rezzies and otherwise running advance recon for this sweet adventure of ours.

James has curled up on the cot, and he's staring into space. He looks tired. His color is James-like, which is never so great. I'm not sure how to monitor a change. I worry that he's parked for good now, that the powerful laws of the late afternoon, which seem to visit men of a certain age, will be pulling him down into some bottomless, mood-darkening sleep, from which he will wake crankily, trumpeting his exhaustion, denying that he ever slept.

"Are you going to be napping?" I ask him, as neutrally as I can. "Because . . ."

"No, I'm not going to be *napping.* Are you kidding me? Here?" He has a way of shouting in a whisper. It's his evacuation shelter whisper, I guess, although it has caught the attention of certain of our neighbors, who might want to scooch their cots somewhere else, come to think about it.

Yes, I want to assure them. *We will be like this all night, whispering our special brand of kindness at each other, so pull up a chair and put your heads in our asses. That's where the view is best.* Perhaps that's one way to secure our area and erect a kind of privacy barrier.

"Maybe you should get up?" I say.

"Jesus, Alice, I've been driving for hours. I can't relax for a minute?"

"Yes you can, and even longer. Take all the time you like. I would just like to know your plans so I can plan accordingly."

"What," he hisses. "Are you going to go out and meet some friends? Go out to lunch, maybe?"

We have a different strategy when it comes to the timing of our emotional broadcasts. James buckles in public, and a hole opens in his neck, or whatever, and out comes his sour message for me and the world. One feels that he is emboldened in a crowd. It is possible that he does not see them as human, and thus fails to experience shame when he debases himself in their midst. Like masturbating in front of a pet. Whereas I frequently wait until we are alone, and then I quietly birth my highly articulate rage in his direction, in the calmest voice I can manage. I certainly have my bias, but it is possible that neither style is superior, and that a level silence in the face of distress or tension is the ultimate goal. Silence, in the end, is the only viable rehearsal for what comes after, anyway. I mean way, way after. And one certainly wants to be prepared. One wants to have practiced.

"Not here, James," I say, as brightly as I can.

"What you mean is not anywhere, right, Alice? Not anywhere and never?"

Not bad. He is learning. Although I do not doubt that he will share his feelings with me when we find some privacy.

We head out to the car and talk this through. The cots will be here as a last resort, although it feels odd using the word "resort" with respect to such a location. James feels that we should start driving because there will be plenty of other people with our same idea, all of them racing to find the closest hotel room. It's kind of the plot of *Cannonball Run,* except the people are old, they drive very slowly, and some of them just might die tonight. Eventually, James explains, if we go far and fast enough, we should find some part of this hellish country not affected by the storm, with plenty of empty beds. He would like to express confidence now, I can see that. I imagine that he wants me not to worry. If only he could do it without making me worry so much more.

The roads might still be packed, he says, and who knows about the weather. Around us there's a fringe of rain and the sky is black and there's that sound, a kind of pressurized silence, as if the orchestra is just about to start playing. The conductor will tap his baton and all hell will break loose. We figure we should get out of here, head further inland, and maybe there will be some food and a nice clean bed in a room where we can lock the door. It sounds decadent to me, and delicious, and I sort of cannot wait. We are a team, and it feels like we've just broken out of jail together.

We pull onto the highway and I check the news on my phone. "They are calling this storm Boris."

"Boris," he says flatly, as if I've just told him the name of a distant star.

"What's the thinking there?" I wonder.

"They needed a B name."

"Yes, well then, Boris, of course."

"And they practice a kind of diversity."

"Yeah?"

"I don't know. I'm sure they want to be inclusive."

"Not to trigger anyone by using a regular name?"

"Boris *is* a regular name," says James. "In several parts of the world. With massive populations. Possibly more regular than John, worldwide."

"Then let the storm go bother them."

"I'm sure there are people named Boris over here."

"Oh I'm sure. I bet their cocks stink."

"What is wrong with you?" James is grinning. I don't think he minds my moods when they're not directed at him.

"Plenty. I'm hungry and you won't let me eat. We just have to drive and drive. I'm going to hurl myself from the car."

James smiles, and he pretends to do math, wetting his finger and tabulating an imaginary problem in the air in front of him. "Fifty," he says.

"What?"

"I definitely think that's at least fifty times that you've threatened to jump from a moving car. At least since I've known you. I can't be sure about the time before that, but something tells me you had a penchant for it in your early years, too."

He may be right. I don't care to reflect too far back, particularly on the threats I may have needed to utter in certain stifling situations as a youth, which, one should not be surprised, very often occurred when I was a passenger in a car. I used to think about it more seriously, imagining myself rolling like a weevil, but finally free of torments. And of course the most delicious part of the fantasy was what would happen in the car after I ejected. The shock, the panic, the deep, abiding respect. Even the jealousy. Someone had finally done what everyone else could only dream of.

"Boo-ya," I say. "Perhaps a more intuitive name."

"Beelzebub."

"Bitch face."

"Bronwyn."

"Bald Mountain."

"Boredom." And we both laugh.

"Boredom the storm is barreling down the coast. Boredom brings destruction in its wake. Coastal villages still recovering from the deadly effects of Boredom."

The road is kind of gross. There's a wild, erratic rain, as if some man with a bucket, hiding in a ditch, is occasionally hurling water at us, like from an old film set. We have the news on, and we've texted some friends. Everyone is everywhere. A few of them did opt for the cots back at the shelter. *What could it hurt,* they wrote. *And they've come around with snacks!* Our plan is to push to the next town, but it's hard to see how that happens in this rain, in this darkness. It's two hours or so in normal driving conditions, and looking at James, squeezed into an awful, tense ball behind the wheel, gnashing his teeth like a cartoon character, it's hard to feel that he has two more hours of driving left to give. Poor thing. This is the statistic that is looking to claim our aging, musty bodies: the danger that befalls people in flight from other danger.

"I'm happy to drive," I say.

"You don't like how I'm driving?"

Okay, well, see. "I'm offering to help."

"I'm good. I'm great."

Sure you are. James is like some harassed sea creature, hiding behind a rock. I rub his neck, smooth down the back of his hair. I need my driver alive. My poor, poor driver. By taking care of him I take care of myself.

"Thanks," he says. "That feels good. If only I could see. I mean, right? I feel like I'm playing a video game. What you could do is call some hotels or motels up ahead, to see if we can get a room."

There's a Holiday Inn and a Motel 6 in the next town. Both lines are busy when I call. I keep trying, and meanwhile I pull up the map on my phone, but my signal is getting spotty, a single bar flickering in and out, and the image of where we are never quite comes through. It's loading and it's loading and it's loading. I see our blue dot, moving slowly over the screen, but there's no terrain beneath it, just a gray block, as if we're floating in space over some bottom-less void.

James pulls over at a gas station and we get chips. Lots of them, the sort we rarely allow ourselves at home. All bets are off. I would inject drugs into my face right now. I would drink gas from the car with a straw. Inside the store, the single-serving wine bottles look exceptional to me—golden bottles in their own gleaming cooler, a shrine to goodness—but it's not fair to James, who has to drive. I don't want him drooling. I don't want him jealous. I'd prefer to keep his feelings to a minimum.

We can hardly see anything save the lights and the black slashes of rain streaking past, but the same sign keeps appearing on the side of the road, every mile or two: *Exit 49 Food.* The third time it crawls past, close enough to grab and shake, to possibly dry-hump, I start to salivate. I picture plates of unspecified steaming good-ness. Salty, crunchy objects littered over wet mounds of something achingly delicious, with sauce, with sauce, with sauce. Polenta with stinking gorgonzola, maybe, and a fork-tender bone of meat from some brave animal. A shank, a leg, a neck, cooked for four years in a thick mixture of wines. With tall drinks that fizz a little and work directly on quieting down one's noisy little brain, perhaps even a warm cloudy drink you pour directly into your eyes. James seems to register my reverie and insists again that we keep driving. Have to have to. He slaps the steering wheel. That's why we bought chips, he cries, trying perhaps to sound like a real human being who feels enthusiasm. It's sort of awkward. We have chips, he says more qui-etly. If we stop now we are doomed, goners.

"It's just that it's already kind of late, and I'm pretty hungry," I tell him.

"What are you saying?"

"That it's late and I'm hungry?"

"If you're not prepared to offer a solution then maybe you should not speak."

Well, it's an interesting rule, and I do enjoy constraints around what can and cannot be said. The deepest kind of etiquette. But if you applied such a standard to everyone, the world over, there'd be very little speech. The world would undergo a near-total vow of silence, with a few exceptions. Perhaps that would be a desired outcome. Perhaps a special island could be set aside for the solution-proffering peoples, who would slowly drive each other to murder.

"Okay, sure, I will restrict myself to a solution-based language. Here's a solution. Let's go to a restaurant. That would solve so many problems. The problem of hunger, the problem of exhaustion, the problem of claustrophobia in this goddamn coffin, and the very real threat of escalating discord between two individual passengers."

"Go to a restaurant and then what? Eating will make us tired. Where will we sleep? I hate being the only one who thinks about these things."

"Oh, is it not fair?" I say. And I will admit that my voice dips into a pout here.

"That's right," says James. "It's *not* fair. I didn't want to put it that way."

"Because it makes you sound like a sad baby?"

"You're the one who said it. *You* said it. How does it make *me* sound like anything?"

"Yes, let the record show that I controlled your words and rendered you helpless and unaccountable. I am all-powerful."

James is quiet for a while. The rain is thundering down on us. The wipers are going so fast across the windshield it seems they might fly off the car. When exit 49 suddenly appears, James veers cautiously down the ramp and pulls the car over in the grass of an intersection.

"The record won't show anything, Alice, because there is no record. It's just us. I'm worried about getting stuck out here. That's all this day has been about. I'm trying to get us somewhere so we can get a room and then we can worry about everything else after that. Could we maybe fight later, when we get home?"

"Oh, I'd like that."

"I mean, I don't really feel well, and the fighting is not helping."

I look at him. So much of our relationship depends on him being alive. Almost all of it.

"Darling," I say. "Let's just go sit and eat and relax for a minute. We can still drive after that. We just have to get out of this rain for a minute. And after dinner, I'm driving. No arguments."

We find the restaurant and get a table near the fireplace, which turns out to be just a storage nook for old copper pots. The waiter is a boy. Not an infant, and not exactly a man. "Are you all weathering the storm okay?" he asks, grinning.

Can one say no? I wonder. *No thank you, we are not. We have failed to weather it and now we are here, in your restaurant.*

The food that comes out is not disgusting. Sweet and hot and plentiful, moist in all the right places. It goes down pretty heavily, though, and I feel the day starting to expire, begging to end. James was right. The druggery of road food. We eat in silence, listening to the rain. Both of us look forlornly at the bar, thinking probably that we shouldn't, we mustn't. On the other hand, we could simply pass out drunk here and maybe they'd take us to jail. There are beds in jail. Soap. New people to meet.

A television above the bar shows a woman in a raincoat being blown off her feet. The clip must be on a loop, or else she keeps getting up, saying something desperate into her microphone, and then falling back down again. I'd like to tell her to stay down, just stay down and take it while the wind and rain lash at her flapping back, but she gets up again and the wind seems to lift her. For a moment, as she blows sideways off the screen and surrenders herself to flight, her posture is beautiful, so absolutely graceful. If you were falling from a cliff, no matter what awaited you, you might want to think about earning some style points along the way, just turn your final descent into something stunning to watch. On the

TV there is nothing to learn about the storm, nothing to know. The numbers that scroll across the bottom of the screen are long, without cease, maybe the longest single number I've ever seen. Does this number describe the storm? What are we to make of it?

In the car we think it over. We are too far from a hotel, and plus, the hotels aren't answering their phones. The driving is dangerous, if not impossible. It's not really even driving anymore, it's like taking your car through one of those car washes. We are exhausted beyond belief. I suggest, as tentatively as I can, that it is not unreasonable to think that we could sleep in the car. Each of our seats reclines, like an easy chair, and if we found somewhere safe and quiet to park, we could ride this out until the morning, maybe even sleep well. Then we could drive all day and maybe get somewhere where they have rooms. We'd be rested. The sun might be up. The world might have ended. But at least it would be tomorrow. Tomorrow seems like the only thing that will solve anything, ever. Along comes tomorrow, with its knives, as someone or other said. That's not the exact quote, I'm sure, but the gist of it sounds true.

James seems like he may have given up. "Is that what you want to do? Sleep on the side of the road? In the car?"

"What I want to do is to be alone in a hole, covered in dirt. But sleeping in the car is the next best thing right now."

"Yes, that often is the second choice after live burial."

It starts to sound nice to me, really appealing. Like going to the drive-in, but without the movie. Like going *parking*, which we must have done once, in another life, before our bodies took on water and started to sink, before the spoil grew like a mold in the back of our mouths. "I don't think there's anything wrong with sleeping in the car," I say. "It's going to be more comfortable than a motel, that's for sure, not that there even *is* an available motel, and plus we won't have to worry about the cascade of ejaculate that's been literally sprayed from human appendages around every single motel room in the country. Purportedly."

James seems to think about it. "When I stay in a hotel," he says,

"I do my best to ejaculate on the walls. It's a civic obligation. You have to pull your weight."

"That's a lot of pressure for a man."

"Sometimes I'm not in the mood. I'm cranky and I'm tired."

"That's when you bring out the jar from home?" I ask.

He laughs. "It's good to have it with me. Who's going to know, you know, if the product is older."

"More mature, in some ways."

"Must. Broadcast. Seed," he says, like a robot, and then he mimes the flinging of the jar, splashing its imaginary contents out into space.

It's not really a rest area that we find. It's a scenic turnout, and the view—of the black, bottomless abyss—is pristine. You can see all of it, every dark acre, and if we don't see our own ghostly faces by the end of the night it's because we're not looking hard enough. We park a bit out of the way, under the branches of a mammoth tree, and when we quickly realize that we've just increased our risk of death—because trees seem to seek people out in these kinds of situations—we move over to an open parking space, with nothing threatening above us.

"Fuck that tree," I say. "Way to try to hide your intentions."

We put our seats all the way back and James pulls out a bar of chocolate from the go bag. I want to rub it all over my neck.

"Oh my god, oh my god. You are a genius," I say. "Certifiable."

"I like to think that I have an elusive, almost unknowable sort of intelligence."

"What else is in there?" Now I'm excited.

James peers into the bag, rummaging around with his hand. "That's the end of it," he says. "The rest is just sadness. Sadness and real life."

This is my sweet man. So weird sometimes. So uncommon. And he steered us here, to safety, where we can eat our sweets and surrender to the night and everything will be so goddamn swell in the morning. Even as the rain literally seems to be crushing the car, one hard bead at a time. Not the rain. Boris. Boris is doing this to us, the motherfucker.

The seats are a little bit divine when you tilt them all the way back. A little bit like first class on an airplane, which we only did once, and by accident, because of a mistake by the sweethearts at the gate. It remains a sort of benchmark for comfort outside the home.

"I'm sorry you don't feel well," I say. "Is it related to . . ."

"What?"

"I mean, is it related to anything? I know you went to the doctor."

"I did go to the doctor."

"And?"

"It was really interesting. Really surprising. I found out that he thinks that I am still alive."

"He sounds like a smart man. I would like to meet him. Maybe shake his hand."

James is quiet and I'm not sure I really like it. I listen to his breath and it sounds fine. But then he coughs, and it's such a feeble cough, as if he barely has the energy for it. I don't like it.

"But now?" I ask. "Are you still not feeling so . . ."

James laughs quietly. "Oh, now. I'd like to say that I'm fine now."

"Well, don't hold back, mister. Say that. Make it so." I take his hand.

"I'm fine," he whispers. "I feel wonderful. Better than I have felt in a long time."

His voice is too quiet for me. The fight has gone out of him. Maybe he's just tired.

"Well, don't go and die on me tonight," I say, and I kind of want to punch him.

"Okay."

"You know that's what everyone's thinking, right. Everyone

who's watching this at home? That the couple who has been bickering all day will start to get along, but it will be too late, and then the man will die. That's such a classic plot."

"Oh is that what they're thinking?"

"That's what all the betting sites say. That's where the odds are."

"Does the woman ever die?"

"In situations like this?"

"Are there any other kinds of situations?"

We settle in, and I guess we are maybe trying to fall asleep, but I feel too vigilant. James's hand is warm in mine. It doesn't feel like the hand of a man about to die. It is big and soft and I pull it over to me, get it in close against my chest.

"I can't see you, James. What is the look on your face? What are you thinking?"

"No one is watching this but you, Alice. You're the only one here. No one knows about us. People can't really know."

"Sweetheart, are you okay? Should I be calling someone?"

"I guess I'm a little more tired than I thought I was."

"You must be. You've done all the driving. You got us out of there. You saved us."

He must think I'm joking with him. I wish I knew how to say it better. How come so many things can sound mean and nice at the same time?

"Could we lie together?" he asks.

I crawl over the seat, wrapping up against him. "Yes of course. I mean, in the end it will be more of a his-'n'-hers sleeping arrangement, just because of these weird beds, but let me settle in here with you for a bit. Why not?"

It feels good to snuggle him. Warm and just right. James is thinner than I remember. I can feel his bones.

"Why don't we do this more often?" I say, nuzzling against him.

"Because we haven't wanted to?" James says. He's drifting off. I can hear his voice grow thin. I'm not ready to sleep. Not ready to be alone.

"Hey," I say to him.

"Yeah?"

"Stay awake with me for a little bit."

"Okay."

"Breast cancer."

"What?"

"Breast cancer is picking up speed. Landfall is expected at twenty-one hundred hours."

"Oh. Ha. Yeah. I almost forgot about that. Boris. So weird. Boris."

When James is silent for a while I nudge him. "Your turn," I say.

"Okay. It's so hard to think." His voice trails off and I nudge him again. Then he says, "Maybe we've thought of the best ones already."

"No, we haven't, we haven't. I swear. There are so many more."

"Okay," he says. "But this one isn't so great. Are you ready?"

I say that I am. I lean in close.

"Balls."

I squeeze his hand. "There you go."

"Balls is blowing at forty-eight mph."

"They sure is," I say. "Hurricane Balls rolled in this morning and people are afraid to leave their homes."

James doesn't laugh. I need to leave him alone. He needs his space.

"Beloved," James whispers, and it's the last thing I hear him say to me before he falls asleep. "Beloved is coming," I say to no one, listening to his breathing slow down. "Close your windows. Go down into the basement and don't come out until she's gone."

The Trees of Sawtooth Park

Dr. Nelson wanted me to feel something. In the palm of his hand was a pale yellow mound of powder. He proposed to puff this powder, with his medical straw, into my face. A precisely regulated expulsion of air, he called it. To exhale just so until I was caked in it.

"Just take it passively, if you would, Lucy," Dr. Nelson said. "Relax your face. If possible, relax your head."

"*You* take it passively." I was so not in the mood. I pictured him shamed by animals, dogs with pants at their knees lining up to defile him.

"Too late for me, I'm sure," Dr. Nelson said, touching his face as if he'd just discovered it. "I've had my hand in the cookie jar so much on this one that I can't feel the effects anymore. I can't feel anything, really. I need more subjects."

So do we all, I thought, but tough luck and boo-hoo.

Dr. Nelson was speaking in a high, shitbird whisper, but no one in the office bothered to look. Because ho-hum. Because who really cared? If a so-called scientist hadn't approached you directly at your cubicle for a turn on his chemical merry-go-round, you kept your head down. Otherwise we were just too used to these eureka freaks sprinting through our wing, spritzing us with boutique medicines. Dr. Nelson was just another white coat haunting the office, with scarcely a body beneath. I called him Half Nelson, because he lacked a badge, had no ID, and worked so far off-book that he hardly seemed to exist. Just a little boy in a sweater, with a huge, grotesque brain pulsing behind his dear, dear face.

"Are you ready, Lucy? Sweetheart?" He brought the straw to his lips, poised to administer a puffback.

I wasn't ready, not really.

"There's not a pill or just, maybe, a lotion?" I asked. I so preferred the cold lotion they'd been deploying recently in the drug trials. Cold lotion was better than human touch by a pretty far cry. A kind of finer boyfriend. With one of these newer lotions, applied just so, I could see myself living alone, feeling loved, feeling complete, in the mountains somewhere, very far from here.

"Nope, there is not," he said, speaking around the straw. "And now I'm going to count to three."

I closed my eyes and relaxed as the sandstorm hit, jagged crumbs pelting my face. Holy holy holy it hurt. Some of it went up my nose. It smelled of flowers, but the sweetness turned rancid and started to burn inside my face. It was like I was smelling myself get cooked.

"Jesus, was there glass in that? Did you just fucking spray glass on me?" I groped for my water.

"Hardly," Dr. Nelson mumbled. He always seemed surprised to find that his subjects weren't corpses. That they could speak or shout. He wiped his mouth. "That's just the coarseness of the grit, so that it doesn't spike too soon on you and blow out your levels. We ground it at forty-one on the, uh." And here he whispered something in German. I think. His speech sounded laced with ancient obscenities. He made a gesture to indicate a large machine, pointing to a room down the hall I had no clearance for. I knew the door that led there. It had no handle. It had no code box. No retina thing, either. It was just a slightly cleaner slab of Sheetrock. But what wasn't, when you thought about it.

Dr. Nelson had a big smile on his face. A shit-eating scientist smile. Whatever he blew into me didn't seem to have much of an opening act. I wasn't seizing, and I wasn't writhing on the ground in some kind of unbearable euphoria. My levels, whatever that meant, were pretty much unblown. I felt the same as always. The same, the same, the same. Fuck it all.

I picked some crumbs out of my hair. They were moist, like bread chewed by a baby. "You're such an asshole, Nelson. That was like the least professional medical trial I've ever been a part of. You don't just. That's not how. Jesus, Jesus, Jesus."

"It's not a trial, Lucy, and this isn't really happening," he said. "You were just sitting at your desk when you felt a breeze. Maybe there was dust in it. It could have been anything. It *was* anything."

Good grief, the caution we endured. It was hard not to read it as extreme self-importance. Did anyone anywhere, in the entire world, have a hard-on for corporate espionage when it came to our doomed and mildly illegal experiments?

"Right, of course, right. I just mean that you have no idea what dosage you gave me."

Nelson had his little phone out, which looked like a soft, baby bird, and was already lost in numbers. "I don't want to argue," he said without looking up, stroking the swollen body of his phone with a finger. "Mostly because you're wrong and it would be boring and exhausting to explain why. But I know the dosage down to the milligram. The puffback is actually a precise delivery system, and that's the go-to-market play, anyway."

Dr. Nelson turned theatrically covert. He shaded his mouth with a hand as if he had a secret that people might lip-read from the surveillance cameras. "Ah-choo," he whispered.

"Uh, bless you?" For, like, the fakest sneeze ever?

"No," he said. "Jesus. I mean *the* sneeze. That's the delivery system. This drug will be delivered via sneeze. Or maybe a yawn. Something that one person does to another. Because, well. Beyond that I can't say. You can probably figure out the rest."

Right. I thought about it, and I thought about it, and I abso-lutely couldn't figure out the rest. The rest was an unwritten world

I was not invited to. I was too far down the chain in this puzzle, another mule without the code. Whatever. It hardly mattered. I was talking to a ghost.

"So what will I be feeling?" I asked, and I must have sounded too eager. Mommy just wants new feelings. Please, please, make Mommy feel something.

"Probably we don't want to give you any help with that. Don't want to game the books or whatever they say."

"They don't say that. That's not a saying. Cook the books, game the system, queer the pitch. Anyway, are you that insecure about your work that you can't tell me anything about it?"

He just blinked.

"Medical pathway? Part of brain targeted? Side effects? Give me some crumbs so I can at least make a goddamn biscuit."

I knew his rules. I knew his life. It was pointless to ask. The secrecy was so bone deep here at Thompson that a false narrative of this bit of medical terrorism, him standing at my desk blowing powder over my head, had already been scripted. The dailies, when they came in, would reflect a different scenario entirely, one in which I had not been medically sneezed on by a hulking gray skeleton. Dr. Nelson looked like he didn't eat, and didn't sleep, and didn't really breathe. So much abstention. What, really, was there left to erase except the idea of the man?

"How about you just tell me what you feel whenever you have a minute. Use the logger on the . . ." He pointed at my terminal. "I added an identity for you."

He told me the name of the experiment. It had the word "bear" in it. It had a longish number, with some letters, too, and I instantly forgot it. He told me the name I'd be logging in with: Terry Corbin. For the purposes of the experiment I was a fifty-three-year-old woman, with no medical issues, and a family history of depression. Not so far from the truth. He told me that my fictional background was necessarily scattershot, because he didn't have time to flesh out a real and believable past for me. Because why bother, and bleh, and gross?

"The system requires medical subjects to have a past, as such, but that level of information has no technical bearing."

I blinked at him. When the scientists spoke that way I tended to turn to ash.

"The past isn't interesting. It doesn't matter. Sentimental value only, if that. Legacy software demands it and we comply, but we phone it in and that's been approved all the way at the top. We're not going to make a fetish out of stuff that has already happened. I sort of actually hate the past."

Like, he hated the past on principle, or certain specific things that had happened in the past? And did he hate his own past, which would be understandable—I imagine he was a small, unnoticed figure in his childhood, perhaps frequently set upon by larger children who tried to drink from his body—or was it the past of the entire world that troubled him?

"Thanks for the sexless name," I said. "And the age. Nice. I can practically smell my coffin."

We did this sometimes. We took on guinea personas for Nelson and his crowd before we romanced the FDA with our product. How did we put it when we congratulated ourselves about the work we did? *We inhabited nascent identities to spread the data to a broader population.* Maybe this was deceitful but it felt scarcely more problematic than using a real person. Scarcely. Crowdsourcing worked really well when you could handpick your crowd and rename them at will. You know, like drafting a football team or casting extras in a gladiator scene. It also saved some pennies on testing and it gave all of us in data collection a chance to sample how people would be feeling in the future, if any of this ever, ever, was approved and came to market. Yeah, if. And if and if and if. It was the unspoken word before a good deal of the sentences we punted at each other. And it was usually the last word, too. Along with many of the words in between.

The burning eased off in my nose and I'd shaken the crumbs free. I still felt nothing from the dose. No rush, no sudden clarity, no blast of sorrow. I was not high and I was not sleepy and I had not been put on some teetering edge that could only be soothed with sex or violence or kindness, which was good, because I wasn't sure what the likely outlets were. This chemical friend looked like a quiet actor. Maybe an out-of-work one. The subtler drugs were always harder to bear, ha ha, because they triggered a bottomless disappointment. In me, anyway. Which I was arguably on the verge of feeling anyway, and who wanted a spotlight on the real? Ever. At times like this I realized how much I wanted out of myself, how blitzed and bored I was by my own thoughts and feelings, my own little story. Terry Corbin could have licked me into some new, intriguing shape, but she was turning out to be a fucking dud with limited powers of rescue. I kind of hated her already.

The other option was a placebo. It could always be that. Maybe it always was. In which case I'd just been sneezed on by a creepy man for nothing.

Just then there was an intercom announcement. Possibly in French. I looked at my coworkers, who all groaned at once. People reached for their coats. A crowd started to gather at the window.

I had questions, even though my heart wasn't in it. My heart wasn't really anywhere.

"What's the time frame on this, or whatever? What's the onset and then how long will this shit last?"

Dr. Nelson looked at his watch. "Yeah, uh. Onset is, you know . . . now." He looked at me and blinked. Still nothing on my end, although I hated evaluating my feelings. It was like looking into an empty room, trying to see if the walls were breathing. Sometimes when I scrubbed in as a monkey for these experiments I was already shaking with the blast of the initial dose by now, quivering under my desk, running for the toilet. For some reason, experimental medicine often led to a thunderous shit. Today was different. This drug might as well have been called Status Quo. Who was going to pay for more of the same?

"As far as duration, this one might be pretty long term. We're working on something sustained, and, uh."

"Sustained?"

"Pretty much. That's how we refer to it. It's one of the words we're comfortable with. But I'm not going to get too involved with language right now. The language for this experience will come last." For some reason Dr. Nelson gestured out the window, as if that was where the language would be coming from. I looked in that direction, right into the sun, and for a moment forgot myself, who I was, where I was, what I was doing. Jesus it felt good.

"So this will last a full day? Two?"

Nelson just stared at me. I was playing cat and mouse with a dead man. Both of us were dead, maybe. Which explained the lack of repartee.

"Or what, like, a week? I should have probably asked you that. I have things to do at home. Stuff I have to take care of."

There was, really, nothing of the sort. There was simply a man named Richard at home, my betrothed, and then the two children we had fashioned out of wedlock, using techniques we'd long since forgotten. These days I bent over a chair to receive his anxiety, but this happened merely monthly, and was marked by a great fatigue. The children walked the rooms of our home collecting food. Sometimes they left for long periods of time and returned home, silent and unchanged. They still called it school but Jesus Christ. When the kids slept I thought of examining them, but for what? From time to time I grabbed them and held them and sometimes they grabbed me and held me. I felt very little when I did this, so I did it more, and the children grew quieter and more remote, hanging from my arms like ornaments on a tree. You could almost hear a bell go off when we hugged, as if we were all good little subjects in the great experiment that was our family. You didn't need special glasses to see where it was all going. You could watch a movie in which people like us were burned alive. We had just slightly more agency than stuffed animals. I'm sure there was more to it, but I didn't know what it was.

Dr. Nelson touched my face. "Lucy, sweetheart." He was one

of those men who talked this way, applying human touch that felt both deeply inappropriate and entirely welcome. I allowed it, however cold his hand felt, however much I shivered. Maybe he could undress me. Maybe he could cut into me with a knife and it would seem like chivalry. I think I am only half kidding. There was a funny way that human law seemed kind of arbitrary when it came to the doctors on our wing. Human law, in the end, would have a short half-life—human law could seem so overwhelmingly polite sometimes. He was always kind enough, but in an overcompensated way, as if he'd just come from the killing floor somewhere up north, freshly showered, blood free for the first time in months. Whatever nice thing he did for you was out of guilt for something especially heinous he'd done literally seconds before. Sometimes in the break room we discussed the various doctors, and we had silent ways of singling out the creeps and corpses among them. The ones who were so recently dead that they twitched just enough to seem functional in the world, tripping and stumbling through rooms on their way to the burial pyre.

"It's a moon shot," Dr. Nelson said. "But we're going really more sort of long term with this one. 'Indefinitely' is one of the words we might use. Maybe. We don't know. I mean, we *do* know, but we also are not saying that we know."

"So the dose of nonsense you just gave me, with mysterious effects that you won't reveal, you're hoping it will last, maybe, forever? That wasn't worth mentioning, as a courtesy?"

Dr. Nelson smiled. "You're welcome," he said.

What we were doing that year in St. Louis—it sounds odd to call it that—was tagging the major feelings, sub-tagging the minor ones. This was the mandate at Thompson Lord, the company where we died a little bit every day. Even on the weekends, when we didn't go to work. Because it taunted us on the horizon, brown and long and suspiciously moist. More of an animal reared up on its hind legs than an office building, even though up close it resolved into brick and glass and was just another future pile of rubble for the end-times.

We were giving order to the interior weather system, and whatnot. Telling a story about our moods. The thousand shades of disquiet, was what we called it in the pale halls of Thompson. A system of classification for all the ways to feel. But because the names of feelings are just so unpleasant, destroyed forever by poets and shameless emoters, we swapped in animal names. Bear and wolf and whatever. It was easier. A Noah's ark of the possible tantrums, freak-outs, and moods. With such an approach, we wouldn't box ourselves into some classification corner, or get lost in a subjective hell farm, and anyway it was better to be on the same page with Dr. Nelson and his team, and the middle geeks at the chem lab who had to conjure hormone equivalents of these feelings, using the ass glands of snakes and whatever.

It sounds a bit highbrow, but it was just an intellectual property land grab on the part of Thompson. They were boiling over with money, and as such were obliged to own what could be thought or felt, even if it could not yet be, well, *done,* by which I mean: sold. Because usually that was just a matter of time.

So, own the moods. Break all possible emotions down into chemical states, and simulate those states with drugs. Pretty simple. Then, curate the hell out of people's days. Feed them their feelings second by second, like a DJ. The drugs would have names like Tuesday, Thanksgiving, First Day of School. We'd lose the animal branding and tag the chemical helpers with super-obvious monikers. Then we'd get into blends. Then we'd get into mods and hacks. The word "smoothie" would not be inappropriate. The horizon on all of this was pretty and it was filled with cake.

Except, of course, the tech sucked balls, and there was no agreement whatsoever in the so-called scientific community— "community" is the wrong word for what happened when these cretins got together in an auditorium—over what even constituted a particular emotional state. You wrote a protein poem for this shit, and you sidecarred a timeline of hormones, but the result too often wobbled when you squirted it into a live human body and eventually everything fell out of focus. People bled, they wept, they shat. Human ignorance turns out to be pretty durable, and it played a starring role in our work. The moods, in the end, were like ghosts. Not even. Less credibility.

And if 2014 really was the year of the sensor, as they kept saying on NPR, it had turned into a pretty long and terrible one, approaching one thousand days now. Maybe more. Who was counting? I was, along with lots of people I knew. Sensors in the trees, on the roads, slapped onto buildings, drinking from our necks, sucking up data on us. Sensors on our bodies, in our clothing. Sensors in our face cream. Sensors, yeah, in the water, finally, because water, really, has the broadest access in the world, inside our bodies and out, and how dopey we all were not to see it sooner. Water as the ultimate delivery system for that final frontier of surveillance—the inside of the human body. The data that came back was mountainous. It was crushing. Did the sensors work? Was the data sound, or even remotely reliable? Yeah, no. I mean, no one knew for sure. Or of course we did, and the answer wasn't good.

It sounds pretty high tech, maybe, and it might have been, if it worked. These were the 2010s, after all, a time of hypotheticals and wish enterprises, when people still needed to eat, and the sun still behaved itself.

We fed this data, big and hairy as it was, to a crew over in a building we called the dorm, where beaver-faced children worked the curation. I mean worked the shit out of it. Maybe these wet beasts were of age, but just. And maybe they were human, but, well, also just. And that's being generous. I don't think they slept, and if they ate it must have been liquid food through a very thin straw, or the tiniest nibbles of mush, because their mouths were disturbingly small. Like, how did these kids really breathe out of such pinholes, at least without causing a balloon squeak? How did they stick a toothbrush in there to clean their teeth, let alone administer oral deliciousness to some hulking uncle who needed his emerson drained? Maybe the kids at the dorm were just, uh, small people, horrendously gifted with numbers, but there was something off in their appearance. Everyone kept reasonably quiet about the whole thing, though. Given the speech protocols at Thompson, not to mention elsewhere, you just didn't really say what you were thinking. And if you could help it, you didn't really think what you were thinking, either. I got good at that. My thoughts were going to die with me, whenever that day came. Or maybe my thoughts already had, preceding me to the grave. I wasn't going to get caught out. I wasn't going to get listened in on. I had a few tricks to protect myself.

The house was dark when I got home. Another cold St. Louis afternoon. There was going to be snow, supposedly, and there was going to be a lot of it. Maybe we'd all be buried alive. Everything would freeze and in hundreds of years they'd find us, chilled in position as we tended our homes or pursued our craven desires out on the street, and the story they would concoct—of who we were and what we were doing—would be so splendid. It would be majestic. Everything so small and remote in our lives—our hand-bags, our kitchen tongs—would be rescued from their current uses and gifted with tremendous, almost unbearable power, united to a meaning we could never even imagine. We'd be gods and we'd be animals, we'd be uncanny accidents in the larger trajectory of the universe, anomalies of light. It would almost be worth it, to die that way, and then to be understood through such a profound, new lens. To be upgraded and romanticized and lifted up. Weren't we all just caught in a rehearsal for our fossilization? Stories would be written. Songs would be sung.

I called out into the house. Richard was usually back from work by now. He'd be up to something desperate in the kitchen. A cooking project from one of his books. Save your relationship with this brilliant stew. That sort of thing. The result was usually a cozy bowl of something to eat, and we'd sit together looking out the window at our favorite tree, trying not to argue. The children would be home as well, for sure. They'd be upstairs in their rooms, polishing their privacy until it glowed. You could sometimes see the light under the door. It stood for everything you'd never know about them. Everything you'd never understand.

But there was no one home. No one anywhere. Quiet in the streets and quiet abroad. Quiet inside the home. A pretty quiet world tonight overall maybe. I had the sense that if I turned on the TV it would not be able to penetrate such profound silence. It'd be no match for this hushed world. I'd just see the strange faces on the screen as if they were trapped under water, shouting silently behind the glass. For a moment I thought that if I cut myself open, there'd be no noise in there, either. Just the silent rush of blood, all perfectly muzzled, even as my body hurried about its business, working so tremendously hard, which you rarely got to see, just to keep me alive.

I slept forever. I slept and slept and slept. And I woke to a different world. The snow was piled high up on the windows. Plows rolled down the street pushing so much snow that the parked cars on each side were covered in it, perfect white mounds with nothing visible underneath. I went to wake the kids, but they'd come and gone already. Richard, too. They must not have wanted to disturb me. I was still in my clothes from yesterday. I needed to shower and eat and get the hell back to work.

The phone rang as I was making breakfast.

"How are you holding up?" the caller asked.

"Who's calling?" I said.

"Is this Terry?"

"No."

"Terry, I just wanted to be sure you're okay. With the storm. If you need anything."

I told them it was a wrong number, and they didn't apologize, or say anything. They just held the line and listened. I said that I was hanging up, and they yelled that name again, *Terry*, just as I disconnected.

At work we were on lockdown, of sorts. Not everyone could make it in. I wasn't going to let some weather stop me, plus Dr. Nelson would probably worry if I didn't show up. He'd think I'd died. He'd send a team. They'd need to collect me, clean up, hide the traces. Whatever. None of that was relevant. The buses were running, and all I did was bundle up like crazy, with so many layers that you could have thrown me from a building and it wouldn't have hurt when I landed. "Unbreakable" was the word I kept saying to myself. Unless a car got to me. Unless someone used fire. I pictured myself flung from a window and falling gently into the snow. I'd be fine. I'd stand up and walk it off. Maybe I'd even ask to do it again, just one more time, because you don't get to feel that way very often. You rarely get to feel that you could fall forever, without harm, as the world rushes by you.

In any case, nothing short of a family emergency was going to keep me from going to work. I took the bus with a few other cozy folks, and it was no big deal. Yes, the walking was slow, and yes, you could not hear a thing, not your feet on the ground, not the cars rolling by, but it was gorgeous and I think we should feel lucky when our world is transformed so wholly before our eyes, when everything is changed just by some snow. You live for things like that, and you don't even know it. Then they happen and you almost want to lie down in it, roll around, and pray that it doesn't go away.

They were calling me Terry at the office, and what a big goof that was. They must have seen the name in the logger, and then why not haze the mule with a bit of nicknamery? I smirked at them. I didn't give a shit. Their names were worse. They were lucky if they even had names. I'd seen their bodies hung with needles. I'd seen them breathing through masks, crying at their desks. These were people who were drowning, who would be dead soon. I walked past their cubicles and saluted. Here's to you, people of the grave. Sleep well, my friends.

There was a book of photos on my desk, which I assumed had been left by Nelson. In this stage of a trial he was always showing me pictures and whatnot, and I guess I was supposed to log my reactions.

I looked through the photos, and it was sordid and strange and not at all pleasant, a book of sorrows and loss and mostly unspeakable desolation. Nelson must have been wondering what I could handle, how low he could go. Unbreakable my ass, maybe he was thinking. Would I give in and buckle? I wasn't going to try to control my reactions. It wasn't as if you walked around deciding how to feel. That's not how it worked. You don't have your feelings, they have you.

The pictures were of people with hair, people licked clean. People with faces you wanted to set fire to. People you would fight on the street if you saw them, even if you loved humanity, even if you did not believe in death. However peaceful you think you are, however sweet and nonviolent and angelic—you have a fight in you if only it can get unlocked, and that's what these pictures were doing, testing one's absolute limits, tearing thresholds, one by one. A kind of violation of your own moral line. Pictures, horribly vivid, of people who couldn't smile without showing who they really were, and it wasn't pretty. Just a way that they opened their mouths and showed too much. People with obvious secrets. People with no inner life. And then people with no outer life, either, because they were just dead. Shots of corpses galore, although just before, moments or days or weeks or maybe years before death, but it's all the same in the longer view. Pictures of children. Babies. Landscapes. Parts of the world that could not have existed. Made-up scenery, not just too good to be true, but too horrible to be true. A good deal of that. Someone's nightmare of the world, the sort of thing that makes everyone wish there were no such thing as the imagination.

And then more people, especially ones who could not have existed, which was the worst. Realistic in their features, and all of that, but clearly unreal all the same. Someone's sick idea of what a person looks like. Perversion everywhere, as if we'd only been born to feel the very worst things, and it all begged a pretty big question about why one had to be a person in the first place.

I'd had enough. I looked over to where Nelson usually came from, the hallway, the wall, his whole mysterious wing, but I didn't figure I would see him today. Which didn't mean he wasn't watching.

One time they strapped me to some sensors and the screen lit up with bright bursts of dots not when I spoke, but when I didn't. So I talked and talked, because I didn't care for those points of light. I could go my whole life without seeing them again. So who cares if I had to talk to keep them gone? I'd say what I needed to. We all do things to keep the wolf away.

The rest of the day was mostly chopped up into the usual workaday carcass: lots of data to wing around, and lots of filing. I pounded away at my terminal and I filled the screen with meaning. Lunchtime came and when people asked if I was going to eat I dragged myself after them and sat through the awful, wet gnashing, holding my breath. Later we heard on the intercom that more snow was coming, and it seemed that a decision went around to let us all get the hell out of there early. People cheered, and afterward it was like they'd forgotten to close their mouths. They were showing teeth, walking around, getting their things, bundling up, all the while showing teeth as if they were about to tear something apart with their mouths, if only no one was watching. I kept my head down because after a little while you can't look at people like that. It starts to unravel you. It starts to be too much.

It was early enough in the day that I thought I could catch the kids coming out of school. Surprise them maybe. I stood at the fence with the other parents, and it wasn't clear who was in jail, us or them. We clung to the fence and we watched the door of the school. We looked at our phones. For a moment it seemed that anything could come out of that door: water, mud, animals.

When the bell rang and the children poured out, the parents pressed against the fence, hollering and waving. The children rippled into the playground, scanning the world for their makers. How did you know, looking at these children, some of them so truly lifelike, which ones were yours? The problem wasn't that none of them were familiar, it was that they all were. I knew all of these kids. Their faces, the little way they ran. Some of them fell over and righted themselves and ran on and my heart ached. I stood there as they paired off and ran to hug their parents, and after the dust had cleared none of them had run to me. Not even one. They'd all been spoken for. I was standing here in plain sight and my own little ones were nowhere to be found. I watched the door and waited. The school had gone quiet. Everyone was shuffling away.

There was a man at the fence who widened his eyes at me, as if I was too big to see in one look, too complicated.

"Hey Terry, don't see you here much anymore. How are the kids?"

What did you ever say when people asked you shit like that? You don't say help me I'm dying. You don't say hold me because I'm going to fall. You don't say I cannot really speak to you right now, because if I do the blood will come out and I won't be able to stop it and then we'll all be in trouble. I guarantee it. You just don't do that.

What I did say was that everyone was swell, in their way, and I rolled my eyes, and what a day and wasn't it beautiful, the snow? The man looked around as I pointed, but you didn't need to look around. It was on us, covering us up, and if we stood still any longer we'd be buried for good. I said, wasn't it the most extraordinary thing he'd ever seen?

There were cops at my house when I got home. Outside of the old rotted house, looking in the windows. A couple of young men in uniform. What was my protocol here? Keep walking and circle back around? But didn't that leave my house vulnerable and should I not be protecting the inner contents? Who else would guard the place if not me?

When I walked up, they took off their hats, called me ma'am.

Did I live here, they wanted to know, and what was my name and would I be so kind as to show them some identification?

They came in and we talked and it was not at all unpleasant. This was routine, they said, they were checking in. They were seeing that people were all right. Did I live alone? Was there anyone else in the house?

I offered them tea and apologized. There was just nothing to eat. Nothing nothing nothing, never, no matter how much I shopped. Trucks rolled up and offloaded food, I explained, and the little ones upstairs sucked it down, spitting out not even a bone. There was no way to keep up.

They were okay, they didn't care, they weren't hungry. They just had a question for me, if I didn't mind. Just a question and then they'd be on their way. Was I okay? Did I feel okay? What did I feel?

What did I feel? What a funny thing for a police officer to ask. I half expected a question along the lines of, where were you when, and I was worried a little bit. I thought I might not know. I thought I might not remember. Who doesn't feel that in some tiny, forgotten part of their day they might have done something truly horrible? And then the cops come, and then, well, you find yourself confessing.

But what did I *feel?* What I felt was old, and I shared this with the officers. I cried a little bit right in front of them, and I'm not really bragging. I felt dead. I felt tired. I felt unattractive. I felt no longer intelligent. I felt slightly horny, but in such a nonspecific way that it might just be an allergy, an illness, an excitation of the skin. But really, I asked them, why was anyone ever expected to report accurately on their own feelings? Could either of them do it? If I were to pin them down and ask them to report the truth of themselves? Would they be able to perform? They shouldn't trust me, I said, finally. I was not a reliable source. If they really wanted an answer, they should ask my doctor.

The car that we rode in had a nice comfortable seat in the back. It was more like a bed. We drove through the sweeter part of town and it was almost like we skirted the perimeter of a plunging cliff. You know that feeling—that the car and the road beneath it are themselves just delicately suspended in space, poised to fall? It's like you understand that the road is holding the car up, and the earth is holding the road up, but it's not clear what's holding up the earth itself, and if you pay attention, really really pay attention, you can feel it, the falling. Certain people are terribly attuned to it, and they can't bear it. They try to escape the world as soon as they can. Scientists try to explain this, but you can see it on their faces, the doubt, the sadness. They are more afraid than we are. I looked out the window and only saw sky, the sort that bends into finer clarity where it meets the horizon. A sharpening of the lens, just where you most need it. Where, if you look carefully, and really study it, you might see something important in the distance, something that has been kept from you your entire life.

I knew where we were going. I'd driven this same route myself, many times. It was my favorite part of town and I'd never get tired of it. I got a little bit emotional, I must admit, when I looked at the long, thin trees in Sawtooth Park. I'd seen these things planted when I was a girl. There had been a fire. Nothing serious, but part of town was blackened. The parks were scorched. It wasn't a big deal. Anyone with a computer could look up the details. From space, maybe, it looked like nothing. But for those of us down below it was not nothing. And then they chose a species of tree that was controversial, I guess. Because these trees grew taller without getting thicker, and after a little while they curled, maybe like hair would. And so from above this park was supposed to really look like something. People *ooh*ed and *aah*ed over it. People said it was indescribable, amazing. But who got to look at the park, or really anything, from above? What population took to the air to see the world? A mistake had been made. Our world had been designed for birds, and the people had been forgotten. What about the people? I always wanted to ask. We will never know how beautiful our own world is if we're stuck down here.

In the car, I asked if I could go ahead and lie down all the way. I wasn't tired. It wasn't that. It was mostly because I did not think I could keep looking out of the window, at the people on the streets, marching off the end of the planet. I couldn't do that without really starting to have some feelings that I was fairly sure would not soon go away. Permanent feelings? Maybe not. I don't think there are such a thing. I think that we die, and the feelings go on, they find a new person, and so on, moving from host to host, destroying bodies and soaring away to the next fellow. But probably not forever. That's too big a claim. I'm not comfortable going out on that sort of limb. We just don't know enough.

Dr. Nelson had another clinic, I guess. The secrets people kept! They had beds there. It was all super professional, a real building in a real place with people as real as can be scurrying around looking busy. Sometimes Nelson brought his subjects in, during a trial, for closer study. That is what I figured when I saw this place. The experiments needed to be controlled. You couldn't blame him. You have a subject who's out at large in the city, and how can you possibly begin to collect any reliable data? If you put them in a bed, in a room, with nurses and the whole shebang, your experiment gets tighter. You narrow down your variables. It's just good doctoring, is what it is. Dr. Nelson knew how to swim in this world. He wasn't going to go over the falls. He knew how to keep from disappearing.

They made me comfortable, which I appreciated. It was only late afternoon, but who doesn't like slipping on some pajamas and getting into bed early now and then? Who would really complain about a luxury like that? Especially when it's snowing. To get into bed and be cozy while the world is turning to powder outside. I was in good hands.

This was the part of the study where they sent in people who pretended to know me. I had to hold my ground. They found an older couple, gray-haired and shriveled up. They played a certain role. They showed off a certain kindness. You've seen it before. Compassion and concern, faces twisted into sympathy. Straight out of central casting. I always loved that expression: central casting. Didn't that just mean the whole world, every fucking person? Anyway, here came the two, sweet-faced old-timers. The name "Terry" was on their lips. Of course it was. They'd obviously been briefed. I didn't mind. They approached my bed, smiling, melting with concern, and took my hand. Even fake feelings can feel good when they come down on you—you know there's very little difference. I'll take a hug when it comes. I'll hug right back. I'll feel the warmth of a body, even the bodies of those two old-timers, who got pretty worked up. I'm really not picky. Does it matter if it's a stranger? What I would like to know is who isn't a stranger? Name one person.

The man they called Richard was the biggest stranger of all. My soon-to-be husband. They sent him in and he said his words. He wore a familiar body but it was big on him. It didn't fit. You could see him squirming inside it, trying to get out. Unless you can rip apart someone's body and finally know their secrets, then they are a stranger. It's fine. It's how things are. Stop crying about it, is what I think. You should, you know, hug them, too. Hug whoever you can. You should live with them. You should spend your whole life with them if you want to. Answer to whatever name they call you—does it finally matter? Put down roots and hand over your money and take off your clothes when they snap their fingers. Just don't forget. Don't take your eyes off them for even one second.

The next thing they did was pretty clever. They had two people come at me masked up perfectly. A young man and a young woman, as if someone had taken my kids and rubbed them in life, in time, in years and years. Maybe someone dragged these people from a truck, sprayed them with oldening, and just pulled on them longwise until they grew and were disfigured and were just some typical, sad-looking adults. But with the faces of my children. The unmistakable faces. And someone made those faces cry as they hugged me. I hugged them and they hugged me and I held my ground. It was easy. Someone peeled them away and they sobbed and said goodbye and I said goodbye, too. It was easy.

It got a little bit late, and it got a little bit dark. For a while when it was snowing it was like the snow was so white and so abundant that it would hold the light, well after sunset, and into evening, radiating it back, so the night never got dark. But that didn't last. It couldn't. That was just a fantasy, because the world doesn't work that way. You have to be realistic.

Most of the people cleared out of my room, but the two old-timers stayed, sitting in chairs, keeping their distance. I didn't want to admit it, I didn't want to tell anyone this, but I was getting tired and I wasn't sure how long I could hold on. Maybe if I wasn't in bed, and maybe if that bed wasn't so goddamned comfortable, and maybe if out my window I couldn't see some lights—of the city, speckled and flowering outside—maybe then I wouldn't feel so drowsy. But I was determined to stay vigilant. You have to stand guard. You have to hold your weapon high. I was thinking that even your enemy has to sleep. Your enemy gets tired, too. You can count on it.

They kept trying to offer me water, but what was I, a moron? *Water.* Did they know where I worked? Did they know what I did? *Water.* I remember when I drank water, just a little girl who didn't know better, unlocking the gates myself, pouring it right in. Come and get me! Holy Christ. Here, have some, they kept saying, just a sip, you're thirsty, you must be so thirsty, Terry, and I wanted to reply, Why not just cut me open. Let's dispense with ceremony. I'd hand you the knife myself, if I had one. Just don't treat me like a fool, please. Treat me with dignity. I'm a human being. Have you ever heard of that? Do you know what a human being is? Well, here's a real one, right in front of your face. Stand back and bow down and show some fucking respect. If there's something you want to know, get out your knives and come at me. I'm ready.

Notes from the Fog

My wife, Gin, once knocked gently on my head, as if it were a door. "Hello," she kept saying. "Hello. Who's in there?" She and our therapist, Dr. Sherby, laughed a little about this, so I did too. What fun. Keep knocking on my head like that, like it's a door, or an egg. I wasn't going to be the only one not laughing. That's Human Survival 101. Not that survival is such a prize. But, still, you might as well control your exit. Put your own little spin on how you step away from the show once and for all. I laughed as Gin kept knocking on my head, and I said, as if I might really be answering the door, "Just a minute, I'm coming. Hold your horses. No need to break the house down."

We all just looked at each other. Maybe I wasn't supposed to be in on the joke. Gin stopped knocking and tucked her hands in her lap.

"I'll be right there," I said, in the most distant voice I could manage, as if I were many rooms away—underwater, overseas—crawling toward them as best as I could.

There was nothing wrong with us. We were sweet. We were great. Friends, if that's what you wanted to call them, said we were the perfect couple. To me that meant we were alive. We hadn't died.

We hadn't bled out in the streets. We didn't drag each other by the hair from room to room. We observed holidays and put food on the table and hadn't been pushed from a cliff yet. We couldn't fly, we couldn't live forever, we couldn't fight off disease when it came. But we lifted the kids into the air and let the wind shape them. Not really, not really, but it could feel that way, and who really knew how the kids had ended up so kind, so free of murder in their hearts? It wasn't because of us. Certainly not me anyway.

Those friends, all of them, went the way of the drain. They floated out of their homes and turned to smoke. They rotted in place. None of them lived long, because nobody does. They wandered off into the sunless afterlife, sooner, later, eventually. You can look up their names and you won't learn much. They packed no bags. Their stuff was probably just thrown away.

It was late April, the eleventh year of my marriage, when I was fired from my job as a teacher at Foley Parochial. Mr. Rubins, the chief anxiety machine at the school, called me into his office. Given the hour, lunch, and his initial silence when I walked in, I knew it could not be good. When is it ever good when someone says they need to talk to you? We should all know better. We should run for the woods when our name is called.

At Foley I was a floater. I roamed the lower grades, preaching the sort of science that doesn't involve the human being. It's a personal preference, a diversion from the official curriculum. The human being is a walk-on player in a spectacle that is none of its damned business. Even though we get our hands on everything. Crumple it up, try to mate with it or destroy it.

I taught chemistry, specializing in the wrong turns of science, the shit-crazed detours. You dive for knowledge, and the dive is long. It might take a lifetime. You come up empty at the end, but along the way you've shaped some brains, you've campaigned pretty hard to seat your error deep in the minds of others. It's something I discussed with my students — the little, scrubbed, colorless beings who hated the planet, themselves, each other, and me especially. How every great insight is something to be embarrassed about later. The shelf life of truth, if it even gets on the shelf. What to do with all of our wrong ideas about the world and ourselves.

At Foley I never had my own homeroom group, thank god. A little fake family of sweating puppies who thought I could lick their wounds and vomit food into their mouths. Which is not to say that I do not care for some young people in this world. It is just a question of the role one plays. The costume worn. I had my own young people at home. I poured myself into them when I could.

At Foley I never struck a child, I hurt no one, I said nothing untoward or incorrect, so far as I know. It was my policy to do my job to the letter, then return home. At home I would rest up and restore myself to power, then rinse and repeat. Forever, if need be. Or that was the plan. I had it charted far into the abyss: how I'd survive my sweet term on the planet, gathering spoils and repelling misfortune, how I'd hit my marks and keep from breaching etiquette, hugging Gin close to me all the while. Because without a religion one must have a code. Without a code it's like piloting a body with no bones through life, which some people do, god help them. Dragging a heap of skin from room to room, hoping people see you as a human being when you are only a spill. You've leaked from something larger that is gone now, not even a shadow, and you are all that remains. In the end it is too exhausting to approximate a real person. You deflate. Where your body was there is barely a face. Your skin gets kicked from room to room. Some child wears it, calls it his "shirt."

Mr. Rubins sat me down, offered tea. He spoke of the world. He called it a place for feelings, for fun. He called it a room waiting to be filled by children. A system of linked rooms. Every so often these rooms empty out, and new children flood in, he explained. Some of us work to keep the rooms clean, well decorated, and ready for the next contenders.

The metaphor was problematic, of course. Worrisome. A poet I otherwise do not understand once said that we are disloyal to both things when we say that one is like the other. It is a kind of treason against difference. I hid my concern. It was fine for him to cushion the air with idiocies. I would grant him that favor, just as I might long for it now and then for myself. A time might come when it might be necessary for me to talk this way, too.

"We do our best, don't we," I said.

Mr. Rubins seemed pained. I must have as well. Who does not seem pained, finally, when you examine them closely enough? He looked at me as if I could help him with his task—to destroy me. Poor man. So out of his league. Death was coming soon, anyway, and then he'd rest in peace, or possibly squirm for all eternity in great agony. We don't really know. Our vision of oblivion is clouded. It should concern us more than it does—how little we know, how little we are trying to find out.

Mr. Rubins spoke of people in general. What they need versus what they want. "Education, which is what we are selling here, finally," he said, "makes a guess about this need every day."

An educated guess? I wanted to ask.

"I wake up and I have to make the right choice," he said.

Whereas I wake up and feel no pressure whatsoever, I didn't say. I wake up and decide who among the earth's gorgeous creatures I will make love to. That's how easy I have it. A buffet of fuckery awaits.

It was wrong to feel anger toward him. Maybe it was wrong to feel anything at all. Mr. Rubins was being controlled by people in other rooms, I knew. Not in some alien way, but really, actually. These rooms were off-site, no doubt. Not at the school, maybe nowhere close. They had him on live feed, maybe. They had a mic in his ear, whispering formations, plays, strategies of attack. A wire pierced into the sweet core of his brain. Just so to speak, because I know that's not how it really works. In all of the important ways he was not a real person, but simply a vessel for urges that originated elsewhere. A remote actor. In truth, the very same thing might have been said of me. A carrier pigeon for a set of feelings and ideas that were not mine. Tear away the body and what was left? I felt for a moment that I could stand up and prove what an apparition Mr. Rubins was, just move my hand through his body and wave it around. But perhaps he had the same thought of me, and it was a standoff. Two creatures equally ephemeral, looking to expose each other. A contest of ghosts, swishing through each other like so much wind.

I mumbled something to Rubins about the challenge of doing the right thing, the burden we all faced. And, above all, the responsibility we had to the children.

Mr. Rubins lit up. It was like I had touched him privately. "Exactly!" he shouted. "We have a responsibility to the children, and to their families."

"And to the community," I said firmly, waving my hand at the window. Because, of course, they were out there. They were wandering in the snow. They needed to be told what to do, what to think, what to feel.

I'm not stupid. I can read feelings. He was winding up to shitcan me and why not just get it over with? On his desk were papers he kept gathering to his body. He puzzled over what he saw on them, but we know what that means. I would use a similar tactic if I had an animal in my office who needed to be torn to pieces. I'd have a few of the same little tricks. The artificial face of confusion. The artificial face of concern. Postures of empathy and compassion.

"It comes down to atmosphere," Mr. Rubins said. "The environment here and who is a good fit. It is tough for me to say this, but I also don't think you will be surprised, Jay. I mean, it can't surprise you to hear this."

Oh, surprise. I looked into my past for the most recent example of real, genuine surprise. I used a fucking telescope and scanned that deep, black hole, back to my birth and maybe even before. Where was the surprise? I looked and looked but the field was bare.

"It's a problem of fit, and I'm afraid I'm going to have to let you go."

He blinked at me. I pictured us far above the earth, hanging from an aircraft, me holding on to his hand as he pulled his fingers away. He would let me go and I would fall and the feeling would not be unpleasant.

The central problem was this, he went on to say: the feelings I cause in others. What people feel when they see me and hear me. What they feel, even, when they think of me. It was a situation the school could no longer abide.

"You've gotten some results with these kids, there's no denying that," Mr. Rubins told me.

But I could deny it. I would. To the grave. I'd been part of a *learning outcomes study*. I'd seen brain scans of some kids, before and after their science exposure. All science learning did was take some gray away. Or maybe it added some. I can never remember. In any case there was a color valuation shift in the brains of my children. It's what might have once been called *making a difference*. Certainly there would be a chemical shortcut for this kind of learning soon, if the learning was even a desired outcome. This premise, that we as a civilization would be better off if we knew more—the progress fetish, the growth fetish, the fetish for getting out of bed—might prove short-lived and decadent in the larger picture, the longer historical view. It will possibly be seen as a tenable mistake. Maybe we should all be hiding in our homes until the right technology comes along to absolve us from, well, from most things of this sort. It is awkward to live just before a significant invention comes about.

You have to wonder. When death is solved one day, all of us will be viewed as mules. Brutish, dumb, not really human. Because we let ourselves get old, grow infirm, die. Because we let ourselves feel pain. We experienced pain with a certain resignation and acceptance. Maybe we thought we deserved it. There was even a value system, a kind of morality, around who could hide their pain the best. You were a superior person if you hid it better. You were praised and celebrated when you pretended you were not in agony. Fucking mules.

Mr. Rubins shook my hand. Whatever he said about me was true, but any human being in the world could be reduced to nothing with a few sentences. That's what sentences do. Turn a man or a woman to powder. It doesn't mean that that powder wasn't once packed together to form a beautiful shape.

My classes, as of now, were covered by others, Mr. Rubins told me. I deserved a break. I could go on home. But I should gather my things first, of course. Didn't want to forget that. Remove every trace, Mr. Rubins requested. Which is, you know, what I tried to do. But later you discover that it's not so easy. Traces remain. Not just one's dumb things, but the people we have spoken to, who hold traces of us inside them. Do we remove them, too? Where does it stop?

Some cats were asleep in the road on my way home. Everyone seemed tired. People sat on the sidewalks as if they couldn't wait to collapse in private. Not a lot of people. But here and there. Enough to notice. I steered the car carefully. I was not tired. Not even close. I sensed I would be awake for a long time.

At home I did some math regarding my finances. I'd have my salary for two more months. I had savings for another three. My pension, such as it was, would pay for a bag of apples every few months for one small child. How much longer would we all live, me and Gin and the kids? It was hard to say. A person had trouble coming up with an airtight plan, or even a deluded plan, when basic data of this sort was so hard to uncover. You could fuss with these little life-expectancy calculators on the Internet, but they didn't always kick out real numbers when it came to kids. Little kids especially, cute or not, healthy or not, creeps or sweethearts. Sometimes the sites shut you out if you punched in, say, a very low number in the menu bar for age—as if you wanted to know something illicit. Life expectancy of a nine-year-old. I mean, why not just say? There's math behind everything. It's not a death threat to wonder how long a creature will live. Who has time for shyness?

The upshot was, of course, not enough money. Nowhere close. Maybe that was always the upshot. Maybe that's the definition of upshot. I loaded up the job lists and clicked into the sweet heart of them. I needed to work alone, in a lonely place, where no one would walk or stand. I needed a job inside myself, a way to get paid for sitting in a dark room, money for steering clear of others. I could clean things and fix things, and I could talk to people who didn't talk back. I had a made-up language, with words that mostly sounded like breath gone wrong, the last breaths of an old man, and I could recite that for someone if they paid me. I could use my body against the world, where things were wrong and needed to be changed. Digging and hauling and lifting and pushing. I could climb and I could descend and I could travel on the horizontal, unless someone was hunting me. I could make shapes where there were none and maybe they'd be called houses. I could speak to children, if anyone would allow it. I could not sing and I could not cook for a crowd and I could not laugh on command. I did not, so far as I knew, have a bad back. I knew something about the invisible world—the worms we call molecules—but all of that could change—facts could grow up—and then I'd just be a storyteller, lying about what goes on around us, hoping people believed that untruth reveals a kind of beauty, and not just because it's a medicine against what is real. Maybe it was once true, and maybe it will be true again.

Gin came home and we drank a great deal, because that was the dance style in those days. That was how we fought the night. We roasted the shit out of a chicken and cracked into it like it was a great mythological beast. There was a wine and we put our faces in it, forgetting to breathe. Gin went to the icebox, where she found a frozen old log of something she'd made, bearded in freezer burn, and with my help we sawed into it, making thick yellow discs. Gin kept saying I should trust her, and when these toasted beauties came out of the oven, after ages and ages, they were soft and hot and sweet, and if they burned my mouth they also almost made me cry with pleasure. We attacked a platter of them and left none for the kids. Screw the kids, we were yelling, smashing our glasses against the wall.

The night wasn't going to go on forever, because no one had figured that out yet. Everyone in the world wished for such a thing, begged for it all the time, but it was as if each of us thought that someone else would do the hard work to bring it about, an endless night now and then, an option, invoked even at extreme personal cost, for no morning. I wanted to sit with Gin forever and die in our chairs. Me dying before she did. But just by a second. Me and then her and then I would have to think a bit about the list from there, who would die and when. There was so much more involved.

"They took my kids away," I told Gin. I hated to ruin her night, but she needed to know.

"What? What do you mean?"

"They took them from me. I'm fired."

It probably wasn't possible for Gin to get softer, but she did. You could have seen it on film, and maybe then you'd see proof that she wasn't even really a person. What a small, dull word for what Gin was. How obscene. She softened and she almost transformed into a kind of medicine, not just a creature but a whole atmosphere, designed to soothe and neutralize this sad angry thing that had flown into its airspace. Gin had been tapped for a role and I could see her getting into character. Ms. Sympathy. She might have had the decency to leave the room during this transformation. Of course I might have had the decency not to exist in the first place. How rude to come on the scene like I did. How thoughtless.

"We knew this might happen, Jay," Gin said. She held my hands.

"You did, maybe."

"Oh sweetie."

"I know."

"Oh no. I'm sorry. I really am."

"Oh it's not your fault. I deserve it."

"You don't."

"Well, you're being nice. You're being paid to say that."

Gin got her wild and beautiful look. She grinned and I almost couldn't bear to look at her.

"Ha!" she said. "Not enough. Where's my money, if that's so? Why aren't I rich by now?"

What I did a few days later was to take a special twenty-dollar bill that I'd been given and that I'd saved forever, I don't know why. A mother might have given it to me long ago, I can't remember. I didn't earn it, I know that. It was a gift. A person handed it to me and I had never at that point seen so much money in my life. I just always kept it in my shaving kit, and it had stayed crisp somehow. It was still new money and I probably thought that it had magic, which embarrasses me to admit because mostly I can't stand that kind of talk. I put it in an envelope for Gin and left it on her dresser. Once I used to collect gin bottles, just for their labels, and I'd steam them off and then scissor out her name, Gin and Gin and Gin. I pasted one of these to the envelope so she'd know it was for her. I wanted to write a note and I thought a lot about what I might say. I wrote it all out in my mind. But there was no easy way to get it out of me. I didn't know how to extract it. It was all in there, in me, but I couldn't prove it.

"From me," I wrote, "for you. Because you are very nice."

After Gin died, the children went to live with their aunt in Maroyo County, north of here by not so long. This all sounds pretty vague, but trust me, it wasn't. It really happened and it felt real and there was nothing remotely vague about any of it. Gin's was the fast cancer, which, I hate to say it, is far cheaper, I mean dollar-wise, and possibly on the emotional side, though I am no expert in that sort of tabulation. How do we count the various ways and styles of nothing we feel?

We used our money for her last days. She begged me not to. Once she even said that I was supposed to drive her out into a field and leave her there. It was one of our favorite places, not that I rank things like that: nice places, fun places, places I like. We used to go there before the kids, and then with the kids, and then alone sometimes, when the kids had their own life. Maybe the kids will go there one day without me. Maybe there will be days when no one goes there, when no one is left. One day it won't even be a field. Lava will flow slowly over it.

Gin wanted only a blanket and a thermos of soup and then I was to drive off. It was a favor she begged me to grant. A favor. It really didn't sound like one. We were making pots and pots of healing soups in those days, with the sort of herbs and roots that cost much more, because we knew so little that we were willing to believe a leaf or a root or a seed would make this all go away.

We drove out to the field and I got her set up on the blanket and poured her out a bowl of soup. The day was fair and we didn't think she'd be too cold. How many nights would she last? It was something we didn't want to discuss. I asked her was there anything else and she just put her head on me. It was small and cold. When I held it I didn't feel like I was holding her. That had happened— her body didn't feel like it was hers. She was somewhere else. I held what she had, anyway. The old, finished body she still showed the world. I touched it and tried to keep it from spilling out onto the ground.

Gin said she didn't want her pills or anything. One of the medicines was a cream for her head. She also had a tincture in a dropper bottle, which she needed to squeeze into her mouth in the mornings, that ate flesh—the kind that didn't belong to her, that had invaded her body and grown in her but that was never hers. She was going to have a little bit of time without it all. It made her feel pretty crummy, she laughed, all of that healing. Something about being awake and alive again. Something about not going into a terrible fog. We talked a little of the kids. They knew she was sick but they didn't know anything. Just like me. Gin asked for things and I agreed. She said things and I nodded. I made assurances I could not keep. She predicted that. She knew it. It was like she was talking to me from the future, telling it all to me. Except here I am in the future, and I don't see her anywhere.

I stood up after a while to say goodbye. You have been a good wife, I told her. I am sure I did not deserve you, and I am sure you do not deserve this. We hugged without tears and I went back to the car, but on the way I ducked off the path and threw myself into the grass. It was there that I waited and watched her. She sipped her soup and stared off at the trees on the far side of the field. She had the blanket pulled over her, and she was so small beneath it it looked like no one was there. Like I had just left an empty campground. We both knew this wasn't really happening. We must have. Some things, just a very few things, don't have to be real if you don't want them to. When she suddenly stirred and looked around—for me, I thought, I hoped—when she struggled to try to stand, I ran to her and picked her up and took her home. And that was the end of that kind of talk.

The last of our money was spent on the hole we put her in. A coffin and some flowers and some food for the few people who came by. The children went up north, and I was told to come see them, and I was told to hug them, and I was told to talk to them. I did those things and did those things and did those things. They had a good aunt, a fair aunt, and if the uncle was neither he was so far away that it might not matter. The idea was, I needed to find work, and get us some money, or nothing, and nothing, and nothing. Would someone explain that to them, I wondered. When I saw them they crowded into me—warm and wet and weepy—and we walked around as one body. We tilted and we swayed, we lurched from room to room, and sometimes we fell. We'd need to figure out how to go faster, I told them, with them hanging on to my neck. We had to be smooth and quick, in case something happened and we had to run. That was what a family was now, just this one body that had a lot of parts, and several heads, and it had children's voices and a man's voice, and it was a force to be reckoned with. So until we learned how to do that, until we could glide through the world as fast as a cat, them hanging from me and me carrying them along, we'd have to be apart. Just for a little while.

You can't give up what you never started, said someone from my past. A mother, a father, a friend. Such a long time ago. I remember only the vague outline of their body, and the horrible glow from their mouth when they spoke.

I did little jobs, big jobs, no jobs. Coins came in and I smashed them into bread, into meat. I made a deal with County Electric, and they put me on a schedule of darkness, which killed the lights for days, in exchange for no charges, and they leaked me power when they could spare it. A trickle on a Saturday, that sort of thing. The house would suddenly hum, shuddering back on, and I'd see something wild and terrible in the mirror. Enough light to blind a small animal, I'd think. I'm sure I wasn't the first person to think about bottling it. But what I had was more than enough. I would have been fine with less.

I called the children when I could, and I told them, "Soon." Sometimes, when they couldn't come to the phone, their aunt held the receiver into whatever space they were in, or so I pictured, and I shouted it, hoping they could hear me. Soon! Despite how it sounded, it wasn't a birdcall. It was the call of a man, their father. It was just how he sounded when he needed to reach them. Whenever their aunt said they couldn't come to the phone, which was more and more, I pictured them trapped on the floor, someone sitting on them. Or blanket after blanket after blanket, covering and smothering them. Or they were in a hole and there was no ladder. Or they were in the water, the wrong kind of water—the black and thick kind, where if you try to swim you slip down lower, you sink, and the more you try to swim, which is what I taught them always to do, no matter the kind of water, the lower you got, until you were standing on the dark sand floor of the darkest, blackest ocean. Of course they could not come to the phone. Of course. They needed to hold hands and push off the ocean floor, first. They needed to swim to the surface, like I taught them.

That year the summer had a glitch. A flaw in the calendar, we were told. Like a leap year, but worse. The days would flicker out early, and sometimes, after sunset, would strobe back on, due to some sort of unspent sunlight that was trapped in the higher atmosphere. People thought it meant something but it most certainly did not.

A star came out in late August, and it took a low position in the night sky, and then it started to make a soft, terrible noise. It had some people concerned. Not just in my neighborhood, my town, where concern runs high, where people polish their worry like a stone. This came from people who know what to watch out for, what to worry about—they said it wasn't good. In daylight, in sunshine, a planet should respect our border, I believe. It looked dirty from here. I daresay it had a shit stain across it. Of course this was only a local weather system discoloring the planet. I knew that. Weather, in the end, simply adds a shit stain to a place. Gray sometimes. Sometimes yellow. But still, just a stripe of shit over the people and place. Sometimes the shit is clear and wet. It comes in pellets. I do not know why we call it rain.

The next day the star was gone. We know enough about stars to say that this one was never there in the first place, so it could never leave, and it may be that it's wrong to even call them stars. Whatever one says, or thinks, about stars is no doubt incorrect, and once you follow this line of reasoning, I mean really follow it as if you're stalking it home for the kill, well, reality pulls away a little bit. Like a skin, it just comes off.

Soon after that I went looking for work and I fucking found it. An unbearable amount of work, everywhere I searched. Because everything was broken, torn, crushed. There were faults in the soil, the buildings, the air. The people, especially, needed work—their moods, their appearances, the way they walked. But of course so did the streets and roads. So did the trees. Disarray everywhere, flaws of design. Error, human and otherwise. A shattered state of things. Would I be paid if I fixed some of these things? Made them right? Not for me to say, I knew. Nothing really was for me to say.

I would have to learn to ignore all of this unfinished work, or it would disturb me — so much wrong, so much left undone. We shirk our duties when we open our doors, when we leave our homes. We shirk and shirk. We walk down the street and we ignore jobs, swirling around us, needing to be completed. We pretend we don't see.

The job I finally took required so little of me that I wasn't sure if I was even doing it. It was like getting paid for not dying. I stood and I sat and I walked. I had memories and I had the opposite, when nothing came to me and I listened to music come from the wall — just a piano that sounded like it had been tipped over and kicked to pieces, but was somehow still in tune. The days were driven fast by an engine I could not see. When cars approached, I pressed a button for the bridge, and when they were long gone I pressed that button again. My money began to form a pile and the pile began to glow.

It was October and the roads were already snowy when I finally went to get the kids. The aunt wasn't even there. The kids were packed and clean and all dressed up and they stood apart from me, because we hadn't been practicing our single-body power walk through the terrible terrible world. The team had been on hiatus and now we were back together, I told them. I knew that I looked strange and scary, and smelled like someone from the past. I hugged them anyway and whispered a few of the things I'd been saving up to say. In my pocket was the envelope I'd given Gin. We took that twenty dollars and we went out to breakfast. We got eggs and cakes and there was a sweet pudding served in a long bowl that the three of us shared, as if we were the fanciest horses at the most golden of troughs. We dove our spoons into it and we laughed at how good it was. I had a real coffee and I accidentally cried, which no one saw. That was her money I was spending. It would be gone after today. Would she have wanted us to, as I kept trying to tell myself? I am afraid the answer was no, and no, and no, because she didn't want anything, she wasn't anything, she had no name and no body and her heart did not beat, and I didn't even know how to remember her right.

I took a sort of girlfriend before too long, and I don't use that expression lightly. I actually took her from another man who was asleep at the wheel, just so out of it—as if he were operating his own body with a broken remote control. You could peel off his face and throw it into the woods. I was forty-eight years old. For some reason I was not dead, even though the late autumn season had that smell. Of failure, of the afterlife.

She had a name, and out of respect for Gin I won't mention it here. The children met her and called her "sister," and she never got too close or too far. When it came time to test our parts, I found she fit on me, but we all knew where that could go. She hollered at night, out of nowhere, and sometimes it put me in a terrible crouch. She had her own job, her own life, her own children, and even, somewhere else—a city, a town, a cave, I didn't know—an old, abandoned husband, who didn't know where she was. I thought of him sometimes.

The deal was that she would always call ahead, and what that sometimes meant was that I'd hear my name, and not just my name but the names of the kids, sounding loud and pretty and strong way down the street. You may not know what it's like to hear your name sung out loud, from far away, by someone who has beauty in her throat. Bow your head and imagine it. Sometimes in the morning we'd hear it and we'd go outside and wait in the yard. When she got up to us, out of breath and laughing, she'd always say: I called ahead, did you hear me?

...

I still go down to Foley, the school where I worked. I watch the kids flow in and out. The ones I taught are long gone, now. They are grown, I imagine. Some of them have died, no doubt. Maybe they are buried near Gin. When you're underground, buried dead like that, distances are different. You are close by to the others. This is understood. You can get to them, and they to you. It's not like up here, in the holding room called the world, where you have to walk or drive or fly. Where you might have to swim. Where, maybe, you can't get somewhere else at all, because of mountains, or wars.

At Foley once, I saw Mr. Rubins, walking from his car over to the school. He had his bag and his hat, a newspaper tucked under his arm. He looked the same, not that I had ever really studied him. What impressed me the most was how he walked and waved and smiled, using all the tricks of a real human person. How he clung to the ground and used his body in relation to gravity, as if he weren't a ghost. He could have floated off, he could have melted down, he could have simply collapsed into a heap of clothing, vacating this world forever, but he held it together, even if it was taking all of his loving energy and soon his chest would explode with the effort. I watched him until he disappeared into the school and the bell rang and everything suddenly went incredibly quiet. I admired his technique. He was a spirit to watch.

The children are home. They keep their own secrets. I no longer curate their minds. No one has time. No one has the energy. Isn't that the world now? Listless, cowering in our homes. Beset by paralyzing indifference. Too tired to eat, and waiting for a hammer to the head? Witness the birds. Their exhaustion. Please. Look at them closely for a change and ignore the ruse of beauty. Who can finally be bothered to still pretend we're not moments away from some blistering cremation?

Not that I have specific information. I don't. I have no gift for the future.

You've driven by houses like ours, and maybe you've wondered just how the surrender happened inside. Did the body rot from the head down, as legend would have it? Who gave up, and how? A question that is always relevant. Take a picture of a family, of any family, and that is always the caption.

Before her diagnosis, possibly even the very morning we learned of her cancer, Gin was outside doing something to the old tree. She loved the tree, felt it needed to know that. Loved it but feared it. Fretted forever that it would topple over and crush us. Now the kids and I will sit under it. It leans and sways and it makes a tremendous sound sometimes. The sound of a house getting crushed, the sound of a train slowing down, the sound of the world hurtling through space—all of this noise booming inside this monstrous tree. We will look around, at the other, smaller trees, at the leafy bushes, at anything that might move in the wind, and all of it is just so still, as if someone is suffocating the world with a bag and not even a breath can escape. And yet the tree above us sways and sways, observing its own private wind, moving according to a logic we'll never understand. Sometimes I hope that Gin was right, that this tree is coming for us. Sometimes when the kids get antsy and want to go inside, I hold them close and ask them to wait. Just a little longer, I say, outside in the shade. Just wait with me under the tree here a little bit longer. Something amazing is coming.

Acknowledgments

I am grateful to the editors who first published these stories: Cecilia Alemani, Andrew Bourne, Junot Díaz, Matthew Fishbane, Ben Metcalf, Sigrid Rausing, Paul Reyes, Will Rogan, Nicole Rudick, David Samuels, and Deborah Treisman. Andrew Eisenman read these stories early with great critical care. I am indebted to him for his intelligence and vision. Max Porter, too. Smart and generous readings that always pushed the stories where they needed it most. Heidi Julavits offered crucial readings and critical editorial ideas at every stage of revision. To me there is no sharper reader, not to mention writer, not to mention person.

A special thanks is due to the MacDowell Colony, who provided not just time and space, of the most ideal kind, but some unnameable deeper gift, conducive to work and concentration, that is harder and harder to find.

To Deborah Treisman, thank you for your faith and support and always exacting editorial insights. Many of these stories are much improved because of you.

To Denise Shannon, my one and only agent, thank you as always for your brilliance, candor, and advocacy. I have been so fortunate to be able to work with you for all of these years.

To Jordan Pavlin, thank you for your unerring belief. I am endlessly grateful for your intelligence and loyalty and passion.

And to everyone at Knopf—thank you for sticking by me and offering such a very good home.

This book was set in Hoefler Text, a family of fonts designed by Jonathan Hoefler, who was born in 1970. First designed in 1991, Hoefler Text was intended as an advancement on existing desktop computer typography, including as it does an exponentially larger number of glyphs than previous fonts. In form, Hoefler Text looks to the old-style fonts of the seventeenth century, but it is wholly of its time, employing a precision and sophistication only available to the late twentieth century.